A Broad Church

Deborah Fisher

Unlimited Publishing
Bloomington, Indiana

Tregolwyn
Wales

Distributing Publisher:
Unlimited Publishing, LLC
Bloomington, Indiana
http://www.unlimitedpublishing.com

Contributing Publisher:
Tregolwyn
Post Office Box 11
Cowbridge CF71 7XT
Wales
U.K.
http://tregolwyn.co.uk

Cover and Book Design by Charles King

This book was typeset with Adobe® InDesign™, using headings in Adobe Jensen™, text in Adobe Garamond®.

ISBN 1-58832-009-X

Unlimited Publishing
Bloomington, Indiana

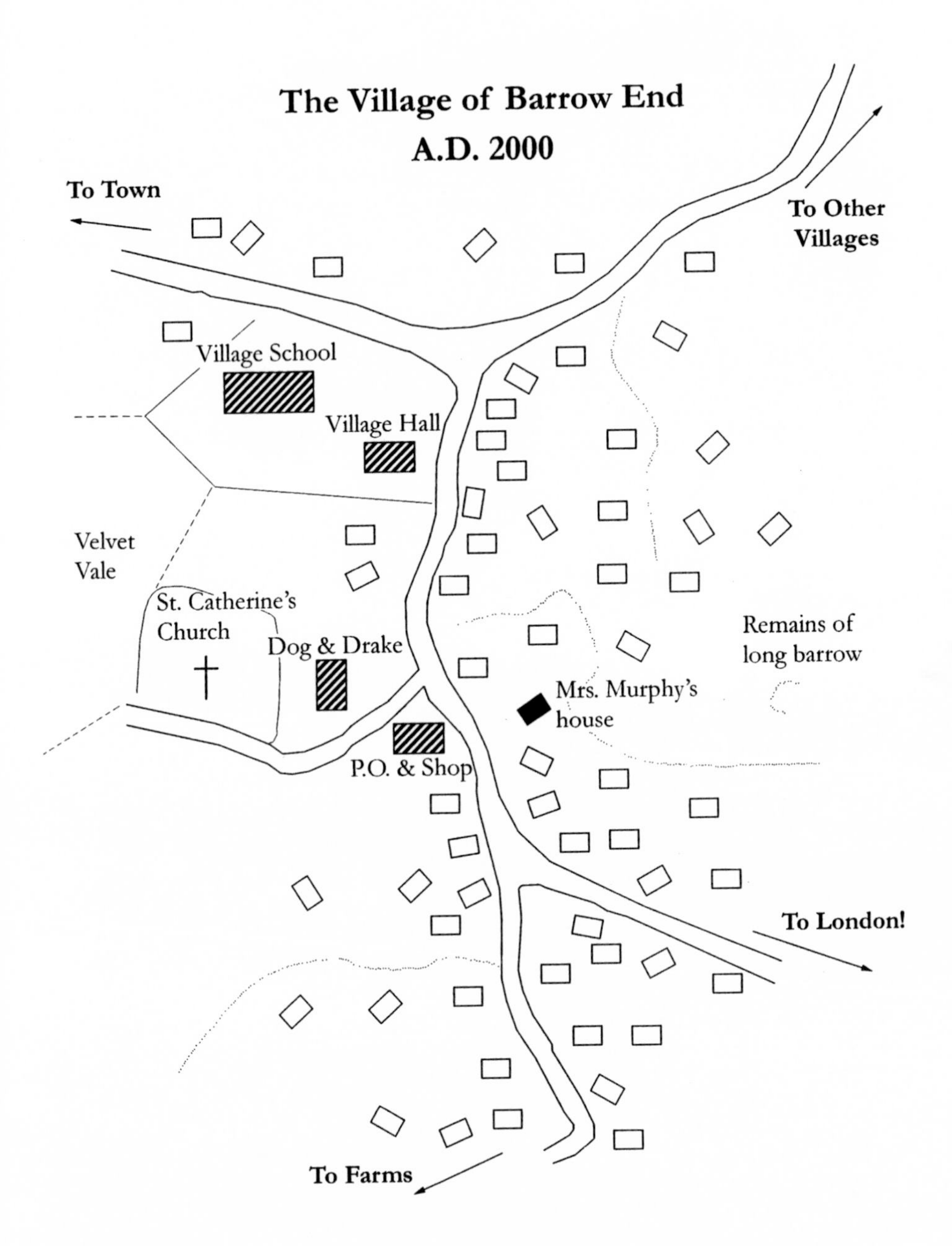
The Village of Barrow End
A.D. 2000
To Town
To Other Villages
Village School
Village Hall
Velvet Vale
St. Catherine's Church
Dog & Drake
P.O. & Shop
Mrs. Murphy's house
Remains of long barrow
To London!
To Farms

Historical Note

The Battle of Barrow End is entirely fictitious, and there was no such person as Sir Henry Kinkade. All other references to the English Civil War are based on fact. The "Re-enactment Society" is of course based on the Sealed Knot—the English Civil War Society.

Chapter I

Touching the Past

"I think it looks very *nice*," said Herbert, contemplating the museum's new Roman exhibit. Praise indeed, I thought.

Jonathan didn't actually say anything, but nodded a couple of times.

Their admiration appeared genuine. One might have anticipated a tinge of envy, or resentment, because I had done something they couldn't. If they felt anything of that sort, they never showed it.

That's not fair. It's wrong to say that the others couldn't have done what I had done, or even that they couldn't have done it as well as I had. Of course they could. It was just that they'd never thought of trying, or if they had thought of it, something—preoccupations, or lethargy, or lack of imagination—had prevented them following through.

In Herbert's case, there was a particular reason why resentment might have come to the surface, because Herbert had been Curator of the District Museum, ever since it opened about fifteen years before. Now I had come along with all my qualifications, and I was unintentionally making him look a little amateurish.

At first, I had been daunted by the prospect of working with him regularly, knowing that he bore a grudge—not against me specifically, but against those who had made the decision to create a permanent post and appoint a professional to it. I hadn't taken Herbert's job as Curator, you understand. He still held that title, but it remained an honorary one. I was actually being paid for my work as "Conservator," and in due course it was understood that I would succeed him as Curator.

If Herbert had told me once, he had told me a hundred times that he had "no ill feeling" about the matter. That was what gave him away. If he really hadn't felt badly used, he would have kept quiet on the subject altogether. Under the circumstances, I could consider myself lucky.

I had, indeed, considered myself lucky when I heard that I had got the job. Having been made redundant from my previous post several months earlier, I was becoming resigned to the idea that I would have to accept something outside my chosen profession when, out of the blue, my mother phoned and told me about the advert she had seen in a local newspaper for someone to run the new District Museum. It was fifty miles from the town where I'd been born, but that was still nearer than London, where I'd been working.

I've just described it as the "new" District Museum, but it turned out not to be a new museum at all. The Liberal Democrats had recently won control of the Borough Council from the Conservatives, and one of their first actions had been to announce, in a blaze of publicity, their plans to improve and enlarge the museum, which they regarded as a potential tourist attraction. A couple of years earlier, archaeologists had dug up a Roman bath-house behind the greengrocer's, and together with random discoveries in odd parts of town, this had led experts to acknowledge that we were living in what had once been one of the most important towns of Roman Britain.

Up until that time, the museum had been housed in a couple of rooms at the back of the public library, which was attached to the Town Hall, in the High Street. It had come into existence as a result of the initiative and sheer hard work of local enthusiasts, of whom Herbert Dyson and his wife, Doris, were the most prominent. They ran the local Historical Society, and had persuaded the Council that a permanent museum was something the town ought to have. Herbert had gone on badgering the authorities until accommodation was offered. He had built up the collection from scratch, and had kept the museum open every weekend with the aid of a band of volunteers.

The newly-elected Borough Council, of course, had no money for a new museum building. The conversion of a derelict house in the town centre was being talked about, but that would be no less expensive, even if they obtained the lottery grant they had applied for. The appointment of a professional—me—was no more than a ruse to deflect the attention of the electorate from this fact. The only immediate result would be extended opening hours, during which I would normally be the only person on duty.

I was expected to carry on without any extra funds, or even any staff. If I wanted a day off, or even a few hours off, I would either have to get a volunteer to fill in for me, or close the museum. The shock of this discovery wasn't enough to deter me, however. Any port in a storm, as they say, and even a poisoned chalice like this one wasn't likely to come my way again, so I accepted the job with alacrity.

Herbert knew that his continued presence had become an embarrassment to the Council. Thankfully, he didn't choose that moment to take umbrage and withdraw his support for the museum. Though I didn't, officially, work *for* him, I recognised immediately that I was going to be dependent on his goodwill in order to do my job. My solution to the problem was to approach him, shyly and deferentially, and ask if he would consider making me Deputy Curator and giving me control of the day-to-day administration, while he continued as the "public face" of the museum. Herbert was shrewd enough to see that this was the best offer he was going to get, and as a face-saving exercise, he accepted.

The situation wasn't without its difficulties, however. To keep Herbert happy, I had to let him have a free hand to go about things in his own way, even when I disagreed. There were certain areas he regarded as his own province. One of these—a task I was more than happy to leave to him—was the recruitment of volunteer helpers and the drawing up of their rota. On this particular Saturday, when the new Roman display was due to be unveiled, they were all on duty.

Verity was more effusive in her praise of the new display than Herbert and Jonathan had been.

"It's wonderful, Rose," she said. She always called me "Rose" for short, as do most of my friends. "You're so clever."

I should have been grateful for the compliment, but it made me rather sad to think she had so little regard for her own ability. Verity wasn't an idiot. She could perfectly well have put together the Roman exhibit, but she genuinely believed herself incapable. She was female, hence, in her own view, helpless when it came to building something from nothing.

Two men had come into the museum that Saturday morning, and they were now in a corner of the main exhibition area, talking to Herbert. They were dressed normally—casually, that is—but one of them was carrying what appeared to be a helmet. I recognised it as something called a "lobster," a type of military headgear used during the English Civil War. It was given that nickname because it bore a resemblance to a lobster's shell. Now *there's* a piece of useless information.

I also thought I recognised one of the two strangers. He had his back to me, but there was something about his stance and his general appearance that took me back in time. Surely it couldn't be him, here, fifty miles away from home?

"Isn't Rose clever?" Verity repeated, addressing Molly, who was passing us on the way to hang up her coat. "Look what she's done with this display! It looked so dull before. Now it looks like the real thing!"

I resisted the urge to ask Verity what she meant by "the real thing." Presumably, she didn't regard the couple of rooms where we worked as a "real" museum. I don't know what that made *me*. Was I simply a feeble substitute for Herbert, who, as I knew perfectly well, still commanded the loyalty of the team of volunteers, though it was getting on for two years since I had supplanted him?

Molly paid scant attention to Verity's effusive comments. The moment she had divested herself of her coat, she went over to Herbert's corner to find out who his visitors were. She couldn't stand mysteries; or rather, she loved them, but she could never wait to find out the solution. She was one of those people who always reads the last page of a whodunnit first.

"Someone from the Re-enactment Society," she informed us on her return. "You know, the people who dress up as Cavaliers and Roundheads. Herbert's trying to get them to do a battle or something, in that field he's so interested in. Near where you live, Rosemary."

I had no difficulty in identifying the field Molly was talking about. For the past few weeks, there had been a strong rumour going around that the current owners of the field next to St Catherine's Church, in the village where I lived, were going to have another bash at getting planning permission for a housing development. Herbert's choice of venue for the proposed re-enactment was no coincidence.

When I first went to live in Barrow End, it was a lovely quiet place. The village is called Barrow End because of the long barrow, a prehistoric burial mound, close to which the first dwellings were built, so many centuries ago that no one can say when the village was founded. The barrow itself is barely visible now, having been gradually worn away by medieval and subsequent farming activity, but the villagers are still proud of its historical significance, and they've never passed up the opportunity to alert visitors and newcomers—like me—to this important local landmark.

As you can tell, the whole area is rich in history and archaeology, and it was pure coincidence that I had happened to end up living within a stone's throw of a historic monument. Not one historic monument, as it turned out, but two.

Chapter 2

Making the Bullets

At the moment when Molly was revealing the identity of our visitors, the younger of the two men—the one carrying the lobster—turned and looked us full in the face, and I saw that it was indeed Joe. Joe Payne. He winked at me, and turned back to the conversation, though he seemed to be taking little part in it.

"Cheeky monkey!" Molly exclaimed, but quietly.

"No, it's okay," I said. "I know him. He was at school with me."

My face felt hot, and I wandered back across the room, ostensibly to take another look at the Roman display. Molly followed.

On a normal Saturday, I would have given Molly a lift to the museum, since she lived about halfway between Barrow End and the town, but she had rung me the night before to say that she was going to be late reporting for duty. Molly was originally from Doncaster, and had joined the museum staff after her husband had left her, alone, in this strange town to which he had brought her a few years earlier. Bouncing back from the blow to her self-esteem, she had set out to rebuild her life without help from anyone, and up to a point she had succeeded.

Jonathan and Verity, like Molly, were volunteer stewards at the museum. In his other life, Jonathan worked as a counter clerk at the DSS. He was passionate about history and archaeology, but had gone straight to work after leaving school at eighteen. You could say that the museum was his university. Verity was his complete opposite, a widow in her sixties, who didn't have another job. For her, working at the museum fulfilled a social need. The same was true of Molly. She was a chatterbox, and it gave her a captive audience. I was very fond of all three of them.

I suppose I fell somewhere between the two extremes. Herbert, Doris and Verity regarded me as a youngster, and visualised me spending every waking moment in frantic social activity—though how they thought I managed this when I was nearly always in the museum, I can't imagine. Jonathan, on the other hand, thought I was a bit of an old fogey, because I didn't go out clubbing and the only pub I ever went to in the evenings was the one across the road from my house.

The village pub was called the Dog and Drake. A battered Victorian sign over its entrance depicted a tired-looking foxhound and a green-headed mallard eyeing one another suspiciously. The pub was situated on the main street of the village, just in front of the church, St Catherine's. Like the church, the Dog and Drake was medieval. They were unquestionably the oldest buildings in Barrow End.

Behind the church was an extensive network of fields, originally the property of two local farmers. One of the farms had been sold in recent years, and the land had been bought by someone who was not in the business of agriculture. Within weeks of the sale, the new owner had applied for outline planning permission for fifty houses.

There was an immediate outcry from the villagers. After much discussion, the local authority turned down the planning application, and the land remained unused for months, until all the fuss had died down. What few of the locals realised at the time was that applying for outline, as opposed to detailed, planning permission is as good as stating an intention of selling the land. It becomes more valuable to a potential developer if they have some choice of what to do with it. The field changed hands again in due course, and the new owners kept horses there for a while. The local residents thought that was the end of their worries.

All this had happened before I arrived in Barrow End. Now, it seemed, the prospect had reared its ugly head again. Herbert was concerned about this, not because he lived in the village—he didn't—but because he believed in maintaining the green belt, and also because that particular field was one of his hobby horses. He had identified it, tentatively, as the site of the Battle of Barrow End.

"Battle" is probably a bit of a misnomer. Like so many Civil War "battles," this confrontation between an offshoot of Parliament's army and a similar number of Royalist opposition, right at the end of 1642, had been more of a skirmish than anything, and certainly didn't involve Oliver Cromwell or the King. Information on the subject was sketchy, with contemporary estimates putting the number of troops involved at anything between two dozen and five hundred on each side.

Personally, I couldn't imagine a thousand men in a field that size, hacking at each other with swords or pikes or whatever they used in the seventeenth century. Early in the Civil War, however—as I discovered when I started reading up on the subject—even the smallest encounter could be decisive. The Royalists had won this particular battle, or skirmish, and their victory had been instrumental in gaining the support of the whole county. In the long run, it hadn't been enough to stop King Charles I from losing his head, but without it the course of the war might have run differently.

Herbert was a real military history enthusiast. Too young to join up before the end of the Second World War himself, he'd done his National Service before it was abolished, and regarded himself as an old soldier. What he lacked in practical experience, he made up for in attention to detail. He could walk over a known battlefield, point out exactly where each army had drawn up its forces, and then explain why things had gone the way they had. I envied him this ability, because, to me, one field looked identical to any other.

So, when Herbert stated categorically that the Battle of Barrow End had taken place in the field next to the church, I didn't question his judgement. In terms of the application for planning permission, though, it didn't seem terribly significant.

Herbert saw it differently. The field had never, as far as we knew, been ploughed. It had always been used for pasture. That meant that there could still be some valuable evidence lying around close to the surface. Herbert's grand scheme was to conduct a full-scale excavation of the field, but he knew this was never likely to be achieved. The next best thing would be to keep the field as it was, so that "archaeologists of the future" (one of Herbert's favourite phrases) would retain the option of carrying out their own investigation when the rest of us are dead and gone.

"Why don't we just climb over the gate and go for a walk round the field?" I asked Herbert, the first few times he mentioned it. "We might find something. You never know."

"We don't have permission," Herbert would always reply. "It wouldn't be right."

Ignoring Herbert's edict, I had walked the field on my own one day, and noticed nothing visible on the surface of the ground to give me any clues. Recognising that I didn't really know what I was looking for, and that even if I had known, I would probably have needed a metal detector to find it, I never repeated the experiment.

Despite my professional interest, I had never really believed in Herbert's idea. Although the exact details of the battle—or skirmish—weren't known, there was plenty of documentation available about Civil War activity in this part of the country, so it wasn't in itself a reason to preserve the field. A battlefield isn't like an Anglo-Saxon cemetery or a Roman villa. There might be a few artefacts strewn around the place, but they won't tell you much about the way people lived during the period in question. The kind of thing Herbert hoped to find might throw light on subjects such as seventeenth-century military equipment, surgical practice, strategy and tactics, but these didn't sound the most riveting topics in the world to me.

My doubts didn't prevent my being intrigued by the news of Herbert's approach to the Re-enactment Society. I'd heard of them before; they had hundreds, if not thousands, of members all over the country. They even had a branch in America. Whatever had given Herbert the idea of a re-enactment of the Battle of Barrow End, it sounded fun. I just wondered how he was expecting to get permission to use that field.

Needless to say, Herbert hadn't asked my opinion before contacting the Re-enactment Society. Over the years, he'd got used to doing more or less what he liked with the museum, and I'd already dropped heavy hints about the desirability of him consulting me *before* he did things rather than afterwards. On this occasion, however, I was disposed to give him free rein. It was a suitable activity for the museum to sponsor, and as long as he didn't actually expect us to make a financial commitment, I couldn't see any harm in the idea. I preferred to believe he had merely forgotten to tell me about the visitors rather than deliberately excluding me from the conversation.

Having offered her titbit of information, Molly had fallen unusually silent, still apparently transfixed by what was going on down at the other end of the room. I did my best to distract her by drawing her attention to the new display.

"We could do with some more photographs of that last excavation behind the greengrocer's," I said. "That Roman mosaic was a major find. People are really into archaeology these days. There's such a lot of it on TV."

Molly murmured agreement, but her attention was elsewhere. She was definitely eyeing up Joe and his companion. It may have been the older man who had captured her interest. Tall and distinguished-looking, probably ex-military, he was somewhere near her own age. On the other hand, she might have been looking at Joe, speculating on a possible teenage romance between him and me.

"What's his name?" she asked.

"Who?" Perhaps I was going too far in my determination to appear indifferent.

"The boy. The one you was in school with."

I dared to look at him again. As if he had sensed my movement, he glanced over at us and smiled, that perky schoolboy smile I remembered.

"He's Joe. Joe Payne."

And no, he was never my boyfriend, I might have added.

"Nice-looking lad," Molly commented.

"Not exactly a lad," I corrected. "He's the same age as me, twenty-eight. And he's married."

Chapter 3

Drawing Up the Battle Lines

I could hardly have denied that Joe was "nice-looking," subjective term though it is. With his curly dark hair and deep brown eyes, he had always turned heads. I'd been mad for him, just like all the other girls at school, but he had never looked twice at me—at least, not in *that* way.

In the sixth form at Colley Hill Comprehensive, when we had achieved some feeble level of intellectual maturity and were both taking History for A-level, Joe and I had at last become quite friendly. Though I had hardly seen him in the years since leaving school, I knew that he hadn't forgotten those days, and would soon come over to talk to me. Yes, of course I was looking forward to it. I could hardly wait.

He had married a girl I used to know fairly well, by the name of Georgina Blamey. She hadn't seemed at all his type, and I'd been greatly surprised when I saw the wedding photograph in the local paper. It would have been about four or five years earlier that I'd seen it, because I remembered thinking that twenty-three was rather young to be getting married—for a man, that is. They aren't usually ready for that kind of commitment at that age. Peter Markham was living proof of that. The Reverend Peter Markham, I should say.

More of our parish priest later.

I DIDN'T GET an opportunity to talk to Joe before lunchtime, but he caught up with me as I was on my way out of the Town Hall. I got the pleasant feeling that he had deliberately broken away from Herbert's clutches when he saw me putting my coat on.

"Rosemary!" he called, grabbing my arm and linking it in his. "My little Rose! I can't believe it! What are you doing here?"

"I might ask you the same question," I replied, coyly. "You don't live round here, do you?"

"No. Still in the old place, more or less. But I go all over the country with the Society. Every weekend in summer. The old bloke wants us to do a battle down here in August, on what he reckons is an authentic site."

"I know. It's just across the road from where I live."

"You don't say!"

"And his name's Herbert. And he's the Curator of this museum, if you don't mind." Even as I said it, I was giggling like a schoolgirl, and at what? Joe's sense of humour had never been sophisticated. The problem was that Joe's personality was irresistible.

"Any decent pubs round here?" he asked, as we dodged the swing doors. "Or do you go home for lunch?"

"Not worth it," I said. "I usually bring sandwiches, but as it happens, I haven't got any with me today." They were in my handbag; I had planned to eat them in the park. "There are a few places on the High Street that do food."

"And beer?"

I took him into the Lamb & Flag. The pubs in the High Street were all much of a muchness, all centuries old and setting out to appeal to the same clientele, a mass of oak beams and horse brasses.

"So," said Joe, drawing up a stool opposite me as we waited for our food order to be delivered, "how have you been?"

"I'm very happy, thank you," I said. "I've got a job I enjoy, and lots of friends. Everything's going swimmingly. *Now*."

Joe took the hint. "Have you been having problems?"

"I was working in London, as you know." This statement was based on the forlorn hope that he had bothered to keep up with my career progress in the years since I'd last seen him. "But I got made redundant, and I was out of work for a couple of months. I was just about to give up on museum work as a career when this job came up."

"Married yet?"

"No." I suspected he had already checked my left hand, but I went through the motions of answering. "Still looking for Mr. Right. I heard about you and Georgie," I added. "Saw your wedding photo in the paper."

"Did you?" He looked embarrassed for all of one second. "Actually, that's all in the past. We got a divorce."

It gave me little pleasure to know that I had been right in thinking he was too young for commitment. Fortunately, the teenage waitress arrived just at that moment with our ploughman's lunches. Joe ogled her retreating rump appreciatively as she walked away from the table. By the time we had sorted out the condiment situation, other topics of conversation had suggested themselves.

"What are you doing now?" I asked. "Are you still in IT?"

"Systems analyst," he replied, keeping his sentences short so that they didn't interfere with his eating.

I felt no awe. Systems analyst is just a posh name for someone who draws flowcharts.

"Are you getting on well?"

"S'all right. Best thing about it is, I get the weekends off."

"Where exactly do you work?"

"I get around a bit. We do feasibility studies for large organisations. Banks, major corporations, government departments. Even did some work for the Inland Revenue recently."

I laughed. It seemed incongruous. Joe had always been a bit of a rebel, when I knew him. Since he'd been forced to earn his crust in a job that was the height of respectability, I sensed that weekends with the Re-enactment Society were now the centre of his world. We moved on to a discussion of Herbert's pet project. I wanted Joe's expert opinion on the battlefield theory.

"Surely," I said, "they wouldn't have held a battle so close to a church? Not with their religious fervour."

It was a question I'd asked Herbert many times before. I just wanted to see if Joe would come up with the same answer.

"Doesn't seem to have bothered them at all," he replied, not interrupting the process of stuffing a half-baguette into his mouth. "They were robbing the plate from churches right from the start of the War—both armies." He paused to grab another sachet of mayonnaise, and ripped it open carelessly. "There's a church at Alton, in Hampshire," he went on, "that's actually got holes in the internal walls, put there in the campaign that led up to the Battle of Cheriton."

"From bullets?" I queried.

"Bullets!" He laughed scornfully at my anachronism. "Balls!"

A green-wellied couple at the next table looked up in dismay from their lasagne.

"Musket balls!" said Joe, grinning in their direction.

They smiled back, nervously, before continuing their meal.

"Herbie was telling me about this planning application lark," Joe went on. "Someone wanting to build houses on a Civil War battlefield, I ask you!" He grinned again.

"Is it definite?" I asked. "I haven't seen the details yet."

"Herbie showed us."

"Don't keep calling him that," I cautioned. "It might slip out while you're talking to him."

"Oh, he won't mind. After all, we are doing him a favour."

We were interrupted again, by the entry into the bar of Joe's older colleague, the one Molly seemed to have her eye on. He sat down, uninvited, at our table, and picked up the menu, whereupon I was sorry that I hadn't dragged Molly along with us for lunch. She could have kept the other man occupied while I concentrated on Joe.

Joe introduced the gooseberry as Nathan Pendragon. What a fantastic name, I thought, and wondered if it was really his own. It certainly sounded right for someone who went around re-enacting historic battles.

"So tell me," I persisted, "how does Herbert expect to get permission from the owners of the field to use it for a battle, when he's intending to oppose their planning application?"

"That's the clever bit," said Joe. "We're doing the dirty work for him. They daren't refuse us permission to use it, because that would put everyone's backs up and guarantee substantial opposition to their application. Raising money for charity and all that. No, they want to appear all-round good eggs by saying yes to us, and they hope that will win them a few brownie points. And just to add icing to the cake, we've persuaded them to let us use their pet horses for the cavalry, in the actual battle. They'll be wetting themselves at the prospect."

Ignoring the mixed metaphors, I continued the argument. "But I don't see what Herbert expects to get out of it. Re-enacting the battle isn't going to prove anything."

"On the contrary," said Nathan Pendragon, "I intend to produce an academic paper on the subject. Possibly even a monograph for one of the

University Presses. I'm going to show from our experiences exactly how the battle was fought, and prove that it was fought in that very field. Call it reconstruction archaeology, if you like."

It was at this point that it was explained to me that Nathan was actually Professor Nathan Pendragon, a world-renowned expert in military history from one of our most prestigious universities. Not quite world-renowned enough for me to have heard of him; but then, military history was never my specialist subject.

"And you're not going to tell Mr. and Mrs. Farmer this?"

"Not just yet," said Nathan, smiling.

Chapter 4

Farmers in Arms

It was ironic that the couple who now owned the field were surnamed Farmer, because they were not, and never had been, involved in farming. They ran a company which manufactured and sold gaming machines, and they had done rather well out of it, thank you very much. The house they lived in dated back to the fifteenth century in parts, and had once been the manor house of the neighbouring village of Oldwick. Indulging my most deep-seated prejudices, I reflected that they probably didn't appreciate their good fortune.

Trevor Farmer was a portly, white-haired man in his late fifties, who wore loud suits and a lot of gold jewellery. His wife, Valerie, who couldn't have been many years younger, was a "natural" blonde, always immaculately coiffured and made up. She wore loud suits and a lot of gold jewellery.

I'd seen them around town, and not taken a lot of notice. Live and let live, that tends to be my motto. You don't have much choice when you work in a museum, or any other job involving contact with the general public.

Not that the Farmers were regular visitors to the museum. I seem to recall she came in once, to ask if we would display a notice about the Hunt Ball. Fortunately, I wasn't the one who had to refuse her. I referred her to Mrs. Challoner for permission to use the notice board, and made sure I caught every word of their subsequent conversation.

Mrs. Challoner was the District Librarian and my boss (her official title was "Head of Library and Museum Services"), and as luck would have it, she was on the spot at the time. Mrs. C pointed out—rather more tactfully than I would have done in her place—that fox hunting was a controversial activity, and we would undoubtedly receive complaints if we displayed such an advertisement, either in the museum or in the library next door.

Valerie Farmer was indignant. Didn't we realise, she asked, the nuisance caused by foxes, what pests they were, and what a good turn the hunting fraternity was doing the community by keeping the fox population under control? That was irrelevant, replied Mrs. Challoner. Whatever our personal feelings might be on the matter, we had to be careful not to offend anyone.

Seeing that Mrs. Farmer was not disposed to give in gracefully, Mrs. Challoner added that, if we displayed an advertisement for the Hunt Ball, we would be obliged to give equal space to any advertisements the hunt saboteurs might wish to put up on the notice board, giving publicity to their own activities. She was sure Mrs. Farmer wouldn't like *that* to happen. When she put it that way, there wasn't much more that could be said on the matter.

After she'd gone, Mrs. Challoner and I exchanged views on "the kind of woman who gives women a bad name." I admired Mrs. C. She was getting on a bit, quite close to retirement, but she didn't take things easy, as so many people would have done in her position. She was one of that generation of women who've had to fight hard for everything they've achieved in the way of a career. She had been made to prove herself two or three times over, and she wasn't going to free-wheel it down the hill towards her sixtieth birthday. I took my hat off to her, or I would have if I ever wore one.

When we went back to the museum after lunch on that Saturday, Herbert decided to share with the rest of us the details of the discussion he'd had earlier with Joe and Nathan. The visitors had left, to drive back to their respective homes and begin putting their plans into operation. At least, that was what Herbert thought. I happened to know that they were still in the bar of the Lamb & Flag.

My uneaten sandwiches didn't go to waste. I was about to throw them in the bin, when Jonathan exclaimed, "I'll have those if you don't want them!" We both went over to Herbert, to hear what he had to say. Though it was late spring, it was a cold afternoon, and the six of us huddled around the electric fan heater to discuss the issue.

The Farmers, Herbert explained, had put in a completely new application, a detailed one, not just a rehash of the old application for outline planning permission put in by the previous owners of the field. That made it more serious, as they were obviously intending to carry out the development themselves, in the foreseeable future. Though the application had been turned down once, it had a better chance of getting through this time. Planning applications have a habit of being re-submitted until they are successful. Councillors know when they're banging their heads against a brick wall.

The Farmers had toned it down a bit—forty houses instead of the original fifty—but anyone could see it was the thin end of the wedge. If one field could be developed, so could the next (which the Farmers also happened to own), and before we knew it, there would be a continuous ribbon of development stretching from St Catherine's to the golf club two miles away (of which the Farmers happened to be leading lights).

Speaking for myself, I didn't want the field to be developed. It wasn't that I minded new houses being built in the village, or more people coming to live there. No, it was the way any development was carried out that was critical. Individual architect-designed homes, with appropriate access, preferably built on land that had no agricultural potential, were okay as far as I was concerned; but a new estate of forty or fifty "executive homes" would kill the atmosphere and charm of Barrow End. I bitterly resented the idea of anyone attempting to force it on us; yet, as one individual, I wouldn't have had the nerve to try and do anything about it.

Moreover, I had a double interest in the application. Being responsible for the District Museum, it was my job to take note of any local sites of historic significance, and that included protecting them where necessary. The question was, where did my professional responsibilities end and my personal interest begin? I could be confident that I wouldn't be asked to comment on the planning application in a professional capacity—the County Archaeologist would do that. This left me with the problem of whether to involve myself in the matter at all, which might lay me open to an accusation of using my position for personal advantage. For once I was glad that I hadn't been appointed Curator over Herbert's head.

Herbert was dead set against the development simply because of his obsession with the field and its history, but, whatever his motives, I was grateful for the energy he was prepared to put into the task of opposing the planning application. He had already decided that he and I were going to knock on every door in Barrow End and make sure that every resident sent a letter to the Borough Engineer on the subject. I didn't relish the idea of door-stepping so many individuals, and would certainly not have considered doing it without his support. You could never be sure how they were going to take it.

WHEN I GOT HOME, later that afternoon, my landlady, Mrs. Murphy, was looking out for me.

"Hello, me darlin'!" she called, as I came into the hall. This was my cue to enter her downstairs flat, through the open door, and go into the little front room where she had been sitting by the window, awaiting my return.

She couldn't get out much, and she liked to hear what I had been doing. I didn't mind. We got on surprisingly well. Mrs. Murphy was an elderly and rather deaf Irish widow who had lived in Barrow End for donkey's years and was reluctant to leave it. Her late husband had worked on one of the local farms, and they had grown attached to the area. Their daughter, Bridget Dunn, was one of the part-time assistants in the public library, which was housed in the same building as the museum.

A few weeks after taking up my new post, in the market town four miles up the main road from Barrow End, I had still been living in a bed-and-breakfast establishment, constantly on the lookout for suitable permanent accommodation. Then Bridget Dunn, having heard of my unsettled state, drew my attention to a golden opportunity. She referred to it as "my mother's flat," which threw me at first. Contrary to my initial impression, she didn't mean that she wanted me to share a flat with her mother. Thankfully, she was talking about a vacant flat in her mother's house.

Bridget lived in town, and couldn't visit her mother every day. On the surface, it may have seemed as though Mrs. Murphy would have been better off in sheltered housing, but she didn't want to start making new friends and getting used to a new environment at her age. Uneasy about the idea of her mother living alone, Bridget had persuaded her to have the house converted into two flats.

Mrs. Murphy herself retained the ground floor, but the upper floor and the attic were available for renting to a suitable person or persons. The idea was that a second occupant would "keep an eye" on the old lady—on a strictly informal basis—and let Bridget know of any problems that might arise. Although Barrow End, as I've already testified, was a peaceful place, Mrs. Murphy sometimes got a little nervous at night, and it would be nice for her just to have the reassurance of "company" in the house.

From the moment Bridget Dunn set eyes on me, I must have seemed an ideal candidate. Museum staff aren't exactly renowned for holding wild parties, and I was no young chick just out of college either. I was in my mid-twenties, quiet and apparently responsible, just the kind of person who could be relied upon not to cause any trouble. (Little did she know.) Being female and alone, I would make good company for Mrs. Murphy. For myself, I admit I hesitated at the thought of taking on responsibility—on however informal a basis—for an elderly lady I didn't even know; but I changed my mind as soon as I saw the flat.

The building work and re-decoration had only recently been completed, and the rooms were spacious and comfortably furnished with the basics. There was room for the few sticks of furniture I possessed, but all the essential items were already there, and I wouldn't have any problems with maintenance. I had a living room and a fair-sized kitchen that looked out onto the street. At the back of the house was my bedroom, with the small but adequate bathroom next to it. Up a little spiral staircase from the landing was the attic, which I had the option of using as an additional bedroom if I had visitors. (I hadn't acquired an extra bed to put in it, but it was nice to know that it was there.) The rent was reasonable, too.

Mrs. Murphy and I had hit it off immediately, despite the age difference. My new landlady was a dear old thing, with a wicked sense of humour. Though it was sometimes exhausting having to repeat things because of her deafness, she was a lot of fun, and in many ways as entertaining a companion as anyone of my own age could have been. But I always had the option of retreating to my upstairs flat when I wanted a bit of peace and quiet. The arrangement worked so well that, as an incentive for me to remain, my rent had never been increased.

Moreover, I had fallen in love with the village straight away. There wasn't much to it. It basically consisted of one narrow winding street with a little shop-cum-post-office in the middle of it (open four and a half days a week). Since I had a car, I did most of my shopping—and Mrs. Murphy's—at the nearest supermarket, on the edge of town, but for the elderly and housebound, the village shop was a godsend. Next to it was the pub, the Dog and Drake.

Down a little lane, behind the street, less than a hundred yards from my new home, was St Catherine's Church. There had once been a Methodist chapel in the village as well, but the congregation had dwindled to the extent that it had closed a few years before and been converted into a domestic residence. Personally, I wouldn't care for the idea of living in a former place of worship, but the man who had moved in wasn't a churchgoer of any variety, and it didn't bother him. At least he didn't have a graveyard in his garden.

At the far end of the street was a small primary school, which served two other villages besides Barrow End. When I was getting ready for work in the mornings, having my breakfast in the kitchen, I would hear the school bus trundle along, bringing the children from the outlying farms, and see its red roof going past the window. A few minutes later, next door's brood would be heard running down the street to make it to morning assembly. They sounded so *happy* at the idea of going to school that, however unpleasant the weather, these morning sounds never failed to cheer me up.

Next to the school was the Village Hall. This was used for all kinds of activities, ranging from the Senior Citizens' Club to the Senior Citizens' coffee morning. No, I'm only joking. There actually was a sort of a social life in the village. There were keep fit classes, Women's Institute meetings, and even a youth club, on a Friday night.

As in so many rural villages, most of the social activity in Barrow End revolved around the church, and that placed a lot of responsibility on the shoulders of the vicar and his wife. The vicarage wasn't in Barrow End at all, but in its sister village, Oldwick, which fell within the same parish. Bob and Jennifer Eaton, the couple who ran the sub post office across the road from my flat, also acted as caretakers for St Catherine's, holding the keys in the unlikely event of a visitor from outside the district wanting to have a look round. It was a shame more people didn't come to see it, because it was—and still is—rather a pretty church. The building is mostly medieval, but with a few Tudor and Victorian additions and some superb stained glass.

When I told Mrs. Murphy that the planning application had been revived, she had plenty to say on the subject. She had, after all, lived in the village for more than fifty years, and had seen numerous changes, few of which she regarded as beneficial. This particular development, however, was beyond the pale.

"Why don't they build the new houses in the town?" she asked, rhetorically. "Why do they want to go and spoil the lovely green fields?" Mrs. Murphy's view of rural life was somewhat romanticised, but the basic sentiment didn't jar with my own.

Herbert was making the assumption that most of the village residents would, like Mrs. Murphy, be opposed to the development, but there were bound to be a few who were actively in favour of it. They might cite the opportunities for improving facilities in the village, or the boost to local employment, as convincing arguments.

Then there would be those who didn't want the development, but couldn't be bothered to say so. The kind of people who complain about things after the event, but when you try to get them to make a stand, they whine that it's hopeless, that you can't do anything to stop "them," that you're wasting your time trying. You can ask such people, you can beg them, you can give them a standard letter of objection and an envelope and a first class stamp, but you can't make them sign it and shove it in the nearest pillar box.

Under the circumstances, I was very encouraged by the response we got when we did begin to call on the residents. Almost all those we actually caught at home said that they thought the development was a horrendous idea and they would definitely be at the public meeting, which Herbert was arranging to hold in the Village Hall. He intended to use this as the platform to launch an action committee, with the aim of ensuring that "his" field would be spared from development in perpetuity. Until then, he and his chosen few—me included—soldiered on without official sanction, but with every hope of success.

Herbert had recruited the entire museum staff to help with the campaign. In addition, he had been busy buttering up Jennifer Eaton, who ran the village store and sub post office. Jennifer's husband, Bob, was a freelance computer consultant, and Herbert hoped his expertise might also prove useful. Though the Eatons might have benefited, in purely business terms, from forty new families in the village, they were quite happy with their existing turnover and saw no advantage in ruining their environment just so that they could spend every weekend in the shop.

Herbert had also been on to the village school and had the headmaster's tacit support for his campaign. The children were greatly excited at the prospect of seeing a "battle" fought on the field. It would liven up their History lessons for the whole term. Next door's kids showed me a collage they were already in the process of making, complete with three-dimensional Roundhead helmets composed of milk bottle tops, perched on the heads of macaroni-faced soldiers.

Mrs. Murphy, when she learned of Herbert's scheme for fighting the planning application, was vociferous in support of our cause. She couldn't get about very easily, but she did her best to help the campaign by displaying a poster in her front window, and offering to let us hold committee meetings in her front room. Her motive for this kind offer was of course that it would allow her to eavesdrop on all our discussions and carry off news of the latest developments to the Senior Citizens' weekly social sessions.

We tactfully declined, and agreed to hold our meetings in a room at the Village Hall, which we were able to have free of charge. The Village Hall Committee, of which Jennifer Eaton happened to be secretary and Bob Eaton chairman, had come to this decision without much difficulty.

Chapter 5
Velvet Vale

The battlefield and its surrounding area had, for some reason, become known as Velvet Vale. Personally, I thought it sounded faintly obscene, like one of those coy euphemisms the Victorians used to use to refer to their private parts. (Perhaps it was something to do with the number of courting couples who had pre-empted connubial bliss in the long grass.) However, since everyone else called it Velvet Vale, I had no choice but to go along with it.

The group we had formed to fight the planning application therefore became known as the Velvet Vale Action Committee. Herbert had, inevitably, been elected acting Chairman, despite the fact that he didn't live in the village. It made sense, in view of his position as the expert on the battlefield theory, but I suggested that it wouldn't be wise of him to make too much play of the fact that he was Curator of the District Museum. My fear was that it might draw attention to my own dilemma. Herbert had many useful contacts, including some councillors he announced he was expecting to support our cause. Unfortunately, the first name he mentioned didn't receive universal approval.

Edward Long was the Conservative councillor for the ward in which Herbert and Doris lived. I've never understood much about Tory politics, least of all what would make someone go in for it in the first place, and Councillor Long had done nothing to make me revise my general opinion of those who do. He was a tall, lugubrious-looking man in his forties. I knew him by sight, only because I'd seen him sometimes in the Town Hall on a Saturday. Some of the councillors held "surgeries" in the upstairs rooms, where individual electors could queue up to voice their concerns about such issues as council tax, education, library services and, of course, planning applications; and he was a regular at these, I'll say that for him.

When Herbert named Councillor Long, several of the committee groaned out loud.

"Not that dry old stick," said Jennifer Eaton. Her husband, Bob, grunted agreement.

"Dry old stick or not," said Herbert, "he could be a very useful man to have on our side."

"Not much chance of that," commented Jonathan cynically. "He does the accounts for Mr. and Mrs. Farmer. I've seen him out with them, in the golf club."

Councillor Long's day job was as an accountant. His practice was in the High Street, just a step away from the Town Hall.

I didn't make much of Jonathan's remark—I was just wondering what he had been doing in the golf club himself. I was about to ask him, when Herbert replied.

"I'm sure Edward Long won't take sides in this matter. He's a man of great integrity."

Why are people of great integrity always so boring, I wondered? Is it because we all need a touch of vice to brighten up our dull lives? Or is it just that we don't like to see someone who's better at self-discipline than we are ourselves?

Ignoring the views of the rest of the committee, Herbert said he would speak to Councillor Long about the matter when he saw him at the mayoral inauguration in a few days' time.

The vicar of our parish, Peter Markham, had also spoken up on Long's behalf.

"Councillor Long's a decent sort," he added. "He audited the accounts for the church restoration fund, and he never charged us for it. He did it as a favour to Hilary." Hilary was the vicar's wife.

Peter had little choice but to be present at the first meeting of the unofficial action committee, but he made it clear after a few minutes that he intended to play no active part in the campaign. This took everyone by surprise. The church was directly affected by the proposed development.

The parish had spent the last couple of years trying to raise a hundred thousand pounds to carry out essential repair and restoration work to the fabric of the building, not to mention the landscaping of the churchyard. The housing development, if it went ahead, would ruin the prospect of St Catherine's from the surrounding countryside, and would be bound to increase noise and the danger of vandalism. The only possible benefit was that it might bring a few younger families into the village who could reasonably be expected to swell the fast-diminishing regular congregation.

But Peter was adamant. "I don't think it would be appropriate for me to join the committee," he said. "As vicar, I really ought to remain impartial."

There was a moment's silence as we all digested what he had said. I was the first to speak.

"I don't think you're going to have much choice in the matter, Peter," I said. "The church is directly concerned in this. Surely the diocese will oppose the planning permission? It did last time."

"Maybe so," he conceded, "but I still feel I should keep out of it personally. Don't forget, the Farmers are my parishioners. That doesn't mean I can't come to your meetings, if you invite me. And of course, Hilary is a free agent."

Hilary Markham looked uncomfortable.

"I'll be glad to be of service in any way I can," she said, unprompted but not looking at all as if she meant it.

I was still studying Peter's face. It wasn't true, except in the most literal sense, that the Farmers were his parishioners, any more than it could have been said that they were patrons of the District Museum. They may have come to church on the odd occasion—not St Catherine's, but the village church at Oldwick for which Peter was also responsible—but they had certainly never been confirmed or taken communion. It was always possible that they were Methodists or Baptists or something, but I somehow doubted it.

Peter didn't usually mince words. I was remembering a conversation that had taken place between the two of us, about six months earlier, in the kitchen of my flat.

"My wife's not going to die," he had said, "and I'm not going to divorce her."

He had avoided my eyes in order to complete his speech.

"And," he concluded, "I'm not going to commit adultery with you again."

It was the word "adultery" that took me by surprise. Not that I hadn't been aware of what we were doing. Nor had I underestimated its significance for Peter, as a clergyman. It was simply that *I* didn't feel like an adulteress. I couldn't associate myself with that woman in the Bible, the one Jesus had saved from being stoned by the mob. It wasn't because I knew that the moral climate had changed and other women did this kind of thing all the time. It was because I felt innocent.

Peter was the only man I'd ever slept with. I'd gone to bed with him for the first time in my third year at college. (It had taken him the previous two years to persuade me.)

There had been no question, at that time, of his going in for the church. Frankly, it was the last thing in the world I could have imagined him doing. When he had first announced his intention of becoming a vicar, after we had both taken our degrees and our romance—if that was what you'd call it—was all but over, my first reaction had been to laugh. It had seemed so unlikely that I was convinced it was some kind of joke.

When my smile had faded, and Peter had reiterated gently that yes, he really did mean it, he felt a calling, and this was what he was going to do with his life, my next reaction was to feel relief. Had we still been an item, I would have faced the prospect of life as a vicar's wife, and that definitely was *not* what I wanted to do.

Don't get me wrong. As a Christian, I have immense respect for vicars' wives. They have a much harder job than vicars, in my opinion, and because they are mere women, no one recognises the extent of their contribution. No way was I going to let myself in for that.

There had been a gap of six years between my split with Peter and our reunion, when he became vicar of our parish. The parish comprised not only Barrow End, but the neighbouring village of Oldwick and the hamlet of Newick. Oldwick had its own church, St Margaret's, and services were held alternately there and at St Catherine's.

It had been a real shock to my system when Peter had turned up in this part of the world, shortly after I did. It seemed that Hilary, the woman he had met and married in the meantime, was originally from this area, and this fact had made them ideal incumbents. To me, it still seemed like yesterday that Peter and I had parted to embark on our diverging careers. Six years isn't that long; but it had taken less than that for Peter's marriage to go sour.

It wasn't *that* obvious to the untrained eye. But I knew Peter Markham, I knew all his little whims and characteristics, and I could tell, almost immediately, that he was unhappily married.

It took a few months for him to confide in me. We began on a friendly footing, old acquaintances meeting again, the intensity of our previous relationship unknown to the rest of the congregation. We described ourselves simply as "old college friends."

Peter got into the habit of calling in to see me at the museum, and before long he started calling on me at home, on my rare days off. Vicars have a lot of spare hours in the daytime, and calling on parishioners is all in the line of duty. Then he started calling at the flat on the occasional evening, sometimes with Hilary but more often without. The danger was immediately obvious, but it didn't seem to stop him. I think part of it was sheer curiosity. He wanted to see if he could still work the old magic. Being a vicar, he seemed to feel, had emasculated him.

No doubt he had plenty of opportunities for flirtation—or something more fulfilling—if that was what he wanted. But that wouldn't have been enough for Peter. He was probably afraid of attracting the attentions of the wrong sort of woman—middle-aged or elderly, spinsters or widows, or at best young mothers. There were plenty of such women around, willing to devote their time to church activities like flower-arranging and coffee mornings. They admired Peter, they idolised him, and they would have done anything for him.

Peter, however, was looking for someone who could appreciate him as a man, not just as a vicar. Admittedly, like his other potential admirers, I was one of his congregation. It had always seemed strange to me that I could so easily separate the Peter I saw in the pulpit, Sunday after Sunday, from the one I knew in private—the one who still told dirty jokes and put his hand on my arm as we both laughed at the punch line. But he continued to think of me as that inexperienced, "normal" girl he had known at university, and he was glad of the chance to slip back in time to his carefree student days.

It had been almost inevitable that we would renew our relationship. I hadn't been serious about anyone since Peter. He was still in my system, and he wouldn't get out until I had taken one last shot at reconciliation.

You must understand that I didn't set out to seduce him. Nothing could have been further from my mind, that evening he finally confessed what a disaster his marriage had been and we tumbled into bed together. I think he was kidding himself that it was all right to let himself go when he was with me, because I was Rose and in some weird way I had belonged to him ever since he had deflowered me at the age of twenty-one. That was certainly how I felt. But I don't think it was really me he wanted, it was just his freedom. He was kicking against the traces.

There was nothing wrong with Hilary, nothing that I could see. On the contrary, she was the ideal vicar's wife. She wasn't, perhaps, a very interesting woman. She was a bit scatty, and she was a few years older than Peter; but all in all, she was exactly the kind of wife he needed.

After it happened, I didn't see anything of Peter for a couple of weeks. The conversation I've been describing happened at our next meeting.

I was cut to the quick by his words. He seemed to be implying that I had built up some kind of fantasy around him, that I was expecting him to leave Hilary or hoping that something would happen to her, so that I could have him back and, presumably, take over the role of chief organiser for all parish social events. And I will admit, it had crossed my mind that it would have been awfully convenient if Hilary hadn't been around. Peter hadn't lost his appeal for me.

But I'm not stupid, and I wasn't stupid then. For a vicar to leave his wife for another woman would be professional suicide. And just think how unpopular the other woman would be. All things considered, you could say I'd had another narrow escape.

Chapter 6

The Mayor-Making

It was the week of the mayor-making ceremony. I had never been to this event before, but it happened that on this occasion I'd received an official invitation. You would think, with all the local government reorganisation that's gone on in the past thirty years, this kind of pageantry would have died out. On the contrary, perhaps *because* of all the change, people cling to it more and more as the years pass.

Cynics would say it's got something to do with the fact that everyone enjoys a freebie, and I was no exception to this rule. My enthusiasm for attending the ceremony definitely underwent a sudden growth spurt when I discovered that we would all get a free tea afterwards. There had to be some advantage in being an employee of the local authority. It certainly wasn't the salary.

I enjoyed the ceremony more than I had expected to. I arrived with Mrs. Challoner, whose name had come out of the hat along with my own, it being the turn of the library and museum service to be represented at this year's inauguration. Herbert and Doris also had invitations to the mayor-making. It was a perk that had originally resulted from their role in the local Historical Society. They were old hands, having attended every annual ceremony since 1977.

I had been impressed by the printed invitations bearing the Borough coat of arms, and I was even more impressed by the printed programmes we were all given, to acquaint us with the order of events. As an innocent newcomer to these occasions, I hadn't expected it to be so complicated as to require instructions. However, when I glanced over the contents, I saw that it was actually all quite straightforward. The programme was more of a souvenir than anything.

Mrs. Challoner and I bumped into Herbert and Doris as we were making our way into the Town Hall about a quarter of an hour before the ceremony was due to start. We had come straight over from our respective workplaces. In my case, this had meant closing the museum early and changing my clothes in the Ladies toilet before leaving the building, because I never wore a suit for my day-to-day duties. I had bought one specially, a plum-coloured outfit with a mandarin collar that would come in handy for meetings and the like. I didn't bother with a hat.

Doris was wearing an elaborate feathered creation on her head, something she had obviously bought for a wedding some time in the distant past and was trying to get her money's worth from. The four of us made our way upstairs to the gallery from which we would view the ceremony. In the ground floor lobby, big round tables were in the process of being laid out in readiness for the tea that would follow.

As we edged our way along the row to which we were directed, with me leading the way, I glanced up and recognised the four people who were already sitting there. The man standing up as he saw me enter was none other than Peter Markham. Next to him, nearest to us, was his wife, Hilary, and on his other side were Trevor and Valerie Farmer.

Embarrassment ruled as far as I was concerned, but Peter showed no sign of awkwardness as he greeted us.

I smiled briefly and insincerely at the Farmers as I said hello to Peter and sat down next to Hilary. I had been taken aback at the sight of my ex-lover, but it seemed the attendance was drawn from a much wider cross-section of the community than I had anticipated.

My embarrassment showed in my opening remark.

"I wasn't expecting to see you here," I said.

Luckily, Hilary wasn't the kind of person to take offence easily.

"The Deputy Mayor invited us," she explained. "Councillor Jones-Davies. He's from Oldwick, he goes to St Margaret's—sometimes. He's asked Peter to be the Mayor's Chaplain next year, when he takes over as Mayor."

Looking more closely at the programme, I noticed that the mayoral inauguration ceremony had distinctly religious overtones, including prayers and hymns. It could have been rather a mournful occasion, but was enlivened by the presence, not only of friends all around me, but also of the new Mayor's grandchildren in the front row of the gallery. As the chain of office was being placed around his neck, a little girl, aged no more than three, shouted out, "Grandpa, Grandpa, what a pretty necklace!"

Most of the audience laughed discreetly at this outburst, and the Mayor himself smiled and acknowledged his granddaughter with a little wave. Afterwards, the incoming Mayor's Chaplain made his contribution in the form of a prayer and a brief "thought for the day," and I noted that he was wearing a very natty outfit, including a biretta on his head.

"Is Peter going to have to be got up like that, next year?" I whispered to Hilary.

"I hope not!" she answered. "I have enough trouble keeping his everyday cassocks washed and ironed."

I glanced past her and observed that Peter wasn't wearing a cassock today. He only wore them for services. It had given me a shock the first time I'd seen him in one, looking so different from the student I remembered in jeans and bomber jacket. Even the dog collar on its own still made me look twice. I had to force myself not to remember that he'd been wearing it that evening at my flat, six months earlier.

After the ceremony was over, we trooped down the stairs for tea. There were no reserved places for this part of the proceedings. Mrs. Challoner made her apologies and went to sit with some senior colleagues from the Leisure Department, while Herbert, Doris, Peter, Hilary and I found a spare table. The Farmers, who had barely acknowledged us when we came in, made no attempt to sit with us, but took pains to choose a table as far away as possible, right over the other side of the room. Already they had recognised us as enemies.

Also seated at their table, I noted, was Councillor Long. The councillors had all been togged out in their ridiculous official robes for the ceremony, but without exception they had discarded them when they sat down to tea.

So Jonathan had been right about the Farmers' close relationship with the councillor Herbert thought was going to be on our side. I wanted to point them out to Herbert, to make it clear to him that it wasn't going to be as easy as he thought; but we were separated by Doris and the Markhams, and I couldn't easily draw his attention to what was going on at the other side of the room.

"Look at that," I muttered to Hilary, who was sitting next to me again. "Herbert must be mad if he can't see what's going on in front of his eyes. Jonathan was right about the Farmers and Councillor Long."

Hilary looked up. After considering the evidence for a few moments, she said, "No, I don't think so, Rose. It looks quite innocent to me." She continued eating. Typical of Hilary, I thought ruefully. She could never see the bad side of anyone.

The tea was marvellous, and I could understand Hilary wanting to concentrate on her cake. As well as sandwiches and vol-au-vents, they had those tiny individual glazed fruit tarts and little cream eclairs. I tried not to make a pig of myself in such exalted company. By this time, we had been joined at the table by Councillor Jones-Davies—a jolly Welshman—and his wife.

I had promised Mrs. Challoner that I would be going back to the museum to pick up my things before the usual closing time, and would lock up the library as well. When I got up to leave, I paused by Herbert and reminded him that he had a few matters to raise with the councillors. I left it up to him to decide whether to waste time on the double-dealing Councillor Long or to try and get the Deputy Mayor on our side. As I stood there by Herbert's chair, I saw Long glance over at us a couple of times. Valerie Farmer was whispering something in his ear.

Chapter 7

Know Your Enemy!

The one major decision to be made when the temporary committee finally got together was the date on which we would call the public meeting in the Village Hall. Herbert had appointed Jonathan as "Press Officer" for the campaign, on the grounds that he had a friend who was a cub reporter on the local weekly paper, the grandiosely-titled "County Examiner." He could, at least, make sure that the meeting was well-publicised. His chum would also come along and watch the proceedings. If they were exciting enough, they might make page five of next week's edition.

Herbert had been insistent that we should invite to the meeting not only the two councillors who represented the ward containing Barrow End on the local authority, but also Councillor Long. There was some controversy over this, but as it happened it was just as well, because Councillor Long was the only one of the three who turned up to the meeting. The local authority could consider itself under-represented, since there were about eighty members of the public present.

To my surprise, the Re-enactment Society had turned out in full force. Most of them were wearing all the appropriate gear. I ought to make a brief digression here, to explain what that entailed.

In real life, there wasn't as much difference as you might think between the two sides in the English Civil War; and this was reflected in the appearance of the members of the Society. The Roundheads didn't have particularly short hair, and the Royalists didn't have particularly long hair. Many of the men were wearing what they call "buff coats," which are big leather jobs—rather nice, actually—and under them they had tunics or jackets in various colours and those lovely white shirts with the big lace-edged collars and loose sleeves. Yum yum. Some of them were wearing or carrying helmets, some just plain hats, in styles ranging from woolly caps to the feathered style with the big brim that you see in old paintings.

On their legs they wore breeches in dull colours, the least interesting component of the ensemble (unless you like looking at men's legs). Some had leather boots on, some were wearing old-fashioned shoes and coloured socks, with or without gaiters, denoting their regiment. One or two were carrying swords, but more as a fashion accessory than anything else. Then there were a couple of girls, dressed as "musketeers," which basically meant doing without the buff coat.

It was no joke, I learned, this musket business. They came in two varieties, matchlock and flintlock, and you had to get a proper shotgun licence in order to own one. The musketeers weren't allowed to use bullets—sorry, I mean balls—for safety reasons, but they did use something called black powder, which made a satisfying bang when set off. I wouldn't have thought they could do much damage, given that they weren't using real ammunition. However, Joe told me about one quite nasty accident when some twit had left the ramrod in the barrel of his musket and had nearly been prosecuted after it sailed through the air and embedded itself in someone else's leg. It was probably just as well to leave it to the girls.

In short, there were no hard and fast rules about costume. Although the Society re-fought battles from the whole eight years of the Civil War, uniforms changed a lot during that time, and you could hardly expect them all to turn up dressed for exactly the right period. As it happened, this was completely appropriate for the Battle of Barrow End, which had taken place very early in the War, at a time when both armies still consisted of a rag-bag of newly-recruited zealots and any uniform at all was a matter of luck.

Joe told me that the Society enjoyed occasions like this, when they could show off to the general public, but that wasn't the only reason so many local members had turned up. They were excited by the possibility of having located an authentic Civil War battleground in their home area, and they were ready to show their enthusiasm for its preservation.

Nathan Pendragon was their unquestioned leader. I saw Molly perk up when he walked in, and I told her to stick with me if she wanted an introduction to this charismatic figure. Professor Pendragon didn't need to appear in costume to make an impression. He was wearing an old tweed jacket with leather patches on the elbows, but he still stood out.

Joe introduced me to some of his other friends, including Wally, a gangling youth with a winning smile and a nice line in breastplates. He wasn't actually wearing armour, I hasten to add. He'd just brought it along to show to anyone who expressed an interest. This was typical of the kind of people the Society members were, always looking for a chance to pass on their enthusiasm to new converts. Wally showed me a lobster which he claimed to have made himself. He was just about to explain the construction process to me in detail when, fortunately, the meeting was called to order.

The guest councillor was seated on the platform, alongside Jennifer Eaton, who was our acting secretary, and Herbert himself. The rest of the committee members had to sit or stand along the walls of the hall. I was standing immediately in front of the serving hatch which linked the main hall with the kitchen, but there were a few stragglers who'd arrived late and I had been forced to move forward to make room for them to stand behind me.

We—the committee, that is—had all been introduced to Edward Long individually beforehand, but there had been none of the smiles and pleasantries that the electorate can normally expect from their representatives on such occasions. Someone got out of bed on the wrong side this morning, I thought, as he grudgingly shook hands with one or two of us. He didn't even seem to recognise Jonathan and me, despite having seen us so often at the Town Hall. Such anti-social behaviour was a mistake on Long's part, because it aroused the committee's immediate hostility.

Being the only local authority representative present, Councillor Long could expect to be pilloried, but I didn't have much sympathy for him. It was a pity Herbert hadn't had more forethought, or perhaps he wouldn't have invited him to address the meeting.

When he got up to make his little speech, putting on his glasses to read from prepared notes, you'd have thought he was addressing the House of Lords.

The rest of the audience might have been less prejudiced against Councillor Long than Jonathan and I were, but it didn't do him any good once he began to speak. He started off by saying that, whilst he could understand the concerns of village residents, he was disappointed that we had chosen to form an independent action committee. The correct thing to do, he insisted, would have been to approach our representatives individually and allow the Planning Committee to come to an objective decision on the suitability or otherwise of the planned development. As you can imagine, that got everyone's backs up.

"Ha bloody ha," somebody shouted from the back of the hall.

Long peered short-sightedly into the crowd. "I beg your pardon?" he said. "Did someone wish to make a comment?"

One of my neighbours, a retired colonel, took up the gauntlet. He stood up in the middle of the rows of seated listeners.

"How can we be certain that the decision will be made objectively, Councillor? In my experience, the term 'objective' is itself extremely subjective."

That's got *you*, I thought.

"The Planning Committee will be in full possession of the facts concerning the application," came Long's po-faced reply. "*All* the facts, including any information that may be outside the public domain."

"Do you mean to say, Councillor, that you might not share all the information influencing your decision with those directly affected by this planned development?" countered the Colonel.

"I can't comment on that at present," said Long, beginning to look flustered. "We haven't yet had the Borough Engineer's report. There may or may not be other factors that I don't know about."

Good on you, Colonel, I thought, gloating over the councillor's discomfiture. The Colonel sat down, looking dissatisfied but ready to give the rest of the audience a turn at baiting Councillor Long.

Another neighbour, a woman, asked about the environmental impact of the development. Long replied that the Borough Council would carry out an assessment and report back on that subject as soon as possible. It hadn't been done on the previous occasion, when the application was only for outline planning permission, because they'd never got that far.

"What about English Heritage?" asked someone else, without getting up. For my part, I was determined to keep out of this discussion.

"We've asked them to comment on the historic importance, or otherwise, of this site," replied the councillor.

I saw Herbert bristle with annoyance. It was the phrase, "or otherwise," that had got to him. To be fair to Councillor Long, it was nothing more than a speech mannerism.

Then Nathan Pendragon stood up. "Professor Nathan Pendragon," he announced, before coming out with his question. A respectful silence descended. "I don't wish to sound condescending, but how can we be sure that the full historic significance of this site is appreciated by the powers that be, when it has only recently been identified as a probable Civil War battleground and no archaeological investigation has yet been carried out to prove its authenticity?"

Long looked uncomfortable again. "You will have to rely on your local authority representatives to take that into account," he said, nervously.

There were rumblings of discontent from all around the hall.

"But this isn't a matter that only affects the local community," Nathan protested. "I don't live in this village. I'm here because I'm concerned about the preservation of an important historic site, possibly one of the few battlefields in Britain that hasn't been damaged by subsequent development. You can't ignore that aspect."

"There are many factors to be considered," said Long, determined not to commit himself.

Nathan sat down. Another of my neighbours immediately jumped to his feet. He was red in the face, clearly angered by Long's impassiveness in the face of opposition.

"We don't trust the council," he said, almost shouting. "They're not interested in our welfare. They're only interested in the financial implications. They're afraid to turn down planning applications in case there's an appeal and it costs them money. That's why none of them have turned up here this evening!"

There were murmurs of agreement, increasing in volume.

"That's unfair," Long began, but the rest of his words were drowned out by the general hubbub.

Herbert got to his feet. "Can we have some order, please?" he shouted. The noise died away gradually. "Councillor," he said, turning to Mr. Long again, "please go on."

"You're all jumping to conclusions," said Councillor Long, coldly. He had the nerve to look around him at the members of the action committee for support. He didn't get any. I glared at him, but it had no effect. He didn't even bother to glare back.

It was quite obvious what he was up to. These people were his cronies. He met them at the golf club, Valerie Farmer and her husband, he even made his professional services available to them; and somehow he expected us to believe that he was impartial.

"Who *is* that guy?" Joe whispered. He had arrived at the last minute, and I hadn't even noticed that he was standing so close to me. "I don't think I like him."

"You're not alone," I whispered back, loudly.

I looked over at Peter Markham, and noticed that he was scowling at us. From where he was sitting, he couldn't actually tell us to shut up, but he clearly wished that we would. Hilary also looked rather annoyed.

"What's up with her?" Joe asked, observing her expression.

I shrugged my shoulders. The meeting was still going on around us.

"There are many other factors to be considered," continued Councillor Long, pompously. "This development will..."

His next words were rendered inaudible by a loud clattering from somewhere behind me. Glancing over my shoulder, I saw that Joe's friend, Wally, was the culprit.

"Sorry, mate!" he exclaimed. "Dropped me lobster!"

Guffaws broke out all around. There was no doubt that the interruption had been deliberate. Long turned scarlet with suppressed anger. By the time anyone was ready to listen to him again, he had completely lost the thread of his argument.

"At any rate," he concluded feebly, "you can all have your say in writing. All objections received by the Planning Committee will be given full consideration."

"Too bloody right," someone muttered, over to my left.

That was, effectively, the end of the public meeting. A couple of people started to try and buttonhole Councillor Long before he left the hall, but he evaded them and made his way out to the car park. The only person he stopped to talk to on his way out was Hilary Markham.

"Disappointed in Edward Long," remarked Herbert, when most of the crowd had dispersed and we were trying to shoo out the remainder, prior to locking up the Village Hall. "Thought he'd have shown us more support."

"I did warn you," said Jonathan. "Local government corruption. It's everywhere."

"Anyway, Herbert," I added, "I thought you wanted him to be impartial."

Herbert looked confused. "Well, naturally I do," he said. "But if he looks impartially at the arguments for and against, he's bound to be on our side."

"Anyone fancy a pint?" asked Joe, with a laugh, addressing the group that surrounded him. At the same time, he put his arm around me.

It must have been the busiest night the Dog and Drake had had since New Year. The bar was full of Royalists and Roundheads, whilst in the lounge, the honest villagers of Barrow End assembled loyally to talk over the evening's entertainment.

I was torn between the two groups, but decided to stay with Joe. One or two of my friends did the same. Jonathan stood alongside me, talking to Wally and Nathan.

"That councillor guy!" said Joe again. "What a toffee-nosed ponce!"

Jonathan nodded, laughing. "Edward Long. He's an accountant."

There were more guffaws.

"Lives with his mother," Jonathan added. "And a right old bag she is!"

It had never occurred to me before that Councillor Long's mother was Mrs. Long. *The* Mrs. Long.

She came into our building regularly, ostensibly to use the library. Sometimes I felt that her only purpose in doing so was to cause as much aggravation as possible to the staff. I certainly don't believe she ever read a book. Bridget had told me all about her various little foibles. Whatever her presenting problem, Mrs. Long seldom spent less than twenty minutes at the issue desk, haranguing whoever happened to be on duty at the time.

If the museum was open, she would often call in on us as well. Our opening hours were very limited, and during the week, I was usually the only person there. As far as Mrs. Long was concerned, that put me at her disposal.

Sometimes she would have a specific query which she felt I, in my official capacity, "should be able to answer" without even needing to consult the reference sources available. It would usually be something way out—the date of an obscure or mythical event, or some historical detail which could be obtained from the appropriate volume only after hours of searching.

I never found out what Mrs. Long did with the information when she got it. Sometimes I thought she was only asking for it as a test of the effectiveness of the museum service. The effectiveness *or otherwise*, as her son might have put it. It certainly wouldn't have occurred to her that she could have done the looking up herself. As far as she was concerned, that was what *I* was there for. Apparently, she did exactly the same kind of thing in the library, but they were usually too busy to devote much time to her. In me, she had a captive audience.

What rankled most of all, however, was the complete absence of any expression of thanks when her query had been successfully completed. If, on the other hand, I failed to find the answer she wanted (which was not necessarily the same thing as the correct answer) she would hold forth for another fifteen minutes or so on various topics, ranging from the inefficiency of the public sector to the curse of socialism. That should have been a clue, I now realised, to the fact that the ultra right-wing councillor for Springview ward was her son.

Mrs. Long was a pain in the neck, but then, so were lots of other little old ladies, *and* little old men. (Admission to the museum was free for senior citizens.) We made allowances for them. Francesca, one of the part-time library assistants, had actually managed to make me feel, temporarily, sorry for Mrs. Long by telling me her family history. The sympathy I felt hadn't lasted beyond her next visit; but the story came back to me now.

It seemed that Mrs. Long had three sons. When the youngest was aged about fourteen, her husband—Mr. Long, whatever his first name was—had committed suicide, by hanging himself in the garden shed. Francesca wasn't sure of the full sordid details—motive, and all that—but it was still a terrible story. Being charitable, I assumed that the experience had contributed to making Mrs. Long the way she was.

Chapter 8
Lady and the Tramp

Jonathan had picked a bad time to draw my attention to the relationship between Mrs. Long and our supposedly helpful local councillor, because she chose the very next morning to make one of her forays into the museum.

"I want a book," she declared, "and they won't let me have it!"

This complaint was made, at top volume, as she entered through the swing doors, and I wasn't exactly sure to whom it was addressed—me or the library staff. When I looked up, there she was, standing by the reception desk, chins a-quiver, turning a look of extreme aggression in my direction as I approached.

The museum wasn't meant to be open to the public that day, but I had been working in a back room, accessioning some bronze hand-axes that a local metal detectorist had donated, and I had unwisely left the door unlocked. There was a big sign on it, saying "CLOSED," but I suppose Mrs. Long had caught sight of me inside and assumed that the sign had been put there on purpose to inconvenience her.

It wouldn't do to make too much fuss over the matter. The same kind of thing had happened once or twice before and I had normally allowed the people in, even if we weren't officially open.

"I'm sorry?" I said, when I had recovered from the shock of seeing Mrs. Long. "What was it that you wanted?"

"I went into the library to get a book," she shrieked. "A book on history! And they won't let me have it! Can't you tell them?"

Though this was really nothing to do with me, I felt I owed it to Mrs. Challoner to try and get to the bottom of the matter. It was just my luck that Mrs. C was at a meeting with the County Librarian, and had left the library under the supervision of Bridget Dunn, my landlady's daughter.

When I entered the library, with Mrs. Long in tow, I saw immediately that Bridget had her hands full with the issue desk. Four would-be borrowers were waiting in line to have their books stamped, and an elderly man was hovering around, obviously waiting for her to be free to answer a query.

"Excuse me," he asked politely, waylaying me as I approached the desk, "can you tell me where the toilet is?"

Having directed him into the Town Hall, I moved on, went behind the desk, and stood next to Bridget. Glancing over to where I had left Mrs. Long, I saw to my regret that she was still there.

"What's with her?" I asked quietly, nodding in the direction of my nemesis. "She says you're stopping her from having a book."

"The old lady was trying to take out a reference book on loan," Bridget explained, disposing of one borrower and moving on to the next. She gestured to a thick volume that lay beside her on the desk. "I couldn't let her have it if I wanted to. It hasn't got a bar code or a label."

I picked up the book and looked at it. It was Debrett's Peerage. Taking it in my hands, I returned to the entrance where she still stood, evidently expecting some result.

"I'm sorry, Mrs. Long," I said, trying desperately to maintain a show of politeness as I repeated what Bridget had already told her. "This is a reference book, and it can't go out of the library."

"But I need to use it!" she protested. "I need to refer to it."

"You can use it here, Mrs. Long," I said. "If you'd just like to sit down at one of the tables, you can use it for as long as you like."

"That's no use to me!" she said belligerently. "I may need it for more than one day."

"Then I'm afraid you'll have to keep coming back," I said sharply. I was already on a short fuse, still annoyed over her son's performance at the public meeting.

"That's no use to me!" she repeated. "This is not good enough!"

I averted my eyes. "Perhaps there's an older edition in the stock room," I said. I wouldn't have made the offer if I hadn't been fairly sure that there was, because I know how annoying it is to be kept waiting by someone who turns out to be unable to help.

"No," she said immediately. "That's no good! I must have the most up-to-date information. It's essential."

At this point, I must own up to a basic flaw in my personality. Had Mrs. Long been more ready to compromise, I would probably have broken all the rules and told Bridget to let her take the book out on a short loan. After all, how many people in our town were ever likely to want to consult Debrett's Peerage? But Mrs. Long was determined not to accommodate me, so I was not going to accommodate her.

"I'm afraid it's the best we can do," I said. "What was it you wanted to look up, anyway?" I hoped that if I changed the subject, it might deflect her wrath.

"I'm writing my family history," she exclaimed, importantly, "and I think I'm related to a Duke!"

How I prevented myself from laughing, I'll never know. I had long suspected that Mrs. Long was gaga. Resisting the urge to ask which Duke, I reiterated that we couldn't allow the book out on loan, but I was sure that the entry she was interested in wouldn't have changed since the old edition, and I was prepared to double-check this on her behalf.

She was still insistent on being allowed to take the book out. We had reached an impasse.

"How about photocopying the page?" I suggested helpfully, failing to observe the warning gestures Bridget was making in the background.

The photocopier had broken down five minutes earlier, and Bridget, being on her own, hadn't had time to ring the service agent.

Mrs. Long blew a gasket when Bridget told her. "This is a disgrace!" she wailed. "The council spends millions on this service..." —I knew *that* wasn't true— "and the best you can do is try and fob me off with a photocopy, and then it turns out it's not working anyway! Why haven't you had it mended?"

"I really am sorry, Mrs. Long," I said. "Apparently it's only just happened, and I didn't know. We haven't had a chance to call the repair man yet. Look, I tell you what we'll do." I was thinking quickly. "As soon as the machine's fixed, we'll make you a copy of the page you want—free of charge—and it'll be waiting for you next time you come in."

"But I need it now!" She sounded for all the world like a child who's had its toy taken away.

"All right, then, I'll get it done this afternoon, and I'll drop it off at your house." Anything for a quiet life, I thought. If necessary, I was prepared to go to the printers across the road, get it copied there, and pay for it myself. There was only one thing I wasn't going to back down on, and that was the principle of allowing a reference book out on loan.

"You're not fit to be in charge of this library!" said Mrs. Long. "I'm going to write to my MP about this!"

After she'd swung out through the exit, Bridget and I looked at each other and shrugged helplessly.

"Don't worry, Rose," said Bridget, stifling a giggle now that it was all over. "It's not the first time she's threatened to do that. Nothing ever comes of it." I wasn't worried anyway, because I *wasn't* qualified to be in charge of the library.

As I went back into the museum to finish my cup of cold coffee, I couldn't help wondering why Mrs. Long hadn't threatened to complain about me to her son, the haughty Councillor Long. It would have given me great pleasure to tell *him* where to get off.

When Mrs. Challoner came back from her meeting, and I told her about the episode, she merely laughed.

"Poor old soul," she said, surprising me. "It must be terrible to have such an empty life that you can't find anything better to do with your time than go round annoying other people."

I wished I could be as philosophical. But incidents like this were two a penny in the public library. That very afternoon, a tramp came in and started creating mayhem. I had to lock myself into the museum, and we soon forgot all about Mrs. Long.

I was toying with an idea I'd had. When Herbert and I went round the householders of Barrow End, trying to rustle up opposition to the planning application, we had met some people who were clearly nervous of the idea of opposing the Farmers. Whether because they knew them and feared their influence, or simply because they disliked personal confrontation, it was difficult to persuade them that action was necessary and that every individual could make a difference.

We needed a way of encouraging these people to lend their support to the campaign without exposing themselves to any retribution from the Farmers. We also needed a way that people from outside the village could express support for the general principle of preserving the green belt.

I thought of a petition. I'd seen the tactic used effectively before, on one occasion, in an industrial dispute at a university where I'd worked in the conservation lab. The students were quite definitely on the side of the striking college staff, but they didn't dare *not* attend college because they had exams coming up. We stood on the doors, picketing, not trying to prevent anyone from coming in, but asking them to sign a petition in support of our cause—which was to oppose cutbacks in the local education budget. It worked well, enabling those not immediately involved in the dispute to show their sympathies without having to put themselves at risk. It might work for the Velvet Vale campaign, I thought.

We would have to word the petition carefully. Instead of a statement deploring this particular planning application, it would have to be a blanket statement opposing any development at all that might damage the environment and detract from the historic significance of the village.

Peter Markham came into the museum later that day. He was quite a regular library user, and often came into the building to change Hilary's books as well as his own. She liked romances, he preferred thrillers and historical whodunnits. Usually he would choose a day when the museum was open, and call in to see me at the same time. Despite everything that had passed between us, he still seemed to enjoy my company.

I was still a little irked with Peter, because of his refusal to participate in the Velvet Vale campaign. While we were chatting, I mentioned my idea of a petition, and he was surprisingly positive. He said he thought it a less confrontational approach than we had hitherto been taking. This was encouraging, coming from someone who fell into the same category as the floating voters of Barrow End, and I resolved to raise the matter with Herbert as soon as possible.

Chapter 9

Divide and Rule

On the Tuesday of the following week, I went down to the sub post office to pick up my copy of the latest edition of the "County Examiner."

"Did you hear, Rosemary, that we've made the front page?" said Jennifer Eaton, handing it across the counter. "There's even a photograph!"

The rather gritty black-and-white photograph was of Herbert and Doris standing by a gate next to a field—which might have been anywhere in Britain—pointing vaguely into the middle distance. "Local historians Herbert and Doris Dyson are fighting to preserve this medieval battlefield," it said. So much for accuracy. Herbert would be frustrated, but to most of the "Examiner's" readers, terms like "medieval" and "seventeenth century" were undoubtedly interchangeable.

It was the headline that was designed to catch the attention, though. "COUNCILLOR TAKES FLAK AT PUBLIC MEETING," it yelled; and underneath, in smaller letters, "DISTINGUISHED MILITARY HISTORIAN SPEAKS OUT."

The "distinguished military historian" referred to was of course Professor Nathan Pendragon, not Herbert Dyson. The events surrounding the public meeting were reported with reasonable accuracy in the paragraphs that followed, which took up half the front page of the newspaper. The author of the report, presumably Jonathan's friend, seemed to derive particular glee from dwelling on Councillor Long's humiliation at the hands of the great British public. Perhaps they had crossed swords on a previous occasion, if you'll forgive the military allusion.

"If we keep this up, the campaign's bound to succeed," said Herbert over the phone, when he called me that evening to check that I'd seen the paper. He was being over-optimistic, I thought.

"There's still a long way to go," I warned. "Everybody will have forgotten this article in a few days' time."

"Of course, of course," he conceded. "But the fight goes on."

Jonathan had less success in his attempts to interest our other local paper, the regional "Evening News," in the issue of the planning application. They had already published a letter from Herbert, giving details of the campaign against the development of Velvet Vale, but more than that they refused to do, and they didn't pick up on the story of the public meeting. It was only much later that we discovered the reason for their reticence.

The "County Examiner" didn't give much information about the "distinguished military historian" who had joined our campaign, but I had already found out quite a lot about Nathan Pendragon from Joe, and more would emerge in due course.

Nathan had spent some time in the British army. That was one suspicion of mine which had proved correct. His reasons for joining up had not been the usual ones, though.

Right from the beginning, Nathan Pendragon saw himself as a military historian. With that end in mind, he set himself on the path that would lead to his chosen career. Since his schooldays, he'd spent his leisure time re-playing major battles and military campaigns on an eight by five foot board, using miniature figures or cardboard counters. He had been an only child, with indulgent, intellectual parents. If he couldn't find a like-minded opponent, he had played against himself.

His hobby didn't quite tell him everything he wanted to know. So, after Cambridge, where (naturally) he picked up a double first, Nathan had gone on to Sandhurst, thence into the army. In parallel with a successful career as an officer, he'd built up a reputation as an expert on various aspects of military history, and in his spare time, he'd earned a Master's degree.

He went from the army straight to Oxford for his D Phil, and never looked back. The oddest thing of all about Nathan, though, was that he detested the whole concept of war. I didn't find out all these facts at once. They revealed themselves gradually, as time went on. In the beginning, Nathan was as much of an enigma to me as he was to everyone else.

Another thing I had been right about was Molly. She started to get silly over Nathan. I could be unkind and say that she was already silly;

but her lack of intellectual prowess wasn't the result of an innate lack of intelligence. It was more to do with belonging to a generation of women who were never encouraged to stretch themselves—the same generation as Mrs. Challoner, who had turned out so differently.

Molly would turn up anywhere she thought Nathan might be. She did her utmost to conceal her feelings. Like most people who have themselves suffered from unrequited love in their lives, I was able to recognise the signs quite easily.

Molly hardly ever referred to Nathan by name; she always called him "that military man," or, when forced, "the Professor." Yet she went out of her way to introduce him into the conversation at every possible opportunity. "Will the Professor be there?" she would ask me, in advance of any event connected with the Velvet Vale campaign. If I answered in the affirmative, she would immediately volunteer her services for tea-making or any other menial duty, despite the tenuous nature of her links with the campaign.

It made me want to cry. Molly was not in any way suited to Nathan, and he never looked twice at her. To be uncharitable, her inability to converse on his intellectual level might not have mattered, had she been more physically attractive. But Molly was an ordinary-looking woman. I could sympathise with her on that score, because I was so average-looking myself. No one had ever noticed me across a crowded room, as far as I knew.

It was on a Wednesday morning that Valerie Farmer came into the museum to see me.

As I've said before, I had only ever noticed her in the building on one previous occasion, and I was confident that she neither knew my name nor had the faintest idea of my involvement with the Action Committee. Wrong, on both counts.

When she walked in through the door, my heart sank. I could tell by the purposeful way she was looking around that she was a woman with a mission, and my sixth sense told me it had something to do with me. I was alone in the museum as usual, and I would have been only too pleased for Mrs. Long, or some other little old lady, to make a nuisance of herself at that particular moment.

But the odds were against me. All was quiet, and there was nothing to prevent Valerie Farmer from speaking to me.

"Are you Rosemary Gardner?" she asked, not quite aggressively but not exactly as though she was going to invite me round to tea.

"Yes," I replied timidly. I was feeling a little fragile that morning. My biorhythms must have been at their lowest ebb. "Can I help you?"

"You're on this so-called Action Committee, aren't you?"

"Yes, that's right." I could hardly deny it.

"You want to stop us getting planning permission for our field."

"It's nothing personal," I protested. "We're just concerned about the preservation of the green belt, and we're also hoping for a proper investigation into the site of the Battle of Barrow End."

"There's no evidence for that, you know," she said, talking to me as though I was mentally retarded. "It's just some wild idea that old man has got into his head. I'm sure there's nothing in it." It didn't seem to occur to her that I might know as much about the subject as she did.

"If you mean Mr. Dyson," I said, my hackles rising, "he's very knowledgeable about military history, and he's got the support of a well-known academic. He's explained the reasons for his theory to me several times, and I certainly think there are grounds for further investigation." I was exaggerating, of course. "I've been personally involved in many archaeological excavations, and I feel obliged to lend support to the campaign, as long as there's any possibility that the site could be historically significant."

That seemed to throw her for a minute. "Oh," she said, back-pedalling quickly. "Well, if there's any truth in it, naturally we wouldn't want to stand in the way of a proper excavation. But that'll be decided when the planning application comes up before the Council. There's no need for all this nonsense about committees and petitions. And holding public meetings! I heard you gave poor old Edward Long a terrible time. He told me all about it."

"I can't take the credit for that personally," I remarked, certain that she wouldn't recognise the sarcasm.

"In any case," she forged on, "you don't even know the detail of the application yet. You haven't even seen the plans."

"It's more the principle than the detail that concerns us," I said.

"Principles are all very well, but they don't put bread and butter on the table," she commented obscurely.

I made no attempt to respond to that, but the brief silence didn't bother her.

"Anyway," she said, "you can tell the rest of your committee that they'll have a pleasant surprise when they see the actual plans. They'll see that the development has been very *sympathetically* designed."

Not by you, then, obviously, I thought.

"Although," she continued, "I gather half the committee don't even live round here."

"*I* live in Barrow End," I said. "I live just across the road from St Catherine's."

"Ah, well," she said, "in that case, we can at least have a sensible conversation about it, woman to woman."

I practised a technique I'd once been taught on a training course. Apparently, if you lean backwards— as far as you can without falling over— it stops you from feeling anger. Luckily, I was sitting down.

"Look, Mrs. Farmer," I said, "I don't mean to be rude, but I'm only one member of the committee..."

"Self-appointed committee," she interrupted.

"Not exactly," I corrected. "We were elected at the public meeting, by the village residents."

"I heard that the meeting was more or less taken over by a bunch of yobs from that Re-enactment Society or whatever you call it."

"The Re-enactment Society were there, certainly. But the bulk of the audience was made up of village residents, and they were the ones who voted the committee into office."

"My husband and I weren't invited to the meeting."

"No one was specifically invited to the meeting, Mrs. Farmer." I was hoping she wouldn't prolong the argument much longer, because I didn't think I could continue to keep my cool, however far back I leaned. "It was a public meeting, and it was given a lot of publicity. You could have come along if you had wanted. No one would have complained. On the contrary..."

"Oh, I've had enough of this!" she said, suddenly showing her less reasonable side. "You can tell your ridiculous committee that they're mistaken if they think they can intimidate us or drive us away."

"No one's trying to do that, Mrs. Farmer..."

"We won't be browbeaten. The planning application will go through, you'll see, and it'll be the best possible thing for the village. We've got a lot of friends on the Council, and we'll have the last laugh."

As I watched the toss of her dyed blonde hair and her bright blue suit retreating through the double doors, it occurred to me that she had been very unwise to say a thing like that. She had as good as implied that she and her husband were going to use their personal influence with certain councillors to get the application passed by the Planning Committee. Mr. Long wouldn't have been too pleased if he had heard her implying that she had him in her pocket—even if it was true.

ALMOST AS SOON as I arrived home that evening, my doorbell rang. It was my neighbour, Colonel Montgomery. He had been looking out for me, he said, to warn me to be on the lookout for "that Farmer woman."

"Too late, I'm afraid, Colonel," I replied. "She came into the museum today, and harassed me for ten minutes or so. I think she was trying the personal approach in the hope that she could charm me out of opposing the planning application. But she turned quite nasty when I didn't give in straight away."

"She came around to my place too," he said. "Loony woman. I told her, 'I'm not going to be intimidated by a jumped-up little madam like you. Who do you think you are?' I said. I told her, 'I've lived in this village nearly all my life. I'm not going to stand back and see it ruined.'"

I could just imagine him saying those words. Everyone in the village called Colonel Montgomery "Monty" behind his back, although, as far as anyone knew, he was not related to the Field Marshal.

Much as I enjoyed the thought, it seemed to me that it wasn't a good idea to get into a slanging match with the Farmers. It would only add credence to their argument that everyone was prejudiced against them, and that wouldn't help our case.

"I wonder who else has had a visit from Mrs. Farmer?" I asked the Colonel.

It wasn't long before I found out. Half an hour later, the telephone rang, and Herbert told me that Valerie Farmer had turned up at his house when he and Doris were busy in the garden. By my calculations, she must have gone there straight from the museum. Herbert himself had barely given her the time of day, but Doris, he said, had been very upset by the confrontation, and had gone inside to avoid being on the receiving end of Mrs. Farmer's insults.

We compared notes, and found that the basic thrust of her argument had been similar, although she presumably hadn't spoken to Herbert in the contemptuous tone she had used when referring to him in front of me. She had even told him that she had spoken to me and I had been "very reasonable about it." This was such an obvious ploy to divide the committee that we laughed together about it.

"I knew you wouldn't have given in to her that easily, Rose," said Herbert complacently, as he put the phone down.

It worried me, all the same. I wondered how many people would be able to resist Valerie Farmer with as little difficulty as Herbert, the Colonel and I had done.

After that little episode, I found it strange that the Farmers didn't revoke the permission they had provisionally given for their field to be used by the Re-enactment Society — especially bearing in mind that the Action Committee was effectively made up of the same people who were organising the battle (the "yobs," as Valerie Farmer called them). I had nightmares about Trevor and Valerie continuing to string us along, then spitefully pulling out of the agreement at the last possible minute, leaving us out of pocket. That wouldn't have helped the progress of their planning application, of course; but by the time the battle was due to be held, the Planning Committee might well have already met to consider the application and it might all be over bar the shouting.

I was reckoning without Professor Nathan Pendragon, who had taken upon himself the responsibility for all direct communication with the Farmers. Nathan had true panache, and a breathtaking charm that could be turned on and off at will, like a tap. For someone like Valerie Farmer, the prospect of having a handsome, single man, not much younger than herself, prepared to flatter her ego was too much of a temptation, and she yielded easily to his blandishments. She was fully aware that Nathan was amongst the most vociferous of her opponents, but she simply couldn't resist him. And she wasn't alone.

Chapter 10

Dress Rehearsal

The second meeting of the Velvet Vale Action Committee took place the following night at the Village Hall. There were eight of us altogether: Herbert and Doris, Jonathan, Hilary Markham, Colonel Montgomery, Jennifer Eaton from the post office, me — and Joe Payne.

Joe had been elected to the committee only because it was thought a good idea to have someone from the Re-enactment Society involved and because Nathan Pendragon—who would obviously have been first choice—didn't have time to do it. Needless to say, it was me who suggested Joe as an alternative.

Joe didn't seem to mind the prospect of driving fifty miles every time we called a meeting. The Eatons had generously offered him a bed for the night whenever he wanted one. So far, he hadn't dropped any hints about sleeping over at my place, worse luck, but I held out some hope that his motivation for continuing to be actively involved was rather more than an interest in military history.

Herbert called the meeting to order at precisely seven o'clock, even though Hilary Markham didn't arrive till ten past.

"Terribly sorry I'm late!" she exclaimed, rushing in breathlessly. She slapped her shopping bag down in the centre of the table, scattering Herbert's carefully ordered papers to the four winds. The bag bulged with a variety of items, which did not include any shopping, but did include an umbrella, some knitting, and a jar of home-made greengage jam, which she took out immediately and put down in front of Jonathan.

"There you are!" she said. "I told you I'd get you some of Mrs. Fearns' jam. That'll put hairs on your chest!" She laughed heartily.

Jonathan looked embarrassed, and spirited the jar away, under the table.

Herbert said nothing, but made a poor job of concealing his annoyance. He cleared his throat.

"Can we get on with the business of the meeting, now that we're all here?"

Up to that point, we had been preoccupied with administrative detail.

"First of all, I want to thank Jonathan for the excellent press coverage of the public meeting. Well done, Jonathan!" Herbert paused, as if he expected everyone to applaud, but we failed to meet his expectation.

"Now," he went on, "to the subject of the proposed re-enactment of the Battle of Barrow End. I've obtained a provisional date of August the twentieth. Will that be all right with everyone?"

"That's a Sunday, isn't it?" remarked Colonel Montgomery.

"Correct!" said Herbert. "I've checked with the vicar, and he's no objection. The thing is, the museum is open all day on a Saturday, and I feel strongly that the volunteers should all have the opportunity to attend this important occasion, so there was nothing for it but to arrange it for a Sunday. In any case, if we'd wanted to have it on a Saturday, we'd have had to wait until next summer, because the Society is fully booked up for this season."

This shouldn't have come as a surprise to me, having seen the enthusiasm with which Joe and his friends went about their dressing up.

Others reacted as I did, however, on finding that the Action Committee had acquired the additional responsibility of organising the re-enactment. At first we were nervous about the financial outlay involved. We simply didn't realise, at that point, that the Re-enactment Society had the potential to earn huge amounts of money for charity in spectator fees, in addition to its obvious role in promoting the study of military history. Colonel Montgomery put everyone's minds at rest by offering to underwrite the exercise to the tune of a thousand pounds, which would help cover the hire of portable toilets, a public address system, and so forth.

The date Herbert had suggested was acceptable to all of us. At that time of year, the museum would normally have opened for a couple of hours on a Sunday, but those of us who worked there agreed that it could be closed for that particular Sunday afternoon. We all felt we would prefer any tourists who might be in the area to attend the battle rather than hanging aimlessly around town. If we held the battle on a day when the shops were closed, it would give them more of an incentive.

The more we thought about it, the more we realised that people from further afield might be tempted to make a special trip to Barrow End for such an extraordinary spectacle. Accordingly, our plans for the day's events started to blossom and became more ambitious.

The next step was to marshal the opposition to the Farmers' planning application. To this end, Herbert suggested inviting the local councillors—the ones who hadn't turned up to the public meeting—to attend our next committee meeting, so that we could bend their ears on the subject and attempt to convince them of the undesirability of the proposed development.

We went on to discuss Valerie Farmer and her attempts to subjugate the individual members of the Action Committee. The only people who hadn't had a direct approach from her, it seemed, were Joe—who lived an hour's drive away—and Hilary. I was surprised that Hilary had escaped Mrs. Farmer's attention, because I would have thought she was the softest possible target. But at the time, I thought nothing of it.

JOE INVITED HIMSELF back to my flat after the meeting. I had expected him to suggest a drink in the Dog and Drake, which seemed to have become his local recently, but for once he seemed quite happy to drink coffee instead of beer. All evening he'd been touting around a plastic carrier bag, which looked quite out of place in his possession.

"Aren't you going to ask me what's in here?" he teased, while I was filling the kettle.

"Okay then. What's in there?" I obliged.

"Your costume."

I thought he was joking, until I looked at him properly and saw that he was completely in earnest.

"What are you talking about?" I asked.

"I've got you a costume, for wearing when we go anywhere with the Re-enactment Society."

My heart leapt. Did Joe really mean "we"? As in, "us"? As in, "me and Joe"?

"Who said I'm going anywhere with the Re-enactment Society?" I challenged, grabbing the bag from him and excitedly pulling out its contents.

"Don't you want to see us in action?" He pretended to be hurt. "We'll be doing a battle nearly every weekend from June onwards."

"It's a nice thought," I said, "and I'd really like to. But you know very well I work almost every weekend. It's our busiest time in the museum. And I've already made arrangements to go away for my summer holidays, to stay with my friend in Scotland. I don't suppose you do battles north of the border, do you?" I remained hopeful.

"I daresay we do, from time to time," he said, looking slightly down in the mouth. "But it's a bit far for me to travel, in the normal way of things."

I wasn't really listening by now. I was holding out in front of me a set of seventeenth-century women's clothing, consisting of a long, voluminous skirt in a forest green, a lace-up bodice in matching material, and a cotton blouse with ties at the neck.

"May as well try them on, eh?" said Joe, observing the covetousness in my face. "Can't do any harm."

"Where did you get them?" I asked.

"Borrowed them from a girl I know," he said, uninformatively. "She's about the same size as you, I reckon. Go on, put them on right now."

Needing no encouragement, I took the clothes into the bedroom. When I had finished changing, and looked at myself in the mirror, I saw an authentic—and rather fetching—seventeenth-century maiden. The period really suited me. At least, I thought so. But what would Joe think?

I opened the door and went out, shyly, into the living room, where he was sitting with his coffee. He jumped up, almost spilling it, and came over to me.

"Cor!" he said, unsuitably, fingering the neat bow on the front of my bodice as though he was thinking about undoing it. "What a comely wench! But you've forgotten the hat."

He felt around in the plastic bag, which I'd thought empty, and pulled out one of those little bonnets, like the Puritan maid used to wear on the food labels. Unable to see myself in the mirror as I put it on, I had to take Joe's word for it that I looked "fantastic." All the same, it would have been tempting fate to ask him what they wore in the way of underwear.

Joe urged me to come along to a battle with him the following weekend. It grieved me to have to turn him down, but Mrs. Challoner was away on holiday and there was no way I could get out of being at the museum on Saturday. The Sunday was my mother's birthday, and I had promised to visit her, so there was no chance that I could attend Sunday's action replay either. Yes, the Society normally staged two battles every weekend in the summer, one on each afternoon, to make the travelling worth while for everyone. It meant camping, usually in a field supplied by whatever landowner was sponsoring the battle.

Joe told me he was travelling up to the next battle on the Friday evening. If I had agreed to go with him, I would have had to make some kind of sleeping arrangements. He didn't specifically ask me to share his tent, but I assumed that was what was on offer. He might have meant it as a come-on, but, with Joe, it could equally well have involved nothing beyond the platonic. He was never easy to fathom, in that respect.

I couldn't help wondering about him and Georgie, why they had split up. It was easy to see how living with Joe might become difficult. On the surface, he was light-hearted and easy-going, but how much of that can you take when you're the one who's got to do the washing and ironing and dust behind the radiators? Shall we just say that I could imagine how Georgie might have felt after a couple of years with Joe?

Having established in a previous conversation that they hadn't got round to having children during their brief union, I was determined not to ask him for any further details. Apart from not wanting to cause him unnecessary pain—and there must have been some pain involved, good as Joe was at disguising it—I didn't want him to see that I was interested. He might have guessed how I had felt about him, when we were younger, but he was never going to hear it from me.

As to what I felt about him now, that was another story altogether.

Chapter II

Proceeding as Planned

We hadn't yet seen the detailed plans of the proposed development, but Herbert rang me at work, a couple of days later, to say that they were now available. The Council was supposed to be making arrangements for them to be viewed by those concerned, but that would involve nothing more helpful than notifying the public that they were available in the Planning Office at the Town Hall. We had permission to put them on display in the museum or the library, but we needed to get them to a bigger audience, as a matter of urgency.

Herbert had approached his friend, Councillor Long, to ask if the plans could be made more accessible to the villagers of Barrow End, many of whom were elderly and unable to make the journey into town easily. Long, for once, appeared sympathetic, and agreed to ensure that the plans were put on display in the Village Hall one evening, to give everyone an opportunity to examine them and have the detail explained.

I trooped down to the Hall with everyone else to see the plans. It wasn't exactly a meeting, because there were no speeches and there was no debate; but afterwards, I felt it had been a turning point in our campaign. The atmosphere in the hall was one of impending doom, rather than hostility to the councillors present. That's *councillors*, in the plural.

With Edward Long on this occasion was another of the Conservative faction from the Borough Council, a woman named Sally Maplethorpe. She was about the same age as Valerie Farmer, whom she resembled in many respects, except that Sally Maplethorpe's hair was dyed an unconvincing raven black where Valerie's was dyed blonde. Mr. Long had obviously felt he needed reinforcements before he could face the villagers of Barrow End again. I saw him looking nervously at me out of the corner of his eye, and I turned away to talk to someone else. He must have been expecting us to give him another hard time, but he really needn't have worried on that score.

Not many lay people know how to read an architect's plans, and I freely admit that I'm no different. It's extremely difficult to make the mental connection between what you see on paper and what you can expect to see when you look out of your living room window. There were several different ways of looking at what was in front of us: there were side elevations and front elevations and artists' impressions, as well as the basic ground plan.

One thing was certain, however. These houses were going to be little boxes, with virtually no gardens.

The clever part was that the Farmers weren't proposing to build on the whole field at once. No, they could claim to have been sensitive to local concerns, by leaving half the area undeveloped and consequently available for "recreational use." What this really meant, as everybody knew, was that they would wait a couple of years, allowing children to play on the grass in the meantime, then fill it up with more houses and possibly a fish and chip shop.

It was bad enough even without that prospect. I couldn't quite go along with Colonel Montgomery's view that this kind of development would attract "the wrong sort of people" to the village, because I couldn't blame anyone for wanting to come and live at Barrow End. But the prospect of so many people arriving all at once did concern me.

I'm older and wiser today than I was on that evening. In those days, I'd never owned a house myself, and I couldn't have put my reservations about the development into words, as I now can. People are thoughtless when buying houses, especially if they're buying for the first time. A young couple starting out in life will take the best opportunity that presents itself for getting a foot on the bottom rung of the housing ladder. As a result, they generally end up paying over the odds for a tiny, badly-designed house which answers to the literal definition of "detached" but is in actual fact crammed right up against another, almost identical, dwelling.

Some people don't mind this. Some even enjoy the feeling of intimacy it engenders. Others quickly come to regard their new house as a stepping stone on the way to affording the house they really want, and feel no real attachment to it or pride in it.

Despite these misgivings, I was trying hard to keep an open mind. Surely some of the newcomers would want to be active in the community, to attend church, to send their children to the village school and youth club? From that point of view, might it not be a good thing?

But after looking at the plans, I found myself filled with gloom and despondency. Seeing it in black and white made the development somehow seem inevitable, and I began to wonder why we were bothering with opposition at all. The Farmers had gone much further than the previous would-be developer, presenting their detailed plans without going through the interim stage of obtaining outline planning permission. They were clearly hoping to present us with a fait accompli.

Though the Farmers themselves were not present, Edward Long was once again coming across as their advocate, rather than the impartial representative he should have been. When people asked him questions, he gave what I felt were evasive answers, and refused to give a view on the desirability *or otherwise* of the development. I heard him getting drawn into an argument with the Colonel, and deliberately absented myself. I went to the pub instead.

THE MEMBERS of the Re-enactment Society who had already visited Barrow End had taken to the Dog and Drake in a big way. They liked a pub they could effectively take over, where the landlord was welcoming and the locals didn't look down their noses. A mixed group of Royalists and Roundheads soon took to visiting regularly, usually on a Wednesday or Thursday night, and sometimes holding meetings in a corner of the bar—planning their next engagement, or whatever.

Occasionally, they would get a bit boisterous, especially if Nathan Pendragon wasn't there to keep them under control, but things never got so out of hand that a discreet shushing from the landlord couldn't maintain the equilibrium. He was more than happy for the Society to adopt his pub as a temporary headquarters, as long as they didn't drive away the regular customers.

Instead of going straight into the pub, I took a quick stroll down the lane alongside it, towards the church. When I got to the lych gate, I leaned against the churchyard wall and stood for a few moments looking over into Velvet Vale, trying to visualise its future as a housing estate. It was a glorious evening, with pink and yellow clouds surrounding the setting sun. There were three ponies in the field, peacefully grazing—one black-and-white, one brown and one a sort of creamy golden colour. It must be so nice, I thought, not to have any cares in the world, not to be bothered what field your owner puts you in as long as there's plenty of grass. What else matters? I left them to it and wandered back up the lane, in despair.

I had hoped to see Joe in the pub that evening, mainly because I knew he would be able to cheer me up when I came in looking dejected. There had only ever been an outside chance of his turning up, despite the phone calls Herbert had made to ensure that everyone knew it was the night for the viewing of the plans in the Village Hall. Joe had already told me that he didn't expect to be able to make it. Energetic and dedicated as he was, he couldn't come all the way to Barrow End every time something came up. He had other commitments. I wondered, but didn't dare ask, whether they included a woman.

Nathan had come in Joe's place, and he and I entered the bar of the Dog and Drake together on that evening. Wally was there too, but no other members of the Society. Nathan hadn't said much when we were looking at the plans, simply because, for him, they were irrelevant. He wanted the development stopped, regardless of what it looked like or the effect it might have on the village. He wanted the precious battlefield preserved, and he would continue to fight his corner whether or not he got any support from the villagers.

The better I got to know Nathan Pendragon, the more I realised what an extraordinary man he was. He was unmarried, though openly heterosexual, and devoted his entire time and energy to what he called "the search for historical truth." Once he had launched into a discussion of this subject and had whipped up his avid listeners into a frenzy of enthusiasm, he would throw them into confusion by playing devil's advocate, echoing Pontius Pilate's question, "What is truth?" and following it up with such posers as "What is history and why study it?"

You have to remember that many of Nathan's followers weren't university graduates like Joe and myself, but boys from working-class backgrounds, with limited horizons, who had joined the Society with the sole aim of spending their weekends drinking, womanising, and practising violence on one another. They didn't even realise that they were getting a free education at the same time. Nathan was teaching them to think for themselves, and that was how he got his kicks. He didn't stop being a teacher just because he wasn't being paid to do it. It was his life.

I think he found the Society members more of a challenge than his university students. When young people were obliged to come to his lectures, they had no option but to listen politely and agree with what he said. Nathan preferred them to listen to him from choice.

On this particular evening, he soon got into discussion with a group of locals on the subject of the historical evidence for the Battle of Barrow End. They were pub regulars, who hadn't bothered to come to the Village Hall to see the plans for the housing development, but who were now prepared to listen attentively to Nathan's mini-dissertation on the preservation of the battlefield because he automatically commanded their respect. One or two of the younger ones were even toying with the idea of joining the Re-enactment Society.

As I left the pub to go back to the flat, Nathan Pendragon was just launching into a spirited account of the charge of the Royalist cavalry.

"On a dismal October day in 1642...," he began.

Chapter 12

Fireworks!

It was a pity Nathan didn't have time to be directly involved with the Velvet Vale Action Committee, because meetings chaired by Herbert Dyson quickly became a very tedious business. Herbert did everything absolutely by the book, and that made for a lot of time spent on talking and not much spent on doing.

He had, however, persuaded the two ward councillors—the ones who had failed to turn up to the public meeting and hadn't even bothered to come along when the plans were on display—to attend our next committee meeting. In honour of this occasion, Nathan agreed to come along too. It was accepted that his personal prestige would add fuel to our argument, and he was much more articulate in defence of Velvet Vale than the rest of us put together, a regular one-man army.

Herbert, to the annoyance of the rest of us, had insisted on inviting Councillor Long yet again, on the grounds that, having been present at the public meeting, he could make sure that his colleagues understood the strength of feeling in the village. Personally, I doubted that his influence would be used to our advantage. It seemed more likely that he would take this opportunity to try and wheedle the committee into more passive forms of protest. That was my gut feeling, but I wasn't pleased to be proved right almost immediately.

During the past couple of weeks, we had got up our petition, and had taken it round every house in the village. We had also placed it in the museum, inviting those interested in preserving the history of the area to record their opposition to any development in Velvet Vale "until a full archaeological investigation has been carried out." I'd been nervous about doing this, even with Mrs. Challoner's blessing, but it had gone quite well. We already had several hundred signatures. I was particularly pleased, since it had been my idea in the first place.

Almost the first thing Councillor Long said at the committee meeting was that he thought the petition was a bad move on our part, and he recommended that we didn't use it to try to "blackmail" (his term) the Borough Council into submission. The rest of us listened, in silent anger, as he tried to water down our protests.

The meetings, as I've said, were rapidly becoming a source of frustration to me, and not only because of Herbert's chairmanship. Despite Jennifer Eaton's experience of acting as secretary to various committees, she wasn't very good at taking minutes. Most of the time, she just sat there without even a pencil in her hand, and only noted something down when Herbert specifically asked her to. When, at the beginning of each meeting, she was asked to read out the minutes of the previous one, her shortcomings showed up, because she would deliver a version so abbreviated that it barely made sense.

You're probably thinking that this is sour grapes because I wasn't made secretary to the Action Committee myself. If I'm honest, I'll admit that I thought I would have made a better secretary than Jennifer, but I didn't really envy her the task, particularly with Herbert being Chair. On this occasion, I contented myself with acting as a kind of unofficial back-up, turning over my copy of the agenda and scribbling down a few notes on the back, just in case we wanted to go back over this discussion at a later date and check what we had agreed. I didn't want anyone to be able to suggest that we'd agreed to drop my—*the*—petition. Edward Long was continuing to argue the point.

"You think we should hold back the petition, then?" Herbert was saying doubtfully when I glanced up.

"Yes, I do," said Councillor Long. He looked straight at me (well, not *straight* at me—over the top of his glasses, actually). "Can we make sure that's in the minutes, please?" he said.

I may not be a rampant feminist, but I chose to take offence.

"Why are you looking at *me?*" I asked, aggressively.

"I thought...," he began, looking bemused. He fidgeted with his glasses.

"You thought, since I'm female, that I must be taking the minutes," I finished.

"*I'm* the Secretary, Mr. Long," said Jennifer quickly, anxious to avoid a confrontation.

Long looked from me to her. "Oh," he said, and, turning back to me, "I beg your pardon."

The meeting continued, but thanks to Long, the atmosphere had turned sour. Herbert called a coffee break.

Jonathan was supposed to be the one making the tea and coffee this evening. Knowing how hopeless he was at anything vaguely domesticated, I felt obliged to follow him into the kitchen and offer my assistance.

"I don't know what Herbert asked *him* for," he said, in disgust, as he brought out odd cups and saucers at random from the kitchen cupboard. "If we're going to have councillors here, we should limit it to the ones that represent this ward."

I have to say that this was rich, coming from someone who lived at the other end of town.

"We do need to get a broad cross-section of opinion on our side," I argued. "Nathan's always saying this is more than a local issue. But I wish Herbert had chosen some other councillor to adopt. Do you think Mr. Long knew that petition was my idea?"

Jonathan shrugged. "Shouldn't think so."

"No, neither do I." I was forced to absolve Councillor Long of that crime, if no other.

The kettle having boiled, Jonathan began to slop the hot water into the cups, in each of which I had neatly placed a teaspoonful of instant coffee while we were talking.

"You should have done the teapot first," I pointed out. "It needs time to brew."

While he was getting on with that, I put the coffees on a tray, with the milk and sugar, and took them into the other room, putting them down on the committee table. It was merely a coincidence that I should have placed the tray directly in front of Councillor Long.

"Thank you, Miss Gardner," he said pointedly, as though trying to make up for his earlier faux pas. It was the first intimation I had ever had that he knew my name. I wasn't mollified.

None of us was looking forward to recommencing the meeting after the break, but it had to be done. We would probably have been more eager to start again had we anticipated the pyrotechnics that were to follow. A good fight always livens things up.

The two ward councillors, Mr. Kingdom and Mrs. Wadham, had been remarkably quiet throughout the first half of the meeting. They had obviously been "got at" from various quarters in advance of hearing our arguments, and were looking for a way out of their predicament. After the break, it was still Mr. Long doing most of the talking, and he was saying nothing that any of us found acceptable.

Now he was going on about the need for us to be sure we had good grounds for opposing the planning application. If the Borough Council turned it down, he reminded us, it could go to appeal, and that would be expensive and risky. As a prompt payer of my council tax, I objected to that line of reasoning.

Eventually it was Nathan who lit the match that set off the fireworks.

"May I say something, Chair?" he ventured at last, after listening patiently to Long's prevarications and excuses for another quarter of an hour.

Herbert deferred to him immediately, looking grateful that Nathan was finally justifying his presence at the meeting.

"It seems strange to me," continued Nathan, in a tone suggestive of exaggerated respect, "that the person doing most of the talking here is the person least directly involved in the matter and who clearly has the least interest in the broader issues. I don't have a problem with Councillor Long *being* here, but I would really prefer to hear the other councillors telling us what they intend to do for the people they represent, the people of this village. Then I think it is for this committee to decide what action to take next in pursuance of the campaign to oppose the development. If the councillors want to remain present while the campaign strategy is discussed, then the Chair may choose to let them. But surely the whole point of this meeting is for the committee to put the arguments to the councillors and then allow them to withdraw, so that we can get on with the real business of the evening." In other words, he wanted Edward Long to go away.

While Nathan was talking, Councillor Long had been getting redder and redder in the face. Herbert was about to protest, perhaps to say that it would be rude to ask the councillors to leave, or something of that sort, but he never got a chance to reply, because Long went straight on the offensive.

"If I'm regarded as surplus to requirements here," he bellowed, addressing Nathan directly, "I don't know what that makes *you*! You don't even live in this county, and when this is all over, you'll go back to your ivory tower and forget all about these people, and they'll be left holding the baby!"

He's lost it, I thought. He's completely lost his rag. He's even mixing his metaphors.

Nathan looked unmoved, but was about to respond when Herbert finally managed to get a word in.

"Now Edward," he said, trying to conceal his own agitation, "you mustn't take offence. Professor Pendragon was invited here by the committee, just as you were, as an expert on the historical significance of the Velvet Vale site. He didn't mean it personally, did you, Professor?"

As placid as ever, Nathan shook his head. It might have ended peacefully, if Joe hadn't then decided to put in his twopence worth.

"Anyway, squire," he interjected, grinning mischievously at Councillor Long, "Nathan and I spend a lot of our time—and money—over at the Dog and Drake, so you can't say we haven't made a contribution to the local economy."

"And what's more," put in Jonathan, laughing, "they're a lot more fun to be with than some of our so-called local authority representatives."

"Jonathan!" exclaimed Hilary, looking shocked.

It was a stupid thing to say. Jonathan had meant it as a joke, not a provocation, but Long didn't understand that. He went ballistic.

"I don't know what's wrong with you people!" he raged, apparently including the whole of the committee under that general description. "You aren't interested in the prosperity of this town at all, you can't see further than the ends of your noses. And as for you lot" —he gestured vaguely towards Joe and Nathan— "all you're interested in is a good..."

We all held our breath expectantly for the climax.

"...knees-up!" he concluded lamely.

His use of such an old-fashioned term set Joe and Jonathan roaring with laughter, and I admit I added a few sniggers of my own.

"Councillor Long," said Nathan, trying his best to conceal a smile, "I think that's most unjust. The Re-enactment Society is a bona fide organisation established specifically for purposes of historical research. If some of our members choose to patronise local public houses in the evenings, I really don't see how that disqualifies them from being taken seriously."

Long was clearly regretting his outburst, but didn't respond to Nathan's comment. He stood up and collected his papers together ostentatiously. "If you've said everything you wanted to say to me," he snorted, addressing Herbert and avoiding looking at anyone else, "I think I'll take my leave of you now. I have other things to do with my time, and I don't see that there's anything to be gained by prolonging the discussion."

"Taking his ball home," said Joe in my ear, just loud enough to guarantee being heard. Long glowered at us both.

"Thank you, Edward, for coming," said Herbert. "I hope you'll bear in mind the comments that have been made tonight."

Long nodded sullenly, and left. Immediately the door had closed on him, there was more unkind laughter. It was probably still ringing in his ears as he got into his car and drove away.

"That was rather rude of you, Joe," said Herbert, reproachfully. "I know Edward shouldn't have lost his temper, but all the same..."

"Point taken, guv," said Joe. "Won't happen again." He smirked at me.

Councillor Kingdom and Councillor Wadham had remained, fidgeting nervously, in their seats, throughout the altercation. Anxious to salvage something from the evening, Herbert began to address himself to them again. Free of Long's influence, and rather unsettled by the violence of the last few minutes, they started to make reassuring noises. They understood our point of view, they maintained, and they would certainly make sure that our arguments got a sympathetic hearing from the rest of the Planning Committee.

Not for a moment were we convinced.

Chapter 13

My Brilliant Idea

That was when I had my Brilliant Idea. My mind had been elsewhere, after Councillor Long stormed out of the meeting. I had been wondering how we were going to repair the damage to our relationship with the local representatives and not come across as a bunch of bolshie troublemakers.

What sparked it off was the mention, by Councillor Wadham if I remember correctly, of the "case" for Velvet Vale as a Civil War battlefield.

"I've lived in this area all my life," she said, "but no one's ever explained to me the case for that field being the site of a battle. Everyone's always said there was a battle somewhere around here, but I don't understand why you believe it should have taken place in that field as opposed to any other."

I had often wondered the same thing myself, and looked to Nathan to provide her with an answer.

"It's a reasonable question," he said, pre-empting Herbert, "but there's no time to go into that at this meeting — and in any case, this isn't the place for it."

Disappointed, I raised a lonely protest. I had heard Nathan explain it so many times in the pub that I knew it would only have taken him a matter of minutes to convince the councillors.

"It's important, though, Nathan," I said. "I wish we could somehow get it across to people, make them understand that we're not just inventing the story as a means of stopping the development. A public lecture, or something."

Nathan's eyes glinted suddenly, but he said nothing.

"That's not a bad idea," conceded Herbert. "We could hire the Village Hall, and invite people along to find out more of the facts behind what we've been saying. It would be good publicity for the re-enactment, as well."

The rest of the committee started nodding in agreement.

"But of course," Herbert continued, hesitantly, "we would need an expert to give the talk. And I hardly like to ask."

Nathan, though he had known all along that he was the only person who could possibly give a coherent account of the Battle of Barrow End that would serve to convince an audience of the rightness of the theory he supported, modestly affected not to understand who was being referred to until Herbert asked him straight out. Then he agreed that he would give a lecture at the Village Hall, on one condition—that we invited Trevor and Valerie Farmer to be guests of honour.

After all, he pointed out, the field belonged to them.

As WAS USUAL with anything Nathan Pendragon suggested, we all saw immediately that it was a pretty smart move. To exclude the Farmers would have been to invite their displeasure and show ourselves hostile to them personally, despite their tolerance in allowing us to use their field for the re-enactment.

Nathan's strategy was to force the Farmers to acknowledge that their field was the site of the battle. In doing so, they would have to accept its historic importance, and it might weaken their case for pushing the planning application through without a proper archaeological investigation.

He didn't explain all this at the time, of course. He made it appear, in front of the two surviving councillors, as though he had genuine respect for Mr. and Mrs. Farmer and valued their opinion on his theories. The councillors, as might have been expected, received the idea of the lecture with enthusiasm, and went off home feeling that they had salvaged something from the meeting. Anything to put off making a decision.

Nathan's availability was severely limited by his other commitments, so we agreed there and then on a date for the lecture, less than a fortnight away. Herbert was anxious that this might not allow adequate time for preparation, but Nathan waved away any such concerns, saying that the bulk of the material was readily to hand and it would take him no time at all to devise the structure of what he wanted to say.

I was praised by everyone present for having come up with the idea. While we were walking back to my flat, where Joe had left his car, he added his congratulations to those I'd already received.

"Why didn't I think of it myself?" he kept saying.

"Because you're too thick," I retorted eventually, when I was sick of hearing about it.

"You don't mean that!" exclaimed Joe, his perky face momentarily crestfallen.

"Of course I don't mean it," I said, more gently, unlocking the front door and leading him up the stairs.

When we got to the living room door, I did a stupid thing. I turned to him and ran a hand flirtatiously through his dark curls. In response, he put his arms around me, and gave me a great big smacker of a kiss. It wasn't exactly a passionate expression of undying devotion, but it was more promising than anything I'd ever had from him before. It had been stupid of me to get him started down that path. He was getting me all wound up, and my better instincts told me it was for nothing.

"You know," I said, as we went inside, "you were a bit naughty this evening, picking on poor old Councillor Long like that."

"I was, wasn't I?" He grinned. "I'm afraid I can't help myself sometimes. The bloke's such a…" I won't repeat the word he used, but it rhymes with "anchor."

I laughed guiltily, and headed towards the kitchen. Before I had taken two steps forward, Joe's arms came around me from behind, preventing any further progress.

I turned to look into his face. "Don't mess around, Joe," I said. "I'm not going to sleep with you."

I knew exactly how his mind was working, and I'd had enough of being used by men. Joe pretended the idea had never entered his head.

"Don't be daft," he said, attempting to sound the injured innocent, "I wasn't trying to get inside your knickers. You know I'm fond of you. I was just saying sorry for being a bit tactless back there, that's all."

I already regretted what I'd said, but there was no going back. Joe must have thought I didn't want to sleep with him, which was far from the truth. I still fancied him like mad, but I was conscious of an unreliability, a lightness of character about him that I couldn't overlook. It wasn't like it had been with Peter, the knowledge of the impossibility of emotional fulfilment because of an insurmountable obstacle—Peter's wife.

As far as I knew, there were no strings attached with Joe, and that was precisely the problem. He was quite capable of going to bed with me one night, and some other girl the next, and no doubt, during the act, he would make all kinds of protestations of affection. But, as I had come to realise, it would mean nothing.

THE FOLLOWING DAY, I wrote a letter on behalf of the Velvet Vale Action Committee, inviting Trevor and Valerie Farmer to attend a public lecture at Barrow End Village Hall. The lecture would be given by Professor Nathan Pendragon, MA, DPhil, FRHistS, and was entitled, "The Battle of Barrow End: the Historical Evidence."

Strictly speaking, it should have been Jennifer's job, as secretary to the committee, to write the letter, but she had mentioned how busy she was and had said casually that she wouldn't be able to get around to it "for a few days."

Some people have no sense of urgency. With the date of the lecture so imminent, any delay seemed unacceptable, so it was agreed that I should take the task off Jennifer's hands. I took the letter round to Herbert's house to be signed, then I delivered it in person.

The Farmers, as I've mentioned before, lived in what had been the manor house of the village of Oldwick. That's what it was called—The Manor. I was apprehensive about approaching in person because of the danger of being seen by one or both of them and becoming engaged in embarrassing conversation—or more likely, argument—in the process. So I parked some distance from the house.

"House" doesn't seem quite the right word for the place they lived in. The Manor itself was big—at least seven or eight bedrooms, I'd have guessed—but that wasn't all. The extensive grounds, stretching down from the back of the house to the river, had been landscaped, and that wasn't where the Farmers' property ended, either.

They had been buying up land at a feverish rate, helped by the slump in agriculture, to what end nobody was quite sure. It was probably nothing but speculation, because they knew that they would be able to sell the land for a much higher price when there was a turnaround in the local economy.

And, of course, they expected to be able to develop some of it and make money that way. New houses could sell for an astronomical price in this area. When they had succeeded in spoiling the whole district, Trevor and Valerie always had the option of moving somewhere else.

It struck me that they shouldn't have been able to accumulate this kind of wealth so easily. They probably had a nice line in tax evasion going, aided and abetted by their friendly accountant-cum-local authority representative. Edward Long would have called it tax "avoidance," I daresay.

None of the land immediately surrounding the Manor of Oldwick was as yet earmarked for building, except for what the Farmers had constructed on it for their own use. This included various outhouses, a holiday cottage or two (for hospitality to friends), stables, and a garage big enough to house Trevor's Bentley, Valerie's Range Rover, and a couple of smaller vehicles used by their teenage son and daughter.

The locals referred laughingly to the estate as the Ponderosa.

Thankfully, when I arrived on the scene, there was no one about but an odd-job man, who called to me that if I was looking for Mr. and Mrs. Farmer, they were both out. I breathed again, slipped the letter through the door, and made my getaway.

Chapter 14

A History Lecture

The Farmers didn't actually reply directly to my letter—they didn't have enough class to understand that it was required—but they let it be generally known that they were "thinking of coming" to Nathan Pendragon's lecture. Just to make sure, Nathan himself telephoned them the night before, reminding them of the time and place and expressing his sincere wish that they would be able to attend. If I wasn't mistaken, Valerie wouldn't be able to resist that.

We had refreshments lined up for the audience, to ensure maximum turnout and a relaxed atmosphere. Hilary, Molly and I had spent hours making sausage rolls and putting out little bowls of nibbles and plates of biscuits to go with the coffee. Hilary was an expert on that kind of thing, and Molly was doing it mainly in the hope of attracting Nathan's approval. She was over the moon when he came to chat to us beforehand and actually chose one of *her* sausage rolls to sample.

The attendance was as good as we could have hoped, with about fifty villagers turning up, plus a few stray enthusiasts from the local Historical Association, a smattering of Re-enactment Society members out of uniform, and a handful of schoolchildren (all boys, I'm sorry to say). Best of all, there were three local councillors who would have a say in the fate of the planning application. Two of them were Mr. Kingdom and Mrs. Wadham. The third was the Deputy Mayor, Councillor Jones-Davies. For once, Councillor Long didn't put in an appearance. It was hardly surprising, bearing in mind what had happened last time he and Nathan Pendragon had encountered one another.

Actually, I think Nathan was a little disappointed that his sparring partner wasn't there. He would have relished the opportunity to meet Long on home territory, where Nathan was the undisputed expert and could choose whether or not to answer questions from the floor. I was disappointed too. I would have loved the opportunity to let the Councillor see exactly how much attention the committee intended to pay to his advice about the conduct of the campaign.

Joe and I had talked, innumerable times, about the secret of the Re-enactment Society's success, which couldn't entirely be attributed to Nathan and its other leaders—the "Ruling Council," as they were called. After all, there were other such societies, covering other wars, but none of them had anything like the number of members the RS had.

It was something to do with the period, something to do with its glamour and romance. The English Civil War was, of course, possibly the most important war in British history, in terms of the country's religion and constitution. Because it was a civil war, it also affected people directly, forcing them to choose sides. Families were divided by the sword. When you consider the size of the population in the seventeenth century, probably a bigger proportion witnessed the conflict directly than civilians in either of the two World Wars of the twentieth century. But that doesn't explain its attraction in the present day, except for true historians like Nathan.

I've never understood why men like reading about war, in any case. I suppose it's a substitute for indulging the primitive urge to fight. If it's blood and guts you're looking for, there was plenty of that sort of thing during the Civil War. At the Battle of Edgehill, the King's standard-bearer, Sir Edmund Verney, was so determined not to let go of the royal standard that he died with his fist still locked around it. When they got it back, so the story goes, his severed hand was still attached to it.

Any of these things might go some way to explaining the attraction of the English Civil War, but I put the Re-enactment Society's success down to two main things: firstly, the flashy costume, and secondly, the fact that the seventeenth century isn't too close for comfort. By which I mean that you can enjoy the outward trappings of campaign and battle without having to suffer any of the real hardship and violence of the time. Hence the big attendance at this special lecture.

You could tell immediately that Nathan was used to speaking to an audience, because within minutes he had us all in the palm of his hand. Even those who didn't understand what he was talking about were captivated by his swashbuckling prose style. He'd had the good sense to bring along slides—some were of the Re-enactment Society in action, others were of important Civil War sites—to illustrate his explanations. That always makes an evening go more quickly.

In Nathan's case, the slides probably weren't essential. When the time came for our refreshment break, there was a sigh of disappointment from some parts of the hall (mainly the parts with women in). They didn't actually want the lecture to come to an end.

Nathan had promised to take questions from the audience in the second part of the evening, and you could tell that people were looking forward to having their say. He'd had the bright idea of getting us all to write our questions down on pieces of paper, during the interval, so that he wouldn't get too many variations on the same theme. Before starting again, Nathan would eliminate the duplicates, but he would also make sure that the name of each and every person who had asked that particular question was read out, so that no one felt snubbed. He really had a gift with people—if you exclude a certain councillor.

Yes, I admit it. If Nathan had been about fifteen years younger, I could have gone for him in a big way.

Valerie Farmer wasn't immune to Professor Pendragon's charms either. Trevor and Valerie had made a bit of an entrance earlier in the evening. Just as we'd given up on them, when Nathan was about to begin speaking, they swept down the aisle to their reserved seats in the front row. This had been another of Nathan's little schemes to ensure that they didn't have any excuse for not turning up. They sat there like the Queen and Prince Philip, trying to look as though they had an interest in history for its own sake.

It occurred to me that, if Nathan could have assured them that the Velvet Vale site had potential as a tourist attraction, their attitude to it would have changed overnight. Anything that offered the prospect of financial gain was attractive to them. Having seen their house and grounds at close quarters, I couldn't conceive of the kind of greed that wasn't satisfied by what they already owned.

During the refreshment break, the Farmers kept very much to themselves, except for exchanging a few pleasantries with the three councillors, who looked around warily before being seen to respond. They were in a very difficult position, I could see that. They couldn't afford to offend the Farmers; but to go against the wishes of the village residents was tantamount to electoral suicide. Councillor Wadham went to the Ladies three times before the question-and-answer session began. I counted.

When everyone was back in their seats, and Hilary and I had cleared away the leftovers, Nathan got back into position and Herbert started reading out the prepared questions. However silly a question was, Nathan would always begin his answer with some little compliment, such as "That's a very interesting question," or "Now I'm glad someone asked that, because..."

It seemed to me that he had made his case very convincingly during the first half of the evening, and he dispelled any remaining doubts after the break. Trevor Farmer was looking increasingly uncomfortable, but Valerie remained poised, with a fixed smile on her face, until Nathan asked for follow-up questions relating to anything he had said. Valerie raised a hand, and, since she was in the front row, he couldn't very well ignore her.

"I must congratulate you on such thorough research," she began, standing up to make sure that everyone got a look at her outfit, a pink-and-white number that made her look like Shirley Temple (from a distance). Nathan smiled knowingly, but didn't look flattered by her opening comment. He could guess what she was leading up to. "Supposing we accept your theory, that our field..." —she had thrown in that "our" just to make sure that no one in the room failed to understand who she was— "...is the site of the Battle of Barrow End, how does that make it undesirable for it to be developed?"

Coming from her, it was quite an astute question, and one which I thought might cause Nathan a degree of difficulty. I should have known better. He was unfazed by the implicit challenge. Valerie sat down, looking satisfied.

"I'm very glad you asked that, Mrs. Farmer," he said. Then he raised his eyes and voice to make sure that everyone in the hall was listening. "In case anyone here doesn't know, may I mention that this lady is Mrs. Valerie Farmer? She and her husband own Velvet Vale, and it's with their kind permission that the Re-enactment Society is proposing to re-fight the Battle of Barrow End—on its original site—on Sunday, August the twentieth."

"Now some of you may not be aware that Mr. and Mrs. Farmer have made an application for a housing development on this same field. The residents of the village have formed an action committee to oppose that application, and the Re-enactment Society is supporting them in their opposition. Quite properly, Mrs. Farmer is asking the question, 'Why?'"

He cast his eyes around the hall, making sure that his words had sunk home.

"Why indeed? Why should a battlefield be preserved without development? It's not as if there's anything there for the public to see. Or is there? Earlier in the evening, I showed you some slides, copies of photographs I myself took of the field concerned, showing the relative positions of the two opposing forces. I hesitate to refer to them as 'armies,' because the numbers involved were comparatively small. I've already stated that I think there were perhaps no more than two hundred on each side."

It still sounded a lot to me.

"The answer to Mrs. Farmer's question can only be explained in context. The battlefields of Britain, as a whole, are part of our national heritage. Now personally, I'm a pacifist."

If anyone else had made this statement, it would have caused outrage amongst the mainly right-wing voters of Barrow End and its surrounding villages; but Nathan's credentials were impeccable.

"But war is as much a part of history as any other aspect of life. We are living in the twenty-first century. It's getting on for three hundred years since a battle was fought on British soil. That battlefield, at Culloden Moor in Scotland, is rightly recognised as one of the most important historical sites in the country, and receives millions of visitors each year.

"But Velvet Vale is no Culloden, I hear you say. It's just a little field, where a couple of hundred men had a skirmish in an age no one can remember and no one wants to know about.

"Ladies and gentlemen, we come now to the crux of the matter. Are we going to let our heritage be destroyed, whittled away if you like, by individual developments, until there is nothing left? How will we teach our children and grandchildren about the futility of war? How will we teach them about the great constitutional revolution of the seventeenth century? Will we teach them by taking them into some sterile museum to look at things in glass cases?"

At this point he turned to Herbert and apologised humbly, getting a laugh from most of the audience.

"I have nothing against museums," Nathan went on, "but they are no substitute for living history. This solitary field, and the threat to its preservation, are symbolic of the trouble with Britain today. Do we really *need* more houses in this village, Mrs. Farmer?"

I was surprised at his audacity in addressing himself directly to Valerie. It was a rhetorical question, and he didn't give her time to answer.

"Of course we don't. I don't blame individuals for wanting to make use of their assets in a way that brings financial gain. It's not their responsibility to protect our heritage. It's the Government's. And I've written personally to the Prime Minister, and to the Heritage Secretary, to draw their attention to the importance of this issue."

The way he expressed himself, you could almost have believed the Government were shaking in their shoes.

"Now, a few months ago," he continued, "even I was unaware of Velvet Vale. It was thanks to Mr. Dyson here"— Herbert glowed visibly at the compliment— "that I became alerted to the possible existence of an authentic and unspoiled Civil War battlefield in the heart of England. At first I couldn't believe it—that such a thing could have survived. But when I came here and saw the site at first hand, when I studied the documentary sources and the materials which Mr. Dyson had put together over the years, so painstakingly"— he smiled ingratiatingly at Herbert— "I realised that his hypothesis was almost watertight. Further research by myself, carried out under the auspices of my university, revealed the undoubted truth of our conjecture. Velvet Vale *is* the site of the Battle of Barrow End. You've heard the evidence this evening, and I think you must agree it is incontrovertible."

"A few months ago, we didn't know all this, and we could perhaps have been forgiven for allowing this field to be built over. But now, thanks mainly to Mr. Dyson, we do know, and there is therefore no excuse for inertia. We must act *now* to preserve the site. I feel deep regret for any personal inconvenience this may cause to Mr. and Mrs. Farmer, but there are greater considerations at stake here than the rights and privileges of individual property owners. So many of our great battlefields have either been destroyed or are under threat from monstrous motorways, enterprise parks and housing developments—Naseby, Newbury, Edgehill—Dunbar, Brentford, Worcester. And not just Civil War battlefields, but souvenirs of earlier armed conflict—Tewkesbury, Shrewsbury, Stamford Bridge—Lewes, Evesham, Barnet. All gone or severely eroded by development. Are we going to wait until we have nothing left?"

"No!" came the resounding response from the back of the hall. It was the Re-enactment Society. Now I knew why they had come in mufti. No one could be sure which of them were part of Nathan's personal claque and which were residents of the district. Valerie Farmer looked round angrily, craning her neck to try and make out the individual culprits, but there was nothing she could do or say. The time for argument was past, and Nathan had won.

At this point, as though he had been primed, Herbert got to his feet and thanked everyone for coming. Nathan gave a slight bow. There was tumultuous applause, beginning at the back of the hall and rippling right down to the front row. Trevor and Valerie Farmer put their hands together and clapped politely. People began to vacate their seats, but the movement to leave the hall was leisurely, with some stopping to chat to friends and comment on the evening's entertainment. The Farmers were left stranded in their front row seats, unable to beat a path to the door without running the gauntlet of disdain.

It was Nathan Pendragon who came to their rescue. With a courteous gesture, he waved them towards the fire exit, opening it with a flourish.

"Please, allow me!" he said, ushering them out into the balmy summer evening.

I was standing close to the fire door. As the Farmers hurried past, I smiled. It wasn't a spiteful smile—I was merely admiring Nathan's handling of the situation—but Valerie Farmer saw it. She shot me a look of such pure hatred that I almost withered on the spot. By a single thoughtless action, I had made an implacable enemy.

THE SUCCESS of my Brilliant Idea had put me in a really good mood, but I should have known it couldn't last. A few days after Nathan's lecture, Mrs. Challoner came over to the museum, and asked me to step into her office when I closed for lunch.

It had to be something serious for her to do that. The office was tiny, barely big enough for the two of us to sit down, but it was the only place we could go where we wouldn't be disturbed by the library assistants.

Mrs. Challoner tried to force a smile, but I could see she was worried about something. Please, I thought, not another round of redundancies. Worse still, she might be about to tell me that the council had finally shelved its plans for a new museum building.

"I thought it would be better if this came from me, Rose," she said. "I won't beat about the bush. I've had a complaint about your conduct."

I knew immediately that this wasn't the usual gripe from the public about the standard of professional service. The first name that came to mind was that of Valerie Farmer.

"It's to do with your involvement in the Action Committee," she continued.

"I don't see what that's got to do with the museum service," I said.

"Well, indirectly...As Conservator, you're a local authority employee. There's a possible conflict of interests, and it's being said that you shouldn't involve yourself in political issues. The complaint came from a councillor, so I've had to take it seriously."

Edward Long. The swine.

"This is a joke, isn't it?" I said. "The Action Committee isn't political, not in any way. I've got a right to a say in what's happening in the village where I live. For heavens' sake, I've even got a letter from the Borough Engineer telling me how to go about making an objection to the planning application."

Mrs. Challoner's expression was pained. She hated doing this.

"I know that, Rose. Please understand, this isn't coming from me. But I've had a letter from him, and I can't just ignore it."

"What exactly does he say, in this letter?"

"He says you're going too far, that if it comes to a confrontation between the Action Committee and the Borough Council, you'll be put in a difficult position. It's odd, how he's put it, as though he thinks it's for your own good. Reading it, one would almost think he had a sneaking admiration for you."

"He's a nutter!"

Mrs. Challoner laughed. "I don't know about that, but he seems to have got a bee in his bonnet about this. Have you done something to upset him?"

I had a sudden thought. "Do you think he's trying to get back at me because I was rude to his mother the other day?"

Mrs. Challoner looked surprised at the suggestion. "Oh come along, Rose! I'm sure he knows better than that. In any case, she'd probably forgotten all about it herself, before she even got home."

I had to admit that she was right. I thought back to the committee meeting. "No, I know why he's got it in for me. I dared to answer him back in our meeting a couple of weeks ago. He was being rather sexist. You would have approved."

She laughed again. "Rose, you never learn, do you?"

That was when I knew that she was on my side. I thought about asking to see the letter, but then I decided I would prefer not to know what was in it.

"I'm not going to back down," I said. "I don't care what he does. He can get me the sack if he likes, I don't care. I'm not standing down from the Action Committee, and I'm not going to stop campaigning. All I can promise is not to bring it into work with me."

Mrs. Challoner sighed. "That's all I have a right to ask, Rose. But I don't know what to do about answering this letter. Perhaps I should try and talk to him about it."

"I wouldn't bother. He's not worth the effort."

"Don't let it get to you," she said, smiling. "I'd feel a lot better about it if I could be sure you weren't going to do anything silly."

We left it at that. I wasn't sure what she meant about not doing anything silly. If I could have thought of something silly to do, I'd probably have done it out of sheer bloody-mindedness, but I had other things to think about. Over the course of the day, I calmed down, and began to plan for my forthcoming summer holidays.

Chapter 15

A Wet Week

The following week, the weather took a turn for the worse.

I was walking down the High Street in torrential rain, on the way to the bus stop. My car had gone into the garage for a service that morning. I had been due to pick it up at five, but the workshop supervisor had phoned me, only a few minutes before I was due to leave the museum, to say that there was an unexpected problem. There was another part they needed, and they wouldn't be able to get it until the following morning. Would I mind if they kept it in overnight?

What a stupid question! Of course I minded, but it wasn't as if I had any choice in the matter. They offered me a courtesy car, but I would still have had to walk to the garage to pick it up, so I declined the offer. When I got outside and saw how heavily it was raining, I regretted having been so brusque. I waited a little while, in the vain hope that the downpour would let up. Then I remembered I was living in Britain, and set off to throw myself on the mercies of public transport.

I was in a filthy mood by the time I got within a few yards of the bus shelter. It was absolutely throwing it down, and blowing a gale to boot. I couldn't keep my umbrella up, so I was reduced to trying to hold the hood of my coat over my hair, as far as the wind would allow me to, in order to keep dry. I say "keep dry," but my shoes and stockings were already soaked through, and I could feel the edge of my skirt sticking wetly to my knees, under my less-than-adequate coat. It was *supposed* to be summer.

A large, rather flashy, silver car pulled up at the kerb a few feet ahead of me, squirting out dirty water from under its tyres. As I drew level with it, the window lowered itself with an electric whirr. I had to move closer in order to see who was driving.

"Miss Gardner," said Councillor Long, "may I offer you a lift?"

Almost anyone else could have asked me the same question without my taking offence. I'd even have considered accepting a lift from Valerie Farmer. But not Councillor Long, not after his recent behaviour. Several fairly strong reactions coursed through me, but the strongest of them all was a sense of outrage.

Breathless with anger, I opened the car door as if intending to accept his invitation. Resting one hand on the top of the door frame, I looked in at him. He was actually smiling.

"Do you seriously think I would consider getting into a car with *you?*" I shouted.

His mouth dropped open. Before he had a chance to say anything, I had slammed the car door and walked away.

I sat in the bus shelter, watching the streaks of rain against the plastic frame and seething. What an arrogant pig the man was! He had sat there in the Village Hall, drinking our tea, and insulted us all, he had complained about me to Mrs. Challoner—then, a couple of weeks later, he thought he could get round me with fake politeness.

The following Saturday, all the volunteers were on duty, and I regaled Jonathan with the story. He was the only person I'd told about Long's letter of complaint to Mrs. Challoner, and I'd made him promise not to reveal to the rest of the committee that I was in any trouble. Jonathan thought the whole thing was hysterically funny.

"I'll bet his face was a picture!" he laughed. "I'd have loved to have seen it!"

His reaction cheered me up a little, but I didn't tell the others—Herbert and Doris and Verity and Molly—because I doubted that they would see the funny side. Herbert still seemed to be harbouring a residue of respect for Edward Long. I gathered he had known him for a long time. No doubt he would say that my response to such a kind offer had been impolite.

That same morning, I had occasion to go through the lobby of the Town Hall—to use the Ladies' toilet, if you must know—and I spotted the notice of the forthcoming election of councillors on prominent display. I spent some time perusing it, and noted that Edward Long was one of those coming up for re-election. Unkindly, I wondered how much the Farmers were contributing to his campaign expenses.

Though he had been a councillor for as long as I had lived in the area, he was actually one of the most junior members of the local authority, as I now saw. His full name, if you can believe this, was Edward Elgar Long, which I found a bit of a gas. Just like Mrs. Long, I thought, to give her son a pretentious name like that. I wondered what her other two boys were called. Johann Sebastian and Wolfgang Amadeus, possibly?

The same notice also listed the councillors' dates of birth, but when I looked at Mr. Long's, I felt sure that it must be an error.

"Herbert," I asked curiously, as I came back into the exhibition area, "how old is Councillor Long?"

"Edward? Let me see now." He pondered the question briefly, before seeking confirmation from his better half. "Doris!" he called.

Doris stuck her head round the door of the kitchen.

"How old is Edward?" asked Herbert. "Has he turned thirty-five?"

"I don't think so, not yet," replied Doris. "I know he's a little older than Hilary," she added, disappearing again.

"Hilary Markham?" I queried.

"That's right," Herbert confirmed. "I think Edward would be about a year older than Hilary."

I knew that Hilary was coming up to her thirty-third birthday, because Peter had mentioned it in passing. According to the notice in the lobby, Edward Elgar Long was only thirty-four.

"Why do you ask?" said Herbert.

"Oh, nothing. I've only just realised that he was younger than I thought. I took him to be over forty."

"Oh, no." Herbert chuckled. "He's nowhere near that age. He's the youngest of the three boys."

"You know his family quite well, by the sound of it."

"We used to live next door to them, before we moved to the bungalow. Didn't we, Doris? Hilary and her parents lived a few doors further up the road."

"Happy days," mused Doris, coming in with the coffee and putting Herbert's mug down on the reception desk. "Remember how he used to wave to us every morning when he was on his way to school?"

The mind boggled. I could just about accept that Edward Long had once been young, but nonetheless I couldn't picture him in school uniform.

"You know the sad story of his father, I suppose," Herbert went on. Nothing gave him more pleasure than an attentive audience, and he had my full attention now.

"Not the full story," I replied.

"Oh, it was very tragic. Wasn't it, Doris?"

"Don't talk about it, Herbert. It still upsets me to think about it."

You know how you sometimes get that insidious urge to snoop into other people's private business, but it makes you feel so guilty that you can't quite bring yourself to ask. I was torn between wanting Herbert to continue the story, out of sheer curiosity, and not wanting to hear anything that might make me feel sympathy for Mrs. Long and her youngest son.

"Went missing one day," said Herbert laconically. Doris immediately picked up her mug and walked over to the other end of the room, as though she couldn't bear to listen. "Doris was so upset," he commented, his eyes following her. "He was a good man, Dick Long, and a good neighbour. A councillor, too, one of the best we've ever had. But suffered with his nerves. He'd been in the War, you know. As I said, he went missing one day. Hetty thought he'd gone out."

I assumed that "Hetty" was the same person I knew as Mrs. Long. Herbert hadn't paused in his narrative.

"...and when he didn't come back after a few hours, she called the police, thinking he'd been run over or something, you know. But the first thing the police did was to search the house and the garden, and they found his body in the shed. He'd hung himself. Terrible business."

"And his sons were still at school," I concluded.

"No, only Edward. The other two are older, they were already out at work. The eldest one was married, if I remember rightly. The second one got married not long afterwards, leaving Edward at home to look after his mother. Good boy, Edward, always was. He went to university, and did very well. Could have gone to Oxford or Cambridge, but he stayed close by, so that he could go on living at home and keep an eye on Hetty. Once he was qualified, he got himself a position locally, then eventually set up in business on his own. And I'll say this for him, he's been a very dutiful son, ever since."

For the first time, it became apparent why Herbert had shown such loyalty to Councillor Long. We both fell silent, but I doubt if Herbert was thinking the same things I was. I was wondering about the psychological effect on a fourteen-year-old boy of his father's suicide. And the effect on a grown man of knowing he would have to look after his mother for the rest of her life.

It wasn't enough to make me change my opinion of Edward Elgar Long, but I did feel ever so slightly guilty, shortly afterwards, when I revealed Mr. Long's middle name to Jonathan and we giggled over it together.

Chapter 16

Ducks and Drakes

While I was still seething over the business of Mr. Long's letter and my encounter with him in the rain, Herbert rang me to say that the Borough Council had issued its report on the environmental impact of the planning application for Velvet Vale. I went over to his house to see a copy he had managed to get hold of. Needless to say, he had obtained it courtesy of Edward Long.

Councillor Long must have had a sudden brainstorm, because he'd gone into super-helpful mode and given Herbert multiple copies of the report, enough to go round the whole of the Action Committee. It wasn't a very edifying document. There was little detail, only a sketchy account of the environmental factors and a few statements of intent by the Borough Council as to measures to be taken to ensure minimal effect on the environment, in the event of the application being successful. Drainage requirements, vehicle access, colour of roof tiles, that kind of thing. The author of the report seemed to be assuming that the application would be passed.

It wasn't particularly helpful to our cause, but neither was it damaging, except for one small section dealing with the effect on the surroundings of St Catherine's Church. It stated that no objection had been received from the diocese to the application on environmental grounds. I found this difficult to understand, since as far as I could see, the *only* objection the diocese could reasonably make was on environmental grounds. I made a mental note to ask Peter about it, next time I saw him.

Thinking about Peter usually made me think about Joe. I hadn't seen him since Nathan's lecture, and I was missing him. It seemed to me that he might be what I needed at this stage of my life—someone carefree and unconventional, who offered me the chance of a relationship without complications.

At least, it seemed like that when I wasn't with him. When I was with him, I often felt anxious about what was developing between us. What might, on the surface, seem uncomplicated usually has a habit of turning into a web of misunderstandings and hurt feelings.

And anyway, I've never been any good at disguising my emotions. Joe already knew that I fancied him. He couldn't not know. I knew that he fancied me too. That was strange, because I could have sworn he had never been interested in me when we had been friends earlier in our lives. Perhaps he had changed, or I had changed, or we had both changed, enough to make it possible for the feelings to be mutual.

Joe was no longer just a pretty face, either. At school, that was the only part of him that had really interested me—his face. These days, I had more mature tastes, and Joe's skinny teenage body had evolved into something that could satisfy them.

A sixteen-foot pike might look like nothing more than a long wooden pole, but there's a certain amount of strength required simply to carry it upright, let alone use it. Mock battles may not last as long as the real thing, but to participate in one calls for a degree of physical fitness that Joe had achieved. In short, he had muscles everywhere.

I tried not to think about what would happen when the re-enactment was over and Joe disappeared out of my life again. I had no doubt that he would. Whatever happened between us, there was nothing that would make him stay around, once his original motivation—the battle—was no longer there.

It wasn't that Joe didn't have feelings, or didn't care about things. He cared about Velvet Vale. He genuinely wanted to stop the Farmers. But his priorities were different from mine. Marriage and divorce might have changed him, but not in such a way as to make him ready for commitment. Quite the opposite, probably. It would be another ten years before he would want to consider marriage again, and I couldn't wait that long for him.

Sometimes I would go over to the Dog and Drake in the evening, on my own or with friends, just to imbibe the atmosphere that I associated with Joe. Even if the Re-enactment Society weren't in the bar, the place was still redolent of them—their laughter and the intellectual and emotional stimulation they provided, so different from what I could get in the library or the museum. They were so *alive.*

The landlord of the Dog and Drake hadn't been running the pub for long, and I hadn't got to know him very well. I wasn't even sure of his name.

When Herbert and I had gone around mustering the opposition to the planning application, the landlord had confessed to being ambivalent about it. (He didn't actually use the word "ambivalent.") On the one hand, he could see that it would potentially spoil the village, from a purely aesthetic point of view (he didn't use the word, "aesthetic," either). He was also concerned about the possibility of additional noise, vandalism, break-ins, and a flock of under-age drinkers making a nuisance of themselves. He had spent months trying to start up some kind of restaurant trade, encouraging people to think of his pub as a quiet country inn where they could come for a good, reasonably-priced meal and friendly service.

On the other hand, he could see that a new housing estate would make his life much easier from the point of view of attracting custom. He had a wife and two kids to support. He was trying to make a living, and that had to be his first consideration.

I wasn't too hard on him, because I understood his position. On the contrary, I made a point of smiling and being friendly to him whenever we met, in the hope that, when the time came, he would tend to support the faction he was better acquainted with. The Farmers never came into the Dog and Drake.

One evening, I nearly collided with him, as I was negotiating the narrow passage that linked the Ladies' toilet with the bar.

"Meal all right?" he asked casually, as we edged past one another.

I had just treated myself to scampi and chips.

"Very nice, thanks," I said. "You seem to be doing a roaring trade tonight."

"Yes," he said, "thanks to those—what do you call them?—Cavaliers. I don't know what we'll do when they stop coming in here."

Nathan and Wally were both in the bar that evening, with a small group of others.

"Some of them are local. They may keep visiting, now that they've found a congenial landlord."

He laughed, and I realised he didn't know what "congenial" meant.

"You've made them feel at home," I added. "This is the kind of place they like, somewhere with a historic atmosphere."

"Of course, you work in the museum, don't you? This is a very old pub, you know," he commented, as though I wouldn't have noticed.

"Medieval, I should think," I said.

"Sir Francis Drake," he replied.

I did a double-take. "Sir Francis Drake?"

"Yes, he sailed round the world," said the landlord, mistaking my surprise for ignorance. "In the time of Queen Elizabeth. I know, because I looked him up on the Internet."

I was intrigued. "Do you mean that the Drake in the name of the pub isn't just a duck?" I asked.

"That's right. I know because of the sign."

I recalled that the pub sign had recently been replaced, but I couldn't remember the old one being much different from the new one.

"Do you mean the pub sign?"

"That's right. We had it replaced the other day. The one that used to be there was falling to bits. Must have been a hundred years old."

"Really?"

"But the one before that..." he went on. Seeing my interest, he beckoned to me. "Come on," he said, "I'll show it to you."

He led me up the winding staircase, under the heavy beams, to the narrow landing where he and his wife let out a couple of bed-and-breakfast rooms to the occasional tourist. Nathan had taken one, when he came down to give his lecture. At the end of the landing was another, smaller stair, leading up into the roof.

The whole building seemed to be creaking under our weight, as I followed the landlord up this secondary staircase, and into a wide open space, where the roof beams hung threateningly over us.

"Here it is," he said, moving into a dusty corner and dragging out a heavy object, covered with a dust-sheet. "I found it when we moved in. The wife wanted to chuck it out, but I kept it because I thought it might be valuable. But I don't know who to ask."

As he removed the dust-sheet, the sign before last revealed itself. The picture was very faded, but it was clear enough for me to see that the two objects illustrated were not, as on the present sign, a dog and a male duck, but a dog and what looked like a small cannon.

"What on earth is that?" I asked.

"It's a cannon," he said, looking at me as if I was dim-witted. "Like they used to have on ships in Elizabethan times. Like Sir Francis Drake used. I think he must have stayed here or something, and they must have named the pub after him. What do you think?"

I inhaled deeply, extracting what oxygen I could from the musty atmosphere of the loft.

"I think Professor Pendragon ought to see this," I said.

"Who?"

"Professor Pendragon," I repeated, then, understanding his problem, I added, "Nathan."

"Oh," said the landlord, "Nathan!"

It seemed incredible to me that the landlord could have had Nathan Pendragon in and out of his pub for the past couple of months without having discovered that he was a university professor. It seemed he had taken little interest in the conversations going on in the bar, preoccupied as he was with washing glasses and rubbing the names of dishes off the blackboard. When Nathan had been giving his public lecture in the Village Hall, the landlord and his family had, understandably, been at work in the pub. The same was true of the public meeting earlier in the summer.

I went straight down to the bar and called Nathan. Wally came too, and we climbed the creaking staircases once again to reach the attic.

Nathan took one look at the old sign, and said, "That's a drake, all right."

I was puzzled, but Wally turned to me and explained. "It's a type of cannon."

"Ah," I said. "It wouldn't be seventeenth century, by any chance, would it?"

A slow smile was spreading across Nathan's features. "It most certainly would," he said, and turned to the landlord. "I must congratulate you on taking such good care of it."

The landlord preened, and didn't think of arguing as Nathan commanded him to donate the sign immediately to the District Museum, where it would be conserved and put on prominent display. His initial disappointment at hearing that there was no connection whatsoever between his pub and Sir Francis Drake soon dissipated when it was explained to him that what he had uncovered was of far greater historical significance.

It was obvious what must have happened. Some Victorian sign-painter, instructed to produce a new picture, looked at the old one and wondered why a cannon was being shown instead of the "drake" which swam on the village pond. (Yes, there had been a village pond at that time, but it had been filled in at the turn of the century.) Assuming a mistake by the previous painter, he had replaced the cannon that belonged on the sign with a bird—a mallard—of his own devising. With a few brush-strokes he had consigned the history of the building to the dustbin.

"This is brilliant!" Wally was saying, as we took advantage of the drink the landlord had offered us, on the house, as thanks for solving his mystery. "Now we know we've found the site of the Battle of Barrow End."

"Not so fast, young man," said Nathan kindly. "Rosemary, would you please explain to my poor deluded friend why it isn't as simple as that?"

"All the sign proves," I said, "if it proves anything at all, is that there was some military activity around here at about the time of the Civil War. And we already knew that. It certainly doesn't prove that the battle took place in Velvet Vale."

"Quite right," said Nathan. "But you've omitted to consider the question of the dog," he added, mysteriously.

I was at a loss. "Don't tell me there's some item of military equipment called a dog?" I quipped.

Nathan laughed obligingly. "Not as far as I know. You will, of course, recall that Prince Rupert of the Rhine had a large dog which he used to take into battle with him."

"Rupert wasn't at Barrow End, was he?" I asked, hopefully.

"I think we can rule out that possibility," Nathan replied. "At that time, he would have been rather preoccupied with the Battle of Edgehill."

I remembered how Nathan preferred to be asked questions before he offered explanations. "So what does the dog signify?"

"The Mad Dog," he replied. "Sir Henry Kinkade. It was his nickname."

Sir Henry Kinkade had been the leader of the Royalist forces at the Battle of Barrow End.

Nathan didn't seem troubled by the fact that even the oldest pub sign showed, not a man in Cavalier uniform, but an actual dog. That was simply a literal interpretation of the name, he said, in the same way as the mallard was, only older. He theorised that it was a consequence of the villagers wanting Cromwell to overlook their earlier allegiance to the Royalist cause, once Parliament had gained the ascendancy.

We were all in excellent spirits by closing time. As we walked to the car, Nathan continued to talk about the importance of our discovery, which was likely to claim a chapter to itself in his forthcoming book about the Battle of Barrow End. He was, I could tell, slightly frustrated at not having made the discovery of the sign himself. It had never struck him, he kept saying, that the name of the pub could be significant. He had even spent the night there without making any enquiry into the history of the building.

"It just goes to show," he said once again, "that we should never take things for granted. Always remember that, Rosemary. Look beyond the obvious."

"This'll be one in the eye for the Farmers," I said. "And Councillor Long."

Nathan was shaking his head, as he and Wally got into the car. "I wouldn't include that young man in the same bracket as Mr. and Mrs. Farmer."

"I thought you didn't like him," I said.

"Whatever makes you think that?" he asked, through the open window, just before switching on the ignition. "Goodnight, Rosemary."

He left me still wondering whether any sarcasm had been intended.

Jonathan's friend on the "County Examiner" came up trumps this time. The front page article the following Tuesday was headlined, "HISTORIC DISCOVERY IN VILLAGE PUB" and sub-titled "LANDLORD OPPOSES PLANNING APPLICATION." The landlord of the Dog and Drake, thrilled at the thought of the additional publicity, had been easily convinced by Nathan to make a statement to the effect that the proposed development of Velvet Vale would be "a lethal blow to our efforts to preserve our national heritage." It was obvious that Nathan had supplied the words himself.

The landlord had added to the effectiveness of the newspaper report, however, by mentioning that he believed the battlefield to be haunted. He claimed to have seen "mysterious figures" in the field after dark. This particular portion of the story had obviously *not* been supplied by Nathan, who would have scorned the idea of supernatural activity. Though now that I came to think of it, I recalled that the battlefield at Edgehill was supposed to be populated by various military-minded phantoms. It was a toss-up whether the landlord's claims made him sound like a harmless crank or a concerned citizen, but there's supposed to be no such thing as bad publicity.

What the Farmers made of it all I never knew. It was lucky for the landlord that they weren't among his regular customers. There was no way Valerie Farmer would expose herself to the gibes of the Re-enactment Society by entering the pub to harangue those serving there. She just had to grin and bear it.

Chapter 17

What I Did on My Holidays

Towards the end of July I went away for my planned week's holiday, staying with Lucy, a married friend from my college days. Since Lucy remembered Peter Markham very well, as my former boyfriend, I had naturally told her about him coming to live nearby and about our acquaintance having been renewed. However, I had never told her how far the renewal had gone, and I didn't choose this time to do so. As far as I was concerned, it was well and truly in the past.

During the week I didn't think much about the Velvet Vale campaign, but I had been plunged into an atmosphere of nostalgia and I did, inevitably, think a lot about Peter. At this distance in time, I was baffled as to what had ever made me want to recapture the heady days of our student romance. It was one thing to feel a degree of tenderness for someone I'd spent whole nights and days with at a critical time of my life, but quite another to mistake that nostalgic feeling for love. When I looked back on our brief affair—if you could call it that—I felt nothing but shame.

I hadn't meant to hurt anyone, or cause anyone guilt or embarrassment. It shook me that I could have behaved with such casual thoughtlessness in a situation that was potentially shattering for Peter and Hilary. Thank goodness she had never found out about us.

The week away from Barrow End and my job was good for me in lots of ways. I felt happier and more relaxed than I had done for a while, and returned with renewed enthusiasm for the campaign and a determination to turn over a new leaf as far as my private life was concerned.

As soon as I got back in town, I was anxious to learn what, if anything, had been happening while I was away. There was only one major development, and it had no direct relevance to the progress of our campaign. Herbert had decided to throw a party.

He didn't call it a party; he called it a "social evening." Its ostensible purpose was to celebrate the re-enactment of the Battle of Barrow End. By a quirk of fate, however, the only possible date for the party was the Friday evening before the Sunday of the battle. It would be held in the Village Hall. And I, in my absence, had been elected to take charge of the refreshments.

It could have been worse, I suppose. I might have been put in charge of the entertainment or made to stand on the door collecting the entrance fees. In theory, I would be free to enjoy myself as soon as the buffet had been served, which was due to happen at eight o'clock. That meant that I would be frantically busy from seven till nine, first preparing and setting out the food, then clearing away the leftovers and dirty dishes.

There were plenty of offers of help, but the person I'd been counting on most of all—Hilary—had declared herself unavailable. She and Peter were going away on the Friday in question, for a weekend break to celebrate their fifth wedding anniversary, and would only just get back in time for the battle itself. There was no way they could attend the party. Herbert had done everything in his power to find an alternative day and time to accommodate them, but in the end it had proved impossible because of the commitments of the Society members and the rest of the Action Committee.

In the end, Hilary and Peter had refused to allow other people's arrangements to be messed up because of them, and had insisted that the party go ahead without them. Had it not been for that, Hilary would probably have volunteered to take charge of the refreshments herself. As it was, the committee was stuck with me. Once again, I took solace in the thought that, had I been the vicar's wife, I would have had to do this kind of thing all the time.

While we were discussing the arrangements for the party, word came through that the date of the Planning Committee meeting at which the Farmers' application would be discussed had been agreed. It was the day immediately *after* the Battle of Barrow End. That meant that the party, the battle itself, and the planning meeting would follow one another in quick succession. I wished it could have been the opposite way round — the planning meeting, the battle, and then the party to celebrate. That way, if the planning application were passed by the Borough Council, we could at least drown our sorrows.

When I thought further on the matter, I came to the conclusion that things were probably better the way they were. At least the party wouldn't be spoiled by the planning decision, if it went against us. On the contrary, maybe the success of the re-enactment would have some influence on the decision—in our favour. There seemed no doubt that it *would* be a success.

I hadn't heard any more from Mrs. Challoner about Councillor Long and his complaint. When I went back into work, she told me she had decided not to reply to his letter. After some consideration, she'd come to the conclusion that he had no right to try and muzzle council employees, and she wasn't going to go along with it. I must admit I was relieved.

I did see him, though. The school holidays were in full swing, and there were lots of children around, in the library and museum as everywhere else. For the past few months, Herbert had been making preparations for a "Family Activity Day," as an extra fund-raiser.

This was something the museum always did in the summer, but on this occasion Herbert and I had persuaded some of the Re-enactment Society to come down and demonstrate the seventeenth century lifestyle. So, as well as the usual activities, Joe and some of his friends turned up on the Saturday morning and proceeded to show visitors how a housewife in the time of King Charles I would have gone about cooking and cleaning, and how a soldier in the Royalist army would have looked after his equipment.

I didn't participate in this, as I was too busy helping some of the younger children to stick Roman pots together like a jigsaw. This was useful to the museum as well as fun for them, because we had a lot of material left over from various excavations that wasn't wanted by any of the big museums because it was too fragmentary. It wasn't interesting enough, in its present state, to be put on display, but when the kids came to our museum for the day, we would get around to piecing some of it together, and it could then be added to the Roman exhibit.

Believe it or not, the children got quite a thrill out of the idea that their handiwork would be on display in a glass case for future visitors to look at. Quite a few of them used to drag their parents back into the museum a few weeks later to see it again. Some of today's small visitors had obviously been here for the previous activity day, at Easter, because I saw one little boy pointing out to his grandmother the pot he had re-assembled: "That's *my* pot, Gran."

Bridget, my landlady's daughter, called in with her band of offspring, who ranged in age from sixteen to three. The eldest boy went to watch Joe cleaning his armour, and the girls all wanted to see the demonstration of seventeenth-century baking. Talk about sexual stereotyping.

The two youngest were the only ones interested in my Roman pots, and they were very lovable kids. I'd often met them before, when they came to visit their grandmother, so they made a bee-line for me. The little girl, Rhona, who was too young to do anything practical, sat on my knee and played with the "do-it-yourself Roman mosaic" that I'd prepared earlier, while I occupied myself with ensuring that she didn't swallow any of the pieces. Her brother, Patrick, who was six, made a valiant attempt to re-assemble the pieces of a Belgic cooking pot which I'd got out of the store cupboard. I sat there, playing with them and listening to their accounts of end-of-term concerts, and drifted away into a reverie.

I don't quite know what it was that brought me back to the present, but something made me look up, and I found myself gazing straight into the eyes of Councillor Long. He was standing over by the reception desk, talking to Herbert, but he appeared to be looking in my direction. I felt guilty, as though I'd been caught red-handed in some criminal act rather than just chatting innocently to a couple of small children. I tried to pretend I hadn't seen him, but I knew I had failed to disguise my embarrassment.

After he had finished talking to Herbert and gone, I felt almost disappointed. It wasn't that I had wanted him to come over to me and berate me for my recent behaviour towards him, or to remind me of my responsibilities as an employee of the local authority, so I didn't quite know what it was that had got to me. While I had been away, I'd had a lot of time to think, and I wasn't entirely confident that I had dealt with Councillor Long in the most dignified possible way at our last meeting. I didn't care what he thought of me, yet I did somehow feel that I'd let myself down.

The mood didn't last long, not with Joe there. In between demonstrations, he kept coming over to the "Roman area" to chat. He tried to boost my confidence about the party catering by telling me he thought I was a great cook. When I asked how he could possibly know, I realised he had conned me into inviting him round to the flat for a meal.

I knew it wasn't sensible to let him manipulate me like this. No doubt the meal itself would be an enjoyable experience—even if it was cooked by me—but I could foresee exactly how the rest of the evening would progress. Joe would turn up with a bottle of wine and would insist on putting something soppy on the CD player, Barry Manilow or something of that ilk. Then the pair of us would sit down on the settee, his hand would end up on my knee, and I'd have to make the choice between fighting him off and getting myself into a situation I knew I'd regret.

In fact, whatever choice I made, I would regret it. It wouldn't make any difference at all to Joe. He wouldn't go off me just because I refused to go to bed with him, nor would he fall in love with me if I agreed to it. Our relationship would remain much the same as it already was. Under the circumstances, I felt it was better not to make the commitment.

On the other hand, I thought, if I did give in to Joe, I might find that it killed off any remaining mystery attaching to him, and I would be able to get over him quite easily. More easily than I had with Peter, at any rate.

I *thought* I would, but I wasn't sure.

In the end, it all turned out rather differently from what I had expected. There was a short committee meeting scheduled for the following Friday evening, just to discuss the logistics for the re-enactment weekend, and we arranged that Joe would come round to my flat afterwards.

The consequence was that he arrived on time, for once, but he didn't bring wine. He brought beer for himself, and a couple of cans of cider for me. I suppose he remembered that I'd been quite keen on it when we were sixth-formers. He also brought an old vinyl record, which had been a favourite at the school disco in those days. Nostalgia was definitely the flavour of the evening.

I had anticipated that tonight's assault on my virtue would be a mite more subtle than on the previous occasion, but I would have been insulted if he hadn't tried it on at all.

And, of course, he did.

But first things first. The food went down okay. You can't do much wrong with macaroni cheese and salad.

"Have you turned vegetarian?" Joe asked, dismayed at the absence of red meat.

"Listen, Hannibal Lecter, if you want to eat poor murdered animals for every meal, you'll have to go to another restaurant," I joked. "I prefer a bit of variation in my diet. And don't try and tell me you don't like cheese, I've seen you wolfing down a ploughman's in the Dog and Drake, and you nearly always go for the Cheddar."

"Okay, okay!" He raised a hand in submission, pushing a forkful simultaneously into his gob. Then he grinned. "Mmm, this is good."

I opened my can of cider and poured it into a glass. If I couldn't have wine, I was at least going to make some attempt at civilised behaviour.

When we'd finished the macaroni, I got out the strawberry flan I'd made earlier. No, I really had. The strawberries were fresh, and I'd even made the pastry myself.

"You ought to go on that TV programme," said Joe, stuffing it down like there was no tomorrow. "Whassit called, where there are three of them competing?"

"I don't know and I don't care," I said. "Flattery will get you nowhere."

"Well, if I stop flattering you, will that get me somewhere?" he said suddenly.

I didn't reply, but picked up the empty plates and took them into the kitchen.

"Leave the washing up!" he protested.

"I'm going to," I said. "*You're* doing it."

The expression of horror on Joe's face wasn't faked. He soon recovered, however, and went over to the hi-fi.

"Still got your turntable, I'm pleased to see," he commented, taking the record out of its sleeve.

"It's not the same one I had when we were in school, stupid," I said.

"I'm not stupid!" He looked quite hurt for a moment, and turned back to switch on the amplifier. When he looked at me again, the smile was back on his face.

"I'm not too stupid to recognise a pretty girl when I see one, anyway," he said. "Wanna dance?"

Before I even knew what was happening, he had got hold of me and we were in one of those close, drunken clinches that occur at the end of every disco. For a minute or two, I went along with it. Only I wasn't drunk, and I had a pretty shrewd idea Joe wasn't either. Letting myself slip backwards in his arms, I looked up at him and liked what I saw. His hair had grown quite a lot in the past couple of months, and there was plenty there for me to get my fingers tangled in. It was too much of a temptation.

Then he started to kiss me. It was fairly innocuous to begin with, just a few little feathery touches of mouth on mouth, then mouth on cheek, then mouth on neck...I could feel myself becoming light-headed, my logic circuits ceasing to function, my common sense drifting away.

"What next, then?" he murmured, his hand slipping under my skirt and beginning its progress up my thigh.

"Nothing, next," I said sharply, slapping his hand away. "You came here to eat, and you've eaten."

He started to do his hurt look again, but I wasn't in the mood to be placated.

"Look," he went on, seeing my face, "we're both adults..."

"One of us is," I corrected.

"Oh, come on, Rose..."

The music had stopped. I held him at arm's length, and pinned his elbows to his sides.

"Are you telling me you haven't already got a girlfriend?" I asked, forcing him to meet my eyes.

"Well..."

"You have, haven't you?"

"It's nothing serious."

"And is *this* something serious?"

He looked sheepish. "Since you put it like that..." He had another try at winning me over with one of his famous boyish grins. "Look, Rose, I've tried marriage. You'd hardly expect me to rush into it again, would you? I admit, I avoid long-term relationships these days. But I do fancy you. You're really nice, really attractive, and I..."

"I don't want to hear it." I turned away.

Another man would have left at that point, but not Joe. He just laughed it off. "Okay, you win. Let's have another drink."

Much later, after he had drunk too much to drive home and had gone over to the Eatons' for the night, I thought seriously about what had happened. It was possible that I had just missed my last chance of any kind of relationship with Joe. Not definite, but possible.

Did I regret it?

Yes and no. I felt much the same as I had done at the beginning of the evening. Things hadn't gone quite the way I had expected, but the end result had been the same.

The way I saw it, there was a choice. I could keep Joe as a friend. He wouldn't be a very reliable friend, but he was very sweet and a lot of fun. Or I could try and make something else out of our friendship. I could try and get him to make the kind of commitment which he had just told me he wasn't ready to make, and in the process I would risk getting myself in so deep that it was bound to end in tears.

The first option was the sensible one. The down side of it was that I wouldn't get to experience that other side of him, that loving side that I knew was there. I guessed that he would be fantastic in bed, warm, generous, exciting. The trouble was, once I had done it once, I would want to do it again. Sooner or later, Joe would go away, back where he had come from, and he would drop me as easily as he had picked me up. That wasn't what I wanted.

Oh, and guess who had ended up doing the dishes?

Chapter 18

Vicars and Tarts

There was only a week to go before the party, and I was getting extremely apprehensive about my role as caterer.

Hilary, bless her, had helped me devise a list of easy-to-make, guaranteed-to-succeed dishes that could be served up on the buffet. Both Molly and Verity had promised to help with the cooking, serving and clearing. Even Mrs. Murphy had helped out, by offering the use of her freezer. Hilary prepared a mountain of sausage rolls and vol-au-vents which could be frozen and then re-heated just before the party. She brought over several baskets' worth on the previous Friday night, then flitted off to attend a meeting of the parish council before I could complete the job of loading them into the freezer.

I took the baskets back to the vicarage the following evening, but Hilary wasn't there. Peter was on his own in the house.

He looked a little nervous about inviting me in, and I was more than a little nervous about accepting, but somehow we found ourselves alone together in the big old kitchen. It wasn't that I still hankered after him. I've already said I was over that. It just felt awkward.

I hadn't often been inside the vicarage, which was one of those rambling Victorian houses that used to be regarded as ideal homes for the clergy. As I gazed around at the dark cobwebby corners and smelled the musty smell, I was once again thinking about what it would be like to be a vicar's wife, and counting my blessings.

Getting over his initial reluctance, Peter made me a cup of coffee, and we drank it sitting at the big oak table. We kept off sensitive subjects. I told him about my stay at Lucy's and passed on her best wishes, and thereafter we concentrated on the progress of the party preparations. Eventually we moved on to talk about general parish matters.

"Hilary's having a coffee morning on Tuesday," he said. "It's in aid of the NSPCC. I don't suppose you'll be able to come?"

"Tuesday's my usual day off," I answered, "so I suppose I could."

"She'd be very glad to see you," he commented. "She's always saying she gets bored with the same old faces every time."

I had a sudden, horrible thought.

"Valerie Farmer won't be coming, will she?" I asked.

Peter smiled. "I wouldn't think so," he said.

"Thank goodness for that. It would be very difficult to try and keep up a polite front. I know we're Christians and all that, and we have to try and love our neighbour, but really, that woman..."

Peter was still smiling, and I caught a solitary glimpse of the boy I had loved.

"As your vicar," he said, "I can't approve of anything else."

"But go on, Peter," I said, nudging him confidentially, "just between you and me, you don't like the Farmers any more than the rest of us do. Do you?"

He mulled it over. "They're not all bad," he said. "Actually, they've been very generous to the church."

It was a moment or two before I fully took in what he had said. We've established that the Farmers weren't churchgoers, at least not in Peter's parish. I somehow doubted that they were regulars in any church, though no doubt they showed themselves at Christmas and any special services. I had definitely never seen them in the congregation at St Catherine's, regardless of the occasion.

"What church would that be?" I asked, my innocence dissipating fast.

"St Catherine's," said Peter. "They—they made a substantial contribution to the restoration fund."

He looked flustered now, and I began to see what had happened.

"When was this, Peter?" I asked. "Did it happen before they applied for the planning permission?"

"Er...yes, it did, now that you come to mention it."

Of course it did.

"You mean they gave you money for the fund, just before they put in their application to build right next to the church?"

"Not '*just* before,' as you put it. It was some time ago. They contributed it anonymously. They sent me a letter, saying they wished to remain anonymous. I shouldn't really be telling you."

"But you knew it was from them?"

"Of course. They wrote to me, they signed the letter, but they said they would prefer no one to know. Apart from me, that is."

Well, they would, wouldn't they?

"How much was it?"

He weighed up the possibility of telling me a lie before admitting, "Five thousand."

I pondered on the significance of what he had said for a few moments before replying.

"Peter," I said slowly, "do you mean to tell me that you accepted a bribe?"

His face went white.

"It wasn't at all like that, Rose," he stammered. "Not at all. It was the other way round. I didn't even know, at that time, that they were going to make a planning application."

"You could have made an educated guess that they would be putting one in at some future date, though, couldn't you? I mean, why else would they have been so generous? Didn't it seem like a strange thing for non-churchgoers to do?"

"Rose," he protested, "they *gave* me the money. I couldn't refuse it. It was for the *church*."

"So is what the rest of us are doing, Peter. That's for the benefit of the church as well."

"It's all very well for you to say that, Rose, but the church needs money, more money than we can get from the weekly collection. The fabric of the building is falling apart, you know that. There wouldn't have been any church *left* for us to have concerns about if the restoration fund hadn't succeeded in raising the money we needed. And we'll always need more. I couldn't turn down a donation that size. Think what people would have said. It didn't make any difference to my belief that the planning application should be rejected."

"But it stopped you speaking out against it. It stopped you joining the Action Committee."

He looked annoyed. "I told you, I felt I should remain impartial. I meant that."

Another thought struck me. "I suppose that's why there was no objection from the diocese on environmental grounds."

"It had nothing to do with it," he said quickly, and I knew from his tone of voice that it had.

"If they hadn't given you the money," I probed, exploring his conscience, "wouldn't you have behaved differently?"

"No!" He was so emphatic that tiny droplets of spittle shot out from his lips, all over the place. Embarrassed, he grew quieter. "I don't think so," he said.

"You're not sure, though, are you?"

He looked down. "No, Rose, I'm not sure. I seldom am sure about anything. That's what being a priest is all about—not judging people, not taking the moral high ground, recognising that you're as imperfect as everyone else."

He was right. I knew that. It must have been very hard for him. If he had turned down the Farmers' "donation," and people had got to know about it, he would have been taken to task for that decision. I could see exactly why he had acted as he had.

But that didn't make it all right.

"Peter," I persisted, "didn't it occur to you that they were trying to influence you in their favour?"

"No, Rose," he said emphatically. "You didn't see their letter. It quite specifically said that they were making the gift freely to the church, that there were no strings attached, that they weren't expecting any kind of preferential treatment."

"They'd hardly say anything else in a letter, would they? Where is it, this letter? Can I see it?"

"I haven't got it now," he protested. "I passed it on to the diocese, with the money for the fund and the rest of the documentation. In any case, I couldn't show it to you, it was private."

I couldn't argue with that, either. But I wasn't giving in gracefully.

"You know what that donation is, don't you, Peter? It's blood money."

Peter coloured, but didn't respond. I left a few minutes later, feeling that I had been rather hard on him, but reluctant to show any compassion.

When I got home, I spent some time thinking about what I had been told, turning it over and over in my mind and wondering what to do about it.

Joe came round after the pub closed. It was a relief to see him, as it helped take my mind off the immediate problem. I thought of telling him what I'd learned, but it seemed like a breach of confidence. In some ways, it would have been worse to tell Joe than to tell anyone else, simply because Joe didn't know about me and Peter, and Peter—presumably—didn't know about me and Joe. Not that there was anything to know about me and Joe.

(How did that old advertising jingle go, "There are two men in my life..."? To think that I used to envy the woman in that advert.)

Peter could get into trouble over this, I was sure, and he would never have mentioned it if he hadn't been so sure that Rose, his Rose, was to be trusted with the secret. His faith in me was touching. It was also completely unfounded; but I didn't intend to betray him unless there was something to be gained from it, something that would help the campaign.

Since the night of the failed seduction, Joe and I had maintained a friendly distance. When he turned up at the flat that evening, I was pleased at the knowledge that he still had enough of an interest in me to make a social call.

"Joe," I asked idly, while we were drinking coffee, "didn't you say you'd done some work for the Inland Revenue?"

"Yeah, why? Are you in trouble with the taxman? Not been declaring your second income?" He gave a sly grin.

"No, I was just wondering about giving to charity. Aren't there ways you can do it that carry some kind of tax benefit?"

"I believe so. If you're giving a large amount, the charity gets the tax back on it. That's why charities are so keen on covenants and things like that. I only worked on one small part of the computer system, so I couldn't tell you the full detail—and it changes every time there's a Budget. You can get leaflets about it."

"Thanks. You've answered my query."

The conversation moved on to other topics. Joe asked me to come and watch him doing "pike drill" one evening with the Society. As always, I was flattered to be asked, as though it made me someone special, but I knew the truth. I could imagine Joe, checking up on his "other" girlfriend's activities, making sure he never invited us both to be in the same place at the same time. Presumably she was unavailable to watch him drill on this occasion, so he felt safe in asking me. He looked disappointed when I declined; but his moment of disappointment didn't last long.

Chapter 19

Brought to Account

After sleeping on it, I came to a decision. I was recalling something Peter had said, some time before, about Edward Long being the auditor of the restoration fund's accounts. That meant he had his fingers in both ends of the pie, so to speak.

I was going to go and see Mr. Long, in his capacity as the Farmers' accountant. I would confront him with what I knew, and see what he had to say on the matter. I prided myself on the thought that I would be able to tell, simply from speaking to him, how heavily involved he was in the attempt at bribery.

If Long failed to come up with any sensible explanation, I would expose him, and the Farmers, to the press, and I would report the lot of them to the Council, or the Ombudsman, or the Prime Minister if necessary. It didn't matter what they had said in their letter, or how much care they had taken to make themselves look innocent. People would draw their own conclusions. Jonathan's contacts on the "County Examiner" would be only too delighted to print the story, as long as we were careful not to make it libellous, and that would finish the Farmers' chances of getting their planning permission. At least, I hoped it would.

As you can imagine, I wasn't exactly leaping up and down with joy at the thought of approaching Councillor Long. I still felt no guilt about my behaviour to him on the last occasion we'd spoken, but even without that complication, it didn't seem likely that he would make a receptive audience for what I had to say.

If I'd stopped to think more deeply into it, I would have realised that I had a double motive in going to see him. I wanted to show him that I hadn't been intimidated by his action in complaining to my boss. Equally importantly, I wanted to come across as his intellectual peer, not some petulant child who went around slamming car doors.

I had to plan my approach carefully, so that it didn't come across as a threat or an attempt at blackmail. I was quite sure Mr. Long wouldn't respond to that. Whatever else, the bloke had guts, he would face it out and deny everything. No doubt he'd been smart enough to conceal the payment to the Church so that it couldn't be interpreted as corruption. Besides, as he would undoubtedly point out, Peter hadn't actively supported the Farmers. All the same, I decided I wouldn't reveal my strategy to anyone beforehand. Forewarned is forearmed.

The more I thought about it, the more I feared that it would do no good to speak to Mr. Long. But I had this privileged knowledge in my possession, and I had to do something with it.

I entered the accountant's office at four o'clock on Monday afternoon. I hadn't made an appointment. That would have allowed him time to prepare himself. He might not know exactly what I was going to say, but he was a clever man, perceptive despite his political affiliations, and he could make a reasonable stab at guessing, given thinking time. So I wasn't going to let him have any thinking time.

I chose the end of the day partly because the museum was closed and it was easy to finish early, and partly because I reasoned that it would be a thin time for accountants to have appointments with their clients. All the same, I was expecting that he would refuse to see me—and that was assuming he was in his office. But I had a contingency plan. If necessary, I would go to his house, even if it meant having to get past his mother.

Edward Long's office was on the first floor of one of the converted eighteenth-century houses that faced onto the High Street. There was a secretary in the tiny reception area, a middle-aged woman with iron-grey hair. I recognised her, behind her half-moon spectacles, as a regular visitor to the library building, but she didn't acknowledge me. I wasn't put out, as I've found that people often don't recognise one another out of context. Particularly nonentities like museum staff.

"Can I help you?" she said, not exactly exuding welcome.

"I want to see Mr. Long, if he's available."

"Is he expecting you?"

"No."

"He doesn't normally see people without an appointment."

"It's rather important. If he's busy, I'll wait."

I don't know whether he heard my voice, or whether it was merely an accident that Edward Long came to the door of his office at that precise moment and looked out.

He stood there for a few moments, just staring at me. Perhaps he thought I'd come to apologise for my rudeness at our previous meeting, or to confront him finally about the letter he'd sent Mrs. Challoner. I didn't say anything, and I was very careful not to smile.

"Miss Gardner," he said, politely. "Did you want to see me?"

"If it's convenient," I replied, with equal politeness.

He stood aside and pushed the office door wider, so that I could enter. "Please go in," he said. "I'll be right with you."

The receptionist didn't look too pleased at having her authority undermined, but she could hardly object. Mr. Long said something to her quietly, then turned and followed me into the office.

I sat down in the chair that faced his desk. He closed the door on us, and went back to his own seat, behind the desk, making me feel like a child who's just been called in to see the headmaster. I was glad that I had worn my new suit, the plum-coloured one that I'd bought for the Mayor's inauguration.

He sat down slowly, frowning a little. "What can I do for you?" he asked.

Now that it had come to it, it was difficult to find the words. I had thought them all through beforehand, time and time again, but when it came to the crunch, they had deserted me.

"It's about Mr. and Mrs. Farmer," I said.

He looked puzzled. "Yes?" he prompted.

"I assume you knew that they made a large donation to St Catherine's, not long before they applied for planning permission for Velvet Vale."

He sat back so suddenly that his head hit the back of the leather chair with a muffled thud.

"Who told you this?" he said.

"The vicar, Peter Markham. They sent him a letter, saying they wanted to give anonymously to the church restoration fund. It's obvious, isn't it, what they wanted in return?"

"When you say a large donation…?"

"Five thousand pounds."

Long's reaction wasn't at all what I had expected. It wasn't so much the horrified look—I had certainly expected that. It was what he said next.

"Do you have any concrete evidence of what you've just told me?" he asked, first.

"I don't have the letter in my possession," I said. "I doubt if it still exists. But I'll be surprised if a cheque for five thousand pounds can't be traced through the banks involved. I don't think the Church of England would accept a cash payment of that size, even if it were offered. But of course, you audited the accounts for the restoration fund, so you would know exactly what went in and out, wouldn't you?"

He stood up, and came out from behind his desk. My first thought was that he was going to open the door of the office and tell me to get out, but instead he went over to the rows of folders stacked on shelves against the wall and drew one out. It occurred to me that he hadn't yet asked *why* I was telling him all this.

"You know that the Farmers are clients of mine, don't you?" he said, sitting down again with the folder and putting on his glasses.

"Of course. That's why you're siding with them over the planning application," I replied.

He shot me a resentful look. "I suppose you would think that," he said, his voice sharp and bitter. "Try to get a fair hearing for someone, and everyone assumes you're on the take."

"You can hardly claim to be disinterested in the matter."

"I *am* disinterested," he said. "I couldn't care less whether the Farmers get their planning permission or not, provided everybody plays by the rules."

"So you don't care about the people of Barrow End?" I taunted him.

"Barrow End has its own local authority representatives to look after it," he said. "I'm not one of them. All I want is to see the arguments on both sides put fully and fairly, and then the Planning Committee can make a reasoned decision."

It sounded very disingenuous.

"But you're a member of the Planning Committee. That gives you the ability to influence the decision for the benefit of the Farmers."

He looked exasperated. “I will take no part in the decision on Barrow End,” he said. “I’ve already declared an interest in that application, precisely because of my relationship with the Farmers, and that disqualifies me from speaking and voting on that particular application at the meeting.”

It was a good thing he wasn’t looking at me when he said it, because I wouldn’t have wanted him to see how completely he had caught me out. I was gobsmacked.

“I hadn’t heard that,” was all I could manage to say.

“Well, now you have.” He still wasn’t looking me in the face, but continued to leaf through the folder. It seemed to contain receipts and invoices, and I sensed that it related in some way to the Farmers’ business.

Looking at him across the desk, I drew the conclusion that Edward Long made a conscious effort to appear older than he was. The severe haircut, emphasizing every fleck of grey, the conservatively-cut suit and dark tie—he even wrote with a fountain pen, I observed as he jotted something down on a pad near his right hand.

There was something positively impressive about him in this, his natural habitat. He had a gravity and a confidence he hadn’t generally shown at the meetings where our paths had crossed; and something more, a cool aloofness that I envied.

He removed his glasses for a second. For the first time, I noticed his eyes, grey with a halo of green around the pupil. Off-putting.

“Have they declared it? Their... *donation* to the church?” I asked, trying to distract him from my own confusion and still sound as stroppy as I had when I entered his office.

Now I had his full attention. Putting his glasses back on, he looked up from the folder. “That’s confidential,” he said.

“I’m sure they have,” I went on, sarcastically. “I’m sure a financially astute couple like the Farmers wouldn’t miss out on the opportunity to claim back the tax on a donation to a charity.”

I could see he wasn’t going to be drawn into further discussion. He stood up again, and proffered his right hand across the desk. “Thank you for telling me all this, Miss Gardner,” he said. “I’ll have to look into it further.”

I gathered I was dismissed, and stood up, but I didn’t take his hand.

"Think nothing of it," I snapped spitefully, and walked out of the office.

It was the second time I had slammed a door in his face. So much for good resolutions.

IT HADN'T DONE any good at all. In fact, I had given away any advantage, by letting him know that I knew the truth, thus giving him the chance to cover his tracks. Worse than that, we couldn't pin anything on him because he had already declared an interest. So he said. If he hadn't already done it, he would do it immediately I was out of earshot, so that was another avenue closed.

Yet there was something in his manner, something in his reaction to what I had said, that gave me cause for doubt. Was it possible, I wondered, was it just possible that Edward Long, despite being in it up to his neck, hadn't known about the Farmers' little deal with Peter? Could they, in fact, have been using him to add a veneer of respectability to their operations?

There was someone else I could approach, I now realised, someone else who was accountable. Amelia Grundy, the Treasurer of St Catherine's Restoration Fund. I should have gone to her first, to check out my facts, before I made any approach to Edward Long, but I hadn't even thought of it. Typical of me, to rush into things without taking the time to consider all possible alternatives. Amelia would be able to confirm Peter's version of events. More importantly, she could confirm Long's involvement in the whole thing.

She lived over in Newick, the smallest and most remote of the three villages that made up Peter's parish, so she had no interest in the Farmers' planning application. I'd only ever met her half a dozen times, and I hadn't seen her for months. A retired civil servant, she didn't get out much, and she was probably oblivious to what was going on in Barrow End and the potential implications of the Farmers' donation to the fund.

Thinking that there was no time like the present, I drove over to her cottage that very evening, after I'd had my dinner. Newick consisted of no more than a dozen houses strung out on either side of a narrow lane, and Amelia's was the second on the left. The lights were on in her little sitting room, right at the front of the house. She liked to leave the curtains open, so that she could see any visitors before they knocked at her front door.

I saw her through the window as I walked up the path. She was sitting in an armchair, reading by the light of an old-fashioned standard lamp, but she looked up, saw me, and got up from her chair to open the door, before I even had a chance to knock.

She didn't know me very well, and called me "Miss Gardner."

"This is a nice surprise," she said, motioning me to a chair. She seemed to think it was a social call.

I was obliged to make small talk for five minutes or so, before coming to the reason for my visit.

"I wanted to ask you about the church restoration fund," I explained. Miss Grundy looked a little nervous, but not altogether surprised, and she didn't stop smiling. "You kept all the accounts, didn't you?"

"That's right," she said. "Of course, it was wound up some months ago, and I've only got my original hand-written accounts, not the printed copies that went to the diocese. Do you want to see them, too?"

I wondered why she used the word, "too," but at the time I didn't think anything of it. Taking her up on her offer, I noticed how quickly she was able to bring the ledger to hand.

"What I wanted to ask you," I went on, "was how big an individual donation would have to be, in order to be recorded separately."

"That depends," she said, "on whether it came in the form of a cheque, or cash. A collection, for example, from a sponsored walk or something—we did have one of those, didn't we? Yes, I think we did—that would mostly come in as cash, so it would just be recorded as 'Proceeds from sponsored walk.' You see it, there."

I glanced quickly down the columns of figures, until I came to the signature at the bottom. The neat, legible signature of the auditor, Edward Long, followed by the date.

It didn't take me long to spot that the largest single donation shown was the one thousand pounds that my neighbour, Colonel Montgomery, had given the previous July. I pointed to the entry.

"Was that the biggest single donation to the fund?" I asked, trying to sound innocent.

Amelia looked even more nervous than she had at first.

"No, as a matter of fact, it wasn't. It's funny that you should ask. There was a donation of five thousand pounds, but it was made anonymously. It's just shown here under the general heading, Miscellaneous Donations."

"Do you know who made it?"

"No."

"But surely it would have come in the form of a cheque?"

"Yes, but I never saw the cheque. It came through the vicar's bank account."

For a moment, I didn't understand.

"What do you mean?" I asked.

"The donor—the anonymous donor—gave a cheque to the vicar, and the vicar made sure that nobody knew who it was, by paying the cheque into his own personal account, and then giving me a cheque for the total amount, including some cash amounts that people had paid into various collections."

Peter, I thought, how could you be so stupid? Had it never occurred to him that he was laundering money for the Farmers?

"Is that usual?" I asked.

"No." Amelia Grundy looked embarrassed. "I did query it at the time, but the vicar said it was all quite above board. He had a letter from the donor, asking for anonymity, and he said he would pass that on to the diocese with all the other documentation. It sounded reasonable, so I just did as I was told."

I thought for a moment.

"What about the auditor, Mr. Long? What did he say?"

"He didn't know about it."

"How could he not know about it? Didn't he see the cheque?"

"There were a lot of cheques. I don't think he looked at each individual one, there wouldn't have been time. And you see, the five thousand pounds is included in that miscellaneous total. He didn't realise that there was a single donation of five thousand pounds. He just thought it was from various cash collections."

"It's a very large amount."

"Yes, I can remember him asking me about it at the time. I never thought to mention the single donation. To tell you the truth, I had forgotten about it by the time we had that discussion. It only came back to me later."

"It seems strange that he should have been satisfied with your explanation—that it came from collections in cash."

Amelia smiled, and it struck me that she had missed her vocation. She would have made a great confidence trickster, if she'd only had the inclination.

"He's a nice man, Mr. Long. He knew I wouldn't do anything dishonest. He didn't ask many questions, because he knew it made me nervous. I do forget things, more and more, as I get older. But he's always been very understanding. He told me, just now, that I mustn't worry about it, that I hadn't done anything wrong. He said he would make everything all right."

I blinked, in amazement.

"You've just been talking to him?"

"Yes, actually. He only left a few minutes before you arrived. It's strange that you should have been asking all the same questions he was. It wasn't you who made that donation, was it?"

"No, it certainly wasn't!" I realised I had snapped at her, and I tried to soften my tone. "I'm sorry, I mean no, it wasn't me, I don't have that kind of money to spare. But I wouldn't have asked you all these questions if I'd known Mr. Long had already been here."

"Oh, I see. I'm sorry if I've wasted your time."

"No, Miss Grundy, it's me who's been wasting your time."

"That's no problem. It took me a while to remember the full details of what happened. But once Mr. Long jogged my memory, it was easy to repeat it all to you. And I don't get many visitors, so I hope you'll stay and have a cup of tea with me. There's some of my fruit cake left. Mr. Long said it was the best he'd ever tasted."

I stayed for the tea and cake. Under the circumstances, it seemed like the least I could do. And I discovered that Mr. Long wasn't a liar. The fruit cake was the best I'd ever tasted, too.

Chapter 20

The Consequences of My Actions

I stayed away from Peter Markham for a few days after our encounter in the vicarage kitchen. I hadn't gone to church on Sunday morning, and I didn't go to the coffee morning that Hilary was holding on Tuesday, mainly because I wouldn't have trusted myself to be civil to Peter if he showed his face. I was glad they weren't going to be at the party.

For a brief time, I was angrier with Peter than I had been before I spoke to Amelia Grundy. My initial sympathy for his plight had evaporated. Even Edward Long had behaved with a better sense of judgement over this whole business, it seemed; at least he had taken the trouble to investigate when a lapse in procedure was pointed out to him. But then, as I told myself, Mr. Long was an accountant, it was his job to know better. Peter's job was to trust people, and that was exactly what he had done. When you looked at it like that, it was difficult to hold it against him for long.

The week went by, and I spent much of the time preparing my shopping list for Friday night's party. Luckily, I only had to worry about the food and some non-alcoholic drinks. Plenty of other people had volunteered to make sure there was enough booze. Instead of going to the vicarage coffee morning on Tuesday, I used my day off to go to the supermarket and stock up on crisps, nuts and other fall-back items that could be brought out if we ran out of real food. Nothing would be wasted. Any surplus would come in handy after the battle re-enactment on Sunday afternoon.

Herbert had told me that the buffet must be cleared away by nine o'clock on Friday evening "without fail," because he planned to make a speech at that time. We had already discussed how we would recognise Nathan's "contribution to local history." Herbert's speech would be followed by a special "presentation ceremony"; but he told me not to say anything to Nathan about that, so I assumed it was some kind of additional thank you to the Re-enactment Society on behalf of the Action Committee. However, shortly after the approach from Herbert, Nathan himself mentioned a "presentation," and told me not to say too much about it to Herbert, so I concluded that there was going to be a degree of mutual appreciation shown.

Wednesday wasn't a good day. I had been dwelling on the question of the Farmers' attempted bribery so much that I hadn't thought about my other little problem at all. It was pure chance that Mrs. Challoner was off work that day and I was obliged to go through the filing cabinet in her office looking for an invoice that allegedly hadn't been paid.

There wasn't much there that needed to be kept confidential, and she'd always been very open-handed in allowing me the access I sometimes needed to her records. I wouldn't normally have looked in the drawer marked "Personnel" at all, if that dratted invoice hadn't gone missing.

My own name caught my eye, and the letter almost jumped out of the drawer at me. Once I'd seen that it was there, I couldn't stop myself taking a closer look. I reasoned that Mrs. Challoner would have showed it to me anyway, if I'd asked. I'd made a conscious decision not to ask; and yet the opportunity of looking at it in private was irresistible.

The letter was headed, "Confidential" and, of course, was dated several weeks earlier. "Dear Mrs. Challoner," it began. "I feel I must draw your attention to the involvement of your subordinate, the Deputy Curator of the District Museum, Miss Rosemary Gardner, in the activities of the Velvet Vale Action Committee. This committee has been formed with the purpose of opposing a planning application, but instead of confining itself to the matter in hand, one or two of its members have taken it upon themselves to stir up ill-feeling against the applicants and have indulged in confrontational and disruptive behaviour."

"I do not include Miss Gardner in this number, and I recognise that her particular responsibilities at the museum oblige her to take an interest in the preservation of what may turn out to be a site of historic significance. However, as an employee of the local authority, she needs to be very careful about involving herself with elements of society who may not have the best interests of the community at heart. Under section 2.14.3 of the Borough Council's Employee Code of Practice, she is forbidden to take part in political canvassing or campaigning, on pain of dismissal from her post. I would not like to see a promising career blighted, and so I am taking the step of sending this advisory letter."

"I have met Miss Gardner on several occasions and have the utmost respect for her, both personal and professional. However, I feel that she should be given a friendly warning about her conduct. By her present actions, she is not only allowing herself to become publicly associated with political malcontents but may be putting her future prospects at risk. Should it come to a confrontation between the Action Committee and the Borough Council, she will be put in a very difficult position, and I am not sure that I shall be able to protect her from the consequences of her actions. I should therefore be very grateful if you could remind her tactfully of her obligations under the Code of Practice."

The letter was signed by Edward Long.

Mrs. Challoner had described it as an odd letter, and I had to agree. It's always difficult to look dispassionately at something that directly concerns you, but I had the strangest feeling when I was reading that letter.

My first reaction was anger. All the stuff about "political malcontents" and "disruptive behaviour" was guaranteed to get me going. With Herbert as its Chair, the committee could hardly be accused of any such thing. It sounded as though the Councillor had the Re-enactment Society in mind, and all they had been guilty of was a certain amount of high spirits. Did he really feel that way about them, or did he just feel vulnerable because some of them were men of his own age and he was so much the odd one out?

The next thing I wondered was, why had he written the letter at all? The logical thing to do, and probably the most effective in a situation like this, would have been to *speak* to Mrs. Challoner. And I thought I had the answer to that one, too.

Shyness. I recognised it now, as I hadn't done before. Edward Long was a man who couldn't communicate with his equals. In his professional capacity, he was on pretty solid ground. He could talk to people across the desk, as he had talked to me, without any fear of being thought incompetent or stupid. As a councillor, he was also one up on most of the people he came into contact with. He had the power, he had the knowledge, he knew the answers to the questions.

But when it came to someone like Mrs. Challoner, his intellectual equal, and worse still, a *woman*, Mr. Long would have been floundering. As he had been at that public meeting earlier in the summer. As he had been when confronted by Nathan Pendragon. Mrs. Challoner would have argued with him, challenged his opinions, and sent him away with his tail between his legs. So he had written a letter, to prevent her answering back.

What I found most disturbing of all, however, was the bit about protecting me from the consequences of my actions. Why should Councillor Long feel any compulsion to *protect* me from anything? I barely knew the man, and yet he had picked on me, rather than Herbert and Doris, who were old friends of his and also had close links with the local authority. And anyway, what could *he* do to protect me, if it came to it?

It seemed as though his aim was to break my links with the Action Committee, and I couldn't see what purpose that would serve. If this was another attempt to divide and rule, it was a pointless exercise. The Action Committee would carry on, with or without me, and some of the people who might get involved in my place were far more militant than I was. I just couldn't fathom it.

Another thing that struck me, after I'd read the letter over two or three times, was that it wasn't really a letter of complaint—though I could see why Mrs. Challoner had interpreted it as such. The way she had described it to me, it had sounded like an official letter, but now that I'd seen how it was worded, and noticed that it wasn't on the Borough Council's headed notepaper, I realised that Edward Long had done this on his own initiative—or, more likely, at the instigation of the Farmers.

When I'd calmed down a little and thought about things more carefully, I was rather touched by his apparent concern. Maybe he really did believe he was doing this for my own good, saving me from my own stupidity. It was none of his business, and I resented his interference, but it was possible that he was simply taking a paternalistic attitude to a local authority employee.

It struck me then that, if I'd seen the letter sooner, I might not have been so ready to let fly at Mr. Long that day he had offered me a lift in his car. I might have tried to talk to him about it. The words "utmost respect, both personal and professional," kept coming back to me. Even if he had felt the utmost respect for me when he wrote the letter, I was damn sure he felt differently by now.

It was probably just as well that we had an exceptionally busy afternoon, because it stopped me from thinking about it any more. After the day I'd had, I looked forward to an early night, but I had to go down to Mrs. Murphy's flat to pay the rent, and she kept me talking. The consequence was that I didn't even finish eating my dinner till nearly nine o'clock. Then I started watching television, and made myself comfortable on the settee with a glass of white wine. I lay there for a while, and was just thinking about going to bed when a film came on the box that I wanted to see. Mel Gibson. I couldn't turn the set off while his face was on the screen. The film was coming to its climax when my doorbell rang.

I looked at my watch. It was half past eleven. Normally, I would have been in bed by this time. I lifted a corner of the curtain and looked out into the street. At first I couldn't make anything out, then I saw the figure, standing in the middle of the drive. As he looked up at my window, the paleness of his face reflected what little moonlight there was.

Joe.

Chapter 21

Quiet as a Graveyard

I prayed that Mrs. Murphy hadn't woken up, looked out and seen him. She would have had heart failure. For one thing, he was wearing all his re-enactment gear. I went downstairs as quietly as I could, to let him in.

"Rose," he began, in a voice pitched at normal volume. I put my finger to my lips, jerking my head towards the door of the downstairs flat so that he would understand.

"Sorry!" he responded, in a stage whisper.

I led him up the stairs, wondering all the time what he wanted with me at this time of night. I admit, I was hopeful. Just because I'd given him the brush-off once or twice, it didn't mean I didn't want him to boost my ego by trying again.

"Right," I said, closing the living room door on us. "What's up?" A whiff of alcohol caught my nostrils. I sniffed at him suspiciously. "Have you just come from the pub?"

"Of course!" He smiled broadly.

Oh no, I thought glumly. Even if he is that way inclined, it's only because he's drunk. Probably looking for a bed for the night, so that he won't have to drive home. Maybe the Eatons had locked him out.

"Well?" I challenged.

"Aren't you going to offer me a drink?" he asked.

"You must be joking. I think you've had enough already. How are you going to get home?"

"That's just the thing. I'm not going home."

"All right," I said wearily, "I get the picture. I'll make you some coffee. It's a bit late for you to go to the Eatons' now. You can hang on here until you've sobered up, or, if you prefer, I'll ring for a taxi. But you can't..."

"No, no, no, no, no," Joe said, revealing that he definitely was slightly inebriated. "No, no, no, you don't understand. I'm not going home, because I'm on patrol tonight."

"On patrol? What, have the Society introduced night drills or something?"

He chuckled. "In a manner of speaking. You see, we think we're on to something."

I flopped down on the settee and kicked off my slippers.

"Are you going to sit down?" I asked. "Or are you just going to wait until you fall down?"

"I'm not drunk," he protested, drunkenly. "Honest! Scout's honour." He gave a mock salute. I knew for a fact that he had never been in the Boy Scouts.

He fell into one of the armchairs.

"So what's it all about, then?"

"Some of us got together and did a bit of thinking," he said, his tone confidential, "and we reckon there's something going on in that field."

"Yes, of course there is, someone's trying to build houses on it."

"Naw!" He flapped his hand at me scornfully. "Not that. Something else."

"Okay. What?"

"Get us a cup of coffee and I'll tell ya."

Giving in to the inevitable, I got up to make the coffee. Joe followed me into the kitchen.

"You see," he rambled on, "one or another of us goes in that pub nearly every night, and sometimes we see things afterwards."

"I'm not surprised," I laughed.

"No, real things! Lights, that kind of thing."

"And?"

"Well, what do you think? Who'd be out there in the middle of the night?"

I remembered the comments the landlord of the Dog and Drake had made about haunting, and the hairs on the back of my neck stood on end. I searched for a more rational explanation.

"The Farmers keep horses in that field. Someone could be going out there to feed them."

Joe clicked his tongue in irritation. "Naw! Feeding horses at midnight? Why would anybody do *that*? They feed them during the *day*. No, we think they must be doing something they *shouldn't* be doing." His voice had acquired an unusual dipping-and-rising rhythm, thanks to the alcohol.

"Such as?"

"Aha! That's what we've got to find out."

I thought about it.

"Shouldn't you be out there now, then, in case you miss them?"

"Yes. But I came to fetch you."

Now I saw which way this was leading.

"I hope you don't think I'm coming with you."

"Yes, you are, darling. I need your assistance."

I tried not to be thrown by his use of the endearment. With Joe, it meant nothing. "I don't see what use I can possibly be."

"For a start," he said, taking the cafetiere out of my hand before I had a chance to pour from it, "you're going to put this in a thermos flask to take with us."

"You can have it. You don't need me for that."

"Oh, yes, I do. I need back-up."

"Joe," I said, "for goodness' sake, this isn't the sodding Falklands." I'd had a hard day, and he was starting to get on my nerves.

He put his arm around me and pecked my cheek.

"You're a smashing girl," he said. "I knew I could count on you."

After that, how could I have refused?

"JOE, STOP IT, this is ridiculous!" I was whispering, but so loudly that anyone who might have happened to be in the graveyard at midnight could not have failed to hear every word.

I saw that Joe had never changed. He was still that boy I had known at Colley Hill Comprehensive, the one who always wore full school uniform with the exception of one startlingly-coloured item—a pink shirt or bright orange socks—just to catch the teachers' attention. He was still that same boy who had put a real live frog in the cupboard in the French room a couple of minutes before Mr. Barry opened it to get out the textbooks. He was still the one who had kissed all the girls behind the bike shed. Except me.

Now I watched with a pang of nostalgia as he darted out from the shadow of the stone sarcophagus and concealed himself behind a marble cross, a few steps nearer to the field.

He waved his arm, beckoning me frantically over to where he crouched.

"There's definitely someone there," he whispered, when I had come up alongside him. "Look through the gap there, you can see them."

To my surprise, I saw that Joe was right. There *was* someone there, more than one person in fact.

Night hawks. I'd read about them in archaeology magazines. They go round archaeological sites at night with their metal detectors, looking for treasure trove that no one has found as yet.

"We should call the police," I said, quietly. "I'll run back to the flat and phone."

"No, not yet." He caught at my sleeve as I began to stand up, and pulled me back down onto the steps of the war memorial beside him. "We need to know what they're up to."

"They're metal detecting," I said. "It's obvious."

"Is it?" Joe looked again. "Is that what they're doing? How can you tell?"

"Call it an educated guess."

"Oh, damn!" he complained. "I thought it might be something illegal."

"It is," I said, "if they haven't got permission."

"From the Farmers?" he said. Put like that, it showed me things in a different light.

The Farmers owned the land. The metal detectorists, presumably, didn't. Anyone who reported the incident would be doing Trevor and Valerie Farmer a favour.

But I didn't care about that. What I wanted to know was, who were these people and, more importantly, had they found anything in that field?

There was only one way to find out.

"I'm calling the police," I said. It was one of the few times I've wished I owned a mobile phone. "You stay here, just in case they try to make a quick getaway. They must have come by car. Try and get some registration marks or something."

Joe nodded. At last we were on the same wavelength.

I moved cautiously until I was out of the churchyard and in the lane that wound down between the pub and the post office. I glanced into the pub car park as I ran past. There were two cars in the yard, but I was fairly sure they belonged to the landlord and his wife. When I got into the street, I ran, hell for leather, towards the house.

It was no great distance, but almost as soon as I moved out of the shadow of the pub wall, I knew that there was someone behind me. I sensed it before I heard him, but by then it was too late. I felt his breath on my back, I could hear him grunting as he pounced on me and brought me down in a kind of rugby tackle. My legs disappeared from under me and I sprawled onto the road, throwing my hands out in front of me to break my fall. The impact of my body on the tarmac made such a horrible scraping sound that I could barely make out the noise of my attacker's footsteps running away.

I lay there for a few seconds, winded. My chest was painful. The palms of my hands were grazed and bleeding, little chips of gravel embedded in the skin. Despite the fact that I was wearing jeans, I felt the torn skin on my knees as I started to get up.

Whoever it was, he had gone. I stumbled to my feet, feeling not only angry but stupid. I wasn't a hundred per cent sure there had been anyone there. I'd been drinking earlier. Maybe it was a hallucination. Maybe I had just tripped and fallen.

Various wild thoughts raced through my mind as I limped towards the house. Somewhere in the distance I heard a shrill whistle. Some kind of alarm to warn the night hawks to scarper?

I no longer cared whether I woke Mrs. Murphy. It couldn't be helped. Our only chance of catching those people was to get the police there as soon as possible. They had already shown they were capable of violence, by attacking me (if I had been attacked, and hadn't simply fallen over...)

Joe. As I picked up the phone and dialled 999, I thought of Joe, and panicked. If they would knock a defenceless woman to the ground, what would they do to a hefty young man in a Civil War uniform?

He did have one advantage. He was carrying a sword. It wasn't very sharp, only a toy really. But they wouldn't know that.

"Police," I panted into the phone, wondering if I should add a side order of ambulance with that.

Chapter 22

The Worse for Wear

It was half past two in the morning by the time the police left my flat. They had interviewed everyone involved, including Mrs. Murphy, who had been woken by my noisy entry into the house well after midnight. Contrary to my expectations, she was excited rather than alarmed, and kept saying that if she had got her hands on the little booger that had knocked me over, she would have "given him what for." He never realised how lucky he was to escape her retribution.

The police seemed to think the whole story bordered on the absurd, until they realised there was a question of assault. Up to that point, they had been ready to dismiss the whole thing as "not a police matter"; but Joe persuaded them that they couldn't overlook a woman being attacked in a quiet little village, not fifty yards from her own front door. Imagine what the papers would make of an incident like that, he said, meaningfully.

They immediately began taking me seriously, and got statements from me, Joe, Mrs. Murphy, and the landlord of the Dog and Drake, who came across to the house to say that he had—*almost*—witnessed the whole episode. Alerted by a noise outside, he had actually been watching from his bedroom as I got up from the ground and ran towards my front door. He hadn't, unfortunately, got much of a look at my assailant, who had run off a moment earlier, but he confirmed that there *had* been someone there. He had caught a glimpse of a shadowy figure and heard the footsteps running down the lane past the pub, towards the church. Until I heard him say that, I had been seriously doubting my own sanity.

Then they asked me the question that tipped the balance back in the opposite direction. Would I be able to identify the person who had attacked me, in a police line-up? Obviously, I had to say no. Well then, said the sergeant, sounding rather relieved, he doubted if it would come to a prosecution.

I didn't mind too much by now. I was quite satisfied by the thought that they had caught the metal detectorists. They had all their names and addresses. Joe had come up trumps.

They hadn't even seen him until it was too late. By the time I got to my front door, he had doubled round the back of them, and taken the numbers of both four-wheel-drive vehicles parked in the next field. Then he had let down their tyres, and interfered with the starter motors to be on the safe side. Talk about resourceful. Obviously that misspent youth hadn't been without its compensations.

There had been a minor scuffle, when the owner of one of the vehicles, objecting to Joe's presence, had tried to catch him and had chased him round the field. Then, put off by Joe's outlandish appearance and the realisation that they didn't have the law on their side, they had given up the pursuit and sat down to wait for the police to arrive. They couldn't hope to escape detection, and their chances of avoiding arrest were better if they could pretend not to have done anything worse than trespassing.

After the police had left the house, promising to be in touch the next day—or maybe the day after that—to let us know the outcome of their investigations, Joe and I sat in silence for a while, drinking more coffee and generally recuperating from our experience.

"You were bloody brave," he said, condescendingly, as he dabbed antiseptic-soaked cotton wool gently onto my wounds. "Didn't think you had it in you."

"Me? All I did was run for the phone," I simpered. "You were the one that caught them."

My hero.

"Me?" For once in his life, Joe managed to put on a convincing show of modesty. Then he said, "Can I stay the night?"

I HASTEN TO ADD that he slept on the inflatable mattress in the attic. Mrs. Murphy was a very broad-minded woman, for a Roman Catholic, but it would have been an abuse of her trust for me to have fornicated with Joe in her house, on a bed that, technically, was her property. Peter had been very much a one-off in that respect, and I was a different girl now.

In any case, I didn't want to, and neither did Joe. For one thing, we were both too tired. And in the course of the conversation, he had informed me that his girlfriend, Tina, would be coming down the following day, and would be at the party on Friday night.

Joe had been leading me on, there was no doubt about that, but I forgave him. If I had been in love with him, it would have been different. I'm not really sure why I wasn't in love with him. He was still the same old Joe, and I had definitely been in love with him at seventeen. But I wasn't now.

In the morning, I got Joe some breakfast. While he was eating it, I went downstairs to tell Mrs. Murphy that he had been there all night. I told her partly because I didn't want her to be alarmed when she saw and heard him leaving later in the morning, but also because I wanted her to know that it was all above board. That way she had no reason to distrust me. (Thank goodness she didn't know about Peter.)

"He seems a nice young man," she said, fishing.

"He is," I agreed.

"It's about time you found yourself someone," she added.

"I'm afraid you're barking up the wrong tree," I said. "He's spoken for."

"Oh, dear," said Mrs. Murphy. "Ah well, plenty more fish in the sea."

I left before she could bring up the subject of her grandson, Brendan.

Joe was in the kitchen, awaiting my return. "You're never going into work!" he said, as I started packing up my things.

"No reason not to," I replied nonchalantly. Actually, I was rather looking forward to the attention I was going to get from everyone at work when I told them about my mysterious midnight experience.

Joe promised to leave the spare front door key with Mrs. Murphy. I left him, still tucking into his scrambled eggs on toast and reading the Independent. He said he would see me on Friday night, at the party.

Chapter 23

Secret Admirer

I felt a bit groggy all day, mainly because of the lack of sleep, but apart from that I was fine. Writing, using a keyboard, and accessioning pottery were all slightly uncomfortable activities, because of the grazes on my palms, so I stuck to accepting admission fees from the small number of visitors to the museum.

I didn't get the attention I'd been anticipating from my volunteer helpers and my neighbours on the library staff, partly because they had a busy morning and partly because I didn't tell anyone. It was difficult to find a way of working it into the conversation. "You'll never guess what happened to me last night—I got attacked by an unidentified man!" didn't sound quite right somehow. And it would have been unreasonable to expect it to be headline news in the national dailies.

Verity was on duty in the museum with me, but I was reluctant to mention anything to her, even though (or perhaps because) I knew she would fairly overflow with sympathy when she found out. I went to lunch at my usual time, returning at two o'clock to find that the school party had arrived early. Verity was already showing them round the main exhibition area. After they left, all was quiet. Verity went to make a cup of tea, and I sat at the reception desk, flicking through a book on local history which had just come out.

Mrs. Long's strident voice cut mercilessly into my consciousness. Oh please no, I prayed silently, not her, not this afternoon, I can't cope.

The school party had left the swing doors wide open when they came into the museum, so I could see and hear everything that was going on in the library. I looked up and saw her by the issue desk, conducting the usual one-sided conversation with Francesca about how there never seemed to be any new books on the shelves. She seemed to have forgotten about the broken photocopier. Going back to what I was doing, I thought it was fortuitous that I should be in the middle of an activity that contradicted her complaint. If she started on me, I would be ready for her. I'd even give her the new book to take away with her, if she would only leave me alone.

Then I looked up again, and saw that she hadn't come into the library on her own. Her son was standing beside her, looking embarrassed.

Actually, he was looking at me. Staring at me, in fact. He began to walk through the swing doors, towards the reception desk, and I lowered my head, in the hope that he would change his mind and go and bother someone else. When he was still a few feet away, he muttered something that I couldn't catch. It sounded like, "Thank God."

I looked up again to find him right by the desk, towering over me. I didn't say anything.

"Miss Gardner," he said. "I heard you'd been...assaulted. Is it true?" The look on his face could have been interpreted as one of genuine concern.

So the word had got round, despite my reticence.

Looking up at Mr. Long was giving me a stiff neck. I thought of standing up, to give him less of an advantage, but I felt too weak for any kind of confrontation.

"Yes," I nodded. "I was—technically—assaulted last night. But I'm quite all right."

"May I ask what happened?"

"Oh, it was nothing really. Someone pushed me over."

"Where was this?"

"In the village. Not far from my house."

It had already crossed my mind that the Farmers might not have been completely unaware of the goings-on in Velvet Vale, but one thing was quite certain. Edward Long knew absolutely nothing about the circumstances surrounding the previous night's events. He could never have put on such a convincing act of ignorance.

"And were you hurt?" he inquired. The anxious look hadn't gone away.

"Just a few grazes." I held out my hands, palms upwards. "From where I fell." I didn't offer to show him my knees.

He looked even more concerned, if that were possible. "Have you reported it to the police?"

"Yes. But they can't do anything."

"Have they no idea who was responsible?"

"There are several likely candidates. But I didn't see anything. Whoever it was pushed me from behind, and then ran away. I won't be able to identify anyone."

He still looked shocked and confused.

"I see," he said, when he realised I wasn't going to tell him any more of my own accord. "I'm very sorry. But I'm glad you're not injured."

"Thank you." It went against the grain to say it, but I could hardly say anything else. At least it got rid of him.

It was only after he had left the building, dragging his mother with him, that it occurred to me that I had never seen him visiting the library before.

When I got home, there was a message from the police asking me to call in at the station at my earliest convenience. I felt frustrated. I could have gone there on my way home, if I had known. Joe rang while I was having my tea.

"Hey, babe," he said, in a phoney—and not very convincing—American accent, "how ya doing?"

"I'm fine, Joe. And you?"

"Just great," he said, dropping the accent suddenly. "I rang to see how you were, and check that you're okay for tomorrow. Some of the girls are offering to give you a hand with the food."

After putting in a full day at the museum, I had almost forgotten that the party was scheduled for the following evening, and that little old me was supposed to be responsible for the refreshments.

"Oh," I said, unenthusiastically, "yeah, I'll be there. I've got a couple of helpers, so it should be all right. Er, what time will you be arriving?"

"About six thirty," he said. "Or earlier, if I can manage it. Shall I come across and call you when I arrive?"

"I daresay you'll want to park in our drive," I said drily.

"Can I? That would be great. Though, actually, I won't be driving, it'll be Tina."

So I was definitely going to get to see her, the famous Tina. Up to that point, I had been wondering whether she was one of Joe's fantasies, an invention designed to absolve him from the possibility of commitment to anyone else. Specifically, me.

"I suppose that's so that you can get plastered," I grumbled. "What about Tina, doesn't she get to have a drink?"

"She's teetotal," he said, laughing. "Don't I know how to pick 'em?"

As I put down the phone, I sighed.

Just to add insult to injury, a florist's van drew up outside the house on Friday morning, before I had even gone out to work. When the delivery woman rang my doorbell, I assumed that she had made a mistake and the bouquet in her arms was for Mrs. Murphy. My landlady's numerous relatives were scattered to the four winds, and they were always sending her cards and parcels, so why not flowers?

It wasn't a mistake, though. The flowers were for me. And you won't guess who they were from. No, you won't.

They were from Trevor and Valerie Farmer.

"With thanks," said the card.

They were trying to brazen it out. We were expected to believe that they had known nothing about the metal-detecting activity going on in their field in the middle of the night. It was nothing but a face-saving exercise. We had them on the run, all right. Not because the police had caught the metal detectorists and the Farmers had helpfully said they preferred not to press charges against the "trespassers." But because Joe Payne had recognised one of the men he saw in the field that night. It was Valerie Farmer's boyfriend.

It seemed that everyone except me had known about Valerie Farmer's record of extra-marital affairs. Okay, so she wasn't in the first flush of youth, but she was still a lot more attractive than her husband, and she had money. It should have been obvious that she would be on the lookout for new talent. Apparently, it was with Trevor Farmer's full knowledge and co-operation that she had started up a relationship with their part-time gardener. All the same, it was rather careless of them both to think they could get away with employing him to hunt for treasure trove on their land without anyone suspecting their involvement.

I should have explained that Joe didn't actually recognise the man he saw as being a friend of Valerie Farmer. Joe didn't live in the district, so he was as ignorant as I was of local scandal. He only knew the bloke by sight, as a regular drinker in the Dog and Drake. You wouldn't think someone could be so stupid as to go straight from a small village pub to carry out clandestine activities under cover of darkness in the neighbouring field, but that's often how these things work out. The criminal mind isn't any cleverer than average.

Now we've got them, we thought. But when I went to the police station, in answer to the message I'd received, they told me that the Farmers, though they admitted to having employed one of the men found in their field, continued to deny any personal knowledge of their activities. They said they were letting him off because he'd given them such good service.

"'Service' being the operative word," remarked Jonathan, sardonically, when I was telling him about it.

It had crossed my mind to wonder whether Edward Long might have been another of Mrs. Farmer's lovers. I recalled how I had seen them sitting together at the Mayor's inaugural tea, looking very cosy. Much as I disliked the man, I found it hard to believe that he would stoop that low. Since uncovering the secret of his date of birth, I had begun to think of him as belonging to my own generation, even if he didn't act like it. And *she* definitely wasn't.

By the end of Friday, we realised we hadn't made much headway by catching the night hawks. Strictly speaking, the only illegal act that had been perpetrated was the assault on my person, and that couldn't be pinned on an individual, so it couldn't be proved that it was connected with the activity in Velvet Vale. Trevor and Valerie Farmer put the word out that they had been the victims of an attempt to remove any valuable artefacts from the field. That only strengthened their argument for pushing ahead with the housing development. As long as its—possible—historic interest was generally known, they argued, the field would be a target for metal detectorists from all over the country.

They even had the nerve to give the story to the "Evening News," whose editor (another old friend of Valerie's, hence his previous indifference to our campaign) suddenly developed an interest in events at Barrow

End and rang me to ask if I would like my photo to appear in the next edition.

I could picture the headline: "HEROINE FOILS NIGHT RAIDERS: LANDOWNERS EXPRESS GRATITUDE," or something like that. I declined, on the grounds that I was a shy, retiring kind of person and didn't want any publicity.

Everybody knew that it wasn't the first time those men had been over that field with their metal detectors. The reason they had done it under cover of darkness was that any daylight activity would have been observed by village residents, and Herbert would have gone straight round and demanded that any finds be lodged with the museum and reported to English Heritage.

We would probably never know, now, whether they had found anything of interest. The men with the metal detectors, though they admitted being on the field without permission, were adamant that it was the only time it had happened. They insisted that they had never removed any artefacts from the site, other than a couple of Victorian pennies and a belt buckle which the police had reclaimed from their vehicles.

Nathan Pendragon went to the police station and insisted on seeing the belt buckle. It was, as he had suspected, a seventeenth-century belt buckle, of a military design. On its own, it couldn't prove that we had found the site of the Battle of Barrow End, but it certainly supported Nathan's hypothesis. He wrote to the Farmers, on his university's headed notepaper, and asked them to donate it to the District Museum, where he assured them it would be given pride of place next to the old pub sign. Once again, they could hardly refuse.

Chapter 24

Party!

The party at the Village Hall was in full swing. The food I'd slaved to prepare — or at any rate, I'd warmed it up in the microwave and put it out on plates — had been demolished by the revellers, and now they were busy making inroads into the alcohol supply. The landlord of the Dog and Drake had helpfully left a skeleton staff in the pub for the evening and was here in the hall acting as barman. He was very much one of us now.

The talking point of the evening so far had been the landlord's action in getting his pub sign re-painted. Though the existing one had only been up for a few months, he had decided that it was right and proper to acknowledge Nathan's discovery, so he had arranged to have one side painted over. Thus the sign still showed the foxhound and the mallard when you approached from the east, but if you came from the west, you saw a Royalist soldier and a small cannon. It was becoming a mini-tourist attraction.

Had Nathan not been such a tolerant man, and if his lieutenants hadn't been tickled pink at the landlord's gesture, they might have been disposed to criticise the technical detail. The sign-painter was clearly no expert on seventeenth-century costume.

The news about the military belt buckle was also being widely discussed. Jonathan had arranged for an article about it to be featured in the following week's edition of the "County Examiner," but we agreed sadly that this wouldn't be much help in our attempt to influence the planning decision, which would have been made before the paper came out.

There was a kind of disco going on in the main hall, with members of the Re-enactment Society taking it in turns to act as DJ. Most of them were dressed in their full paraphernalia, as usual, but it didn't stop them attempting to dance.

While taking a moment off from my duties as caterer to do the Lambada with Wally, I caught sight of Councillor Long and some of his colleagues, talking seriously to Herbert in a corner of the main hall. I was surprised to see them there, but not altogether displeased. It seemed to me that they were our only remaining hope of getting the planning application stopped, and if they had taken the trouble to attend, there was some hope that they were coming round to our point of view.

I'd cleared away all the used plates and plastic cutlery and deposited them in black bin bags ready for next week's refuse collection. These were now standing in a corner of the kitchen. My duties effectively over, I could take time out to enjoy myself, but I was really very tired. Wednesday night's sleep deficit was catching up with me in earnest.

The room was so full of people (undoubtedly well over the number allowed for by the Village Hall's entertainment licence) that I could hardly breathe. It was very hot, and even though I was wearing a thin, short-sleeved silk blouse, I was perspiring. I retreated into the little kitchen, where I had a right to be.

Although it was very warm in the kitchen, it was certainly cooler than the hall. I didn't want to go outside, because that was where the smokers congregated. I closed the serving hatch to reduce the noise level, opened the tiny window, and splashed my face with water from the cold tap.

From here, I had a good view of people going in and out of the main doors—mostly in—but there were lulls in between times when it was rather peaceful. I left the kitchen door open, and lounged against the sink unit.

I was joined, after about ten minutes, by Edward Long.

"I see you've found a nice little refuge from the crowd," he said, forcing a smile onto his gloomy face.

"I couldn't breathe in there," I explained.

"Nor I," he said. "I was just leaving."

"You're not staying for the speeches?"

"I don't think I'd be very welcome," he said quietly, trying not to look as if he minded.

What did he expect me to say? Yet, for a moment, I felt sorry for him.

"You really didn't know about that donation, did you?" I said, lowering my voice.

"No, I didn't," he said. "But I do now, thanks to you."

"I'm afraid it can't have been very pleasant news for you." Why was I wasting my sympathy on this miserable specimen, I wondered?

"Actually," he said, "you may have saved my career."

I shook my head, not really understanding.

"If it had all gone through," he explained, "I would have been seriously implicated. As their accountant, I was supposed to make sure that the Farmers declared everything. It would have been a breach of professional etiquette to have gone along with something like that. Worse still, since I was auditing the books of the charity they were giving to, how could I have expected anyone to believe that there were donations I hadn't been told about? A stupid piece of carelessness on my part. Trevor and Valerie used me. I've told them to find themselves another accountant immediately."

This didn't sound like a very severe punishment to me, and I resisted the urge to laugh. Besides, I've met accountants before, and any suggestion that they concern themselves with the legality of their clients' behaviour, in my experience, is a joke. What the eye doesn't see, the heart doesn't grieve over. I thought that was their motto.

But when I looked into Edward Long's face, I knew that he was being perfectly honest. How often do you meet a man who prides himself on never telling lies, never misleading, never doing anything underhand or illegal? Okay, maybe there are a few of them around, but look at the experiences I'd had. Peter Markham was a vicar, but it hadn't stopped him sleeping with me and it hadn't stopped him accepting a bribe. And then there was Joe Payne, with a different woman in his sleeping bag every night of the week.

Ironic, wasn't it, that in my determination to dig up dirt and splatter it all over those I regarded as culpable, I had inadvertently delivered the evidence of malpractice into the hands of the most scrupulous person I'd ever met? I realised suddenly that I actually admired Long for his willingness to admit to having been taken for a ride by the Farmers. It was too much to hope that he would go on to sacrifice his professional reputation by helping us to turn the tables on them.

Now that he had started talking, Mr. Long didn't seem to want to stop. "I would have lost all credibility," he went on, "and I would have had to resign my seat on the Council. Though I'm not sure now that I shall allow myself to be re-nominated."

"Why not?" I asked dutifully.

"I'm not sure that I'm very good at it," he said. There was a patchy pink flush on his cheeks and neck.

"What about Peter?" I asked, hurriedly. "Couldn't he get into big trouble over that business of the cheque?"

"*Potentially*, yes," said Mr. Long, treating my query with the solemnity it deserved. "It might be said that he had pocketed some of the money from the Farmers and used the cash collections to make up the amount that went into the restoration fund, since no one else seems to have double-checked the figures." He sighed, as though lamenting Amelia's gullibility. "But in practice"— he looked at me earnestly, and again I felt the urge to laugh— "no one's accusing him of dishonesty, only of foolishness. And *I* can hardly point the finger."

"I'm glad about that," I said wistfully. "I wouldn't have wanted him to get into trouble because I blew the whistle."

"No," he agreed. He looked as if he wanted to say something else, but the words weren't making their way onto his lips.

I couldn't help myself. "I think you should know," I said, "that I saw the letter you wrote to my boss."

"Oh." He gazed out of the window, over the top of my head, in an unsuccessful attempt to conceal his embarrassment. "That was probably the most idiotic thing I've ever done," he said, in a distant voice.

"Did the Farmers put you up to it?" I needed to know.

This was the point at which I could literally see his natural truthfulness struggling to overcome his desire to lie himself out of trouble. The sweat on his forehead was a dead giveaway. He wiped it away self-consciously with the back of one hand.

"They asked me to do it, yes," he said. "But I didn't have to go along with it. Valerie seemed to be gunning for you. You were the person she could get at most easily, being a local authority employee. If I didn't warn you off, I was afraid of what she might do..."

"To you?"

"No." He looked befuddled. "To you," he said. "They've got a lot of influence. I can only ask you to believe that I thought I was acting in your best interests."

The weird thing was, I *did* believe it.

I looked at my watch. It was nine o'clock. The music had stopped, and I could hear a general rustling in the main hall, as the revellers got ready for the presentation ceremony. There had been a stampede of people coming in from outside while we stood there talking, but the flow had stopped and the lobby was deserted.

"I really ought to go in now," I said.

His lanky body was blocking the doorway.

"Just a minute." He seized me by the shoulders.

Looking back on the events of the previous few weeks, it seems ludicrous that I should have had no idea what was coming. And yet, I can honestly say that I had no premonition at all that he was intending to kiss me.

It wasn't a particularly enjoyable experience. He held me, literally by the scruff of the neck, taking a handful of my blouse in his fist to pull me closer. Though I stood, considerately, on tiptoe, he was so much taller than me that he still had to stoop to reach my mouth with his. His other hand came up from my shoulder and caught at my cheek in an effort to press my face more firmly against his.

He didn't have much idea about kissing, either. I could flatter myself by saying that he was so carried away by this impetuous desire for me that he lost control and forgot how to do it, but that wasn't the reason. He just hadn't had a lot of practice.

Eventually he let me go. There was no attempt to repeat the action, or even to make it last, just a sudden release which dropped me back on my heels. He couldn't look at me. Neither of us was breathing steadily.

I was still trying to think of something to say when Joe walked in on us.

"Presentation time!" he announced.

Since Joe didn't seem to have noticed anything amiss, I felt reasonably calm as I walked back into the main hall.

No one followed me. Councillor Long disappeared off into the night, and I stood, with Joe's arm around me, listening to the speeches and trying to concentrate on enjoying myself. It was all above board, by the way. Joe had his other arm around Tina.

She was about as different from me as someone could be and still be female. "Buxom" is the word that springs to mind. It obviously wasn't from Tina that Joe had borrowed the woman's costume he'd given me.

By the way she and Joe were openly canoodling, I suspected that the physical side of their relationship was more than satisfactory, which begged the question of why he'd ever needed to bother to make a pass at me. I put it down to male perversity.

She was a nice girl, all the same. That's nice as in "pleasant to talk to," not as in "sexually repressed." Her friendliness towards me made it difficult to tell whether she was unacquainted with the nature of my relationship with her boyfriend, or whether she knew all about it and just didn't care.

Herbert's speech was going on for longer than was necessary, I thought, and lots of people seemed to agree with me. Everywhere I looked, there were mock yawning gestures and rolling of the eyes. No one complained openly, though, because if it hadn't been for Herbert, this celebration wouldn't have been happening, and neither would the battle.

We didn't know yet what would happen about the planning application, but we were increasingly hopeful that it would be withdrawn or kicked out. According to Herbert, a number of councillors had heard about the metal detecting episode, and were getting cold feet about having promised to support the Farmers. Privately, I wondered if any of them had heard any other rumours.

I had been keeping what I regarded as my trump card up my sleeve — the information about the attempted bribery of the local vicar. But when I looked at it in the cold light of day, what did it amount to? The Farmers had said they were making the donation without prejudice. Peter would say that his decision not to participate in our campaign was a proper one for a vicar to make, and would point to the fact that his wife had been a member of the Action Committee. In any case, he would add, his personal involvement wouldn't have made any difference, one way or the other, to the local authority's decision.

That only left Councillor Long, who would undoubtedly keep to himself the knowledge that the donation hadn't been put through the books properly. After all, to admit that he hadn't picked it up would have been to confess to professional ineptitude and lay himself open to public ridicule. Not a prospect a man like that would relish.

I tried to remember the exact words he had used, in the kitchen. "If it had all gone through," he had said. Was he referring to the planning application, and implying that it wouldn't now go through? But if, as he claimed, he had already declared an interest, then he wouldn't even get a vote. I wished I had questioned him more closely on the subject when I'd had the chance. If only he hadn't distracted me like that.

After Herbert had finished his sermon on the importance of our cultural heritage, he introduced Professor Nathan Pendragon. Although Nathan's speech was probably about the same length as Herbert's, it seemed much shorter. Since he was a very distinguished-looking man, and was wearing full Cavalier uniform, he would have kept the attention of the female half of the audience if he had been reading the telephone directory.

He described briefly his view of the potential significance of the identification of Velvet Vale as the site of the Battle of Barrow End, and explained some of the factors he would take into account when assessing it during the actual battle on Sunday. When he had come to his conclusion, he turned to Herbert expectantly.

"And now I have a very pleasant duty to perform," said Herbert, a little pompously.

"So have I," said Nathan. "You first, Mr. Dyson."

Herbert looked slightly perplexed, but got quickly back into his stride. "I have great pleasure," he said, "in announcing that Professor Pendragon has agreed to become an honorary trustee of the District Museum. I'm sure we're all very grateful to him for everything he's done on our behalf in the last few months, and we look forward to seeing him regularly in the future."

"Thank you very much," said Nathan, making himself heard over the spontaneous applause that broke out at that point. "And I have an announcement of my own to make. In recognition of his outstanding contribution to the study of English Civil War history, the Re-enactment Society has decided to award Mr. Herbert Dyson the honorary rank of Colonel."

Herbert couldn't have looked more overjoyed if he had been told he was getting a knighthood from the Queen. Nathan called to Wally, who carried up onto the stage a replica sword and a rather moth-eaten Cavalier hat, both of which were presented to Herbert. The sword was probably plastic, but it looked magnificent. Nathan plonked the hat onto Herbert's head, and adjusted it to the correct angle.

"Of course," he added, "you won't be fighting in the battle on Sunday, but you certainly look the part."

Then Nathan turned towards me. "Rosemary, would you come up here, please?"

By the time I had recovered from my surprise and wended my way through the crowd to the front of the hall, he had produced, conjuror-style, a large bouquet, which he placed in my arms with a flourish. He said nothing, but gestured to Herbert, who came forward again.

"Rose has played a very important part in the campaign to save the battlefield," he said, "and I want to say a particular thank you to her for all the hard work she's done in making improvements to the District Museum, since she took over as Conservator nearly two years ago. We haven't got our new building yet, but we live in hope. If anyone can make it happen, Rose can."

There was further polite applause. I'm not sure what pleased me more—the gesture of the flowers, or the knowledge that any resentment Herbert had once felt towards me had clearly been overtaken by genuine regard.

"And there's more," he said. One of the rowdies repeated the words, in a mock Irish accent, but Herbert was oblivious to the attempt at humour. "I would like to take this opportunity to announce that I've decided to retire from my post as Curator at the end of this year. Rose will, of course, be my successor."

There was a loud cheer at this news, though I was certain that half the people in the room had no idea of the significance of the announcement, or indeed any idea who I was.

Afterwards Herbert told me, confidentially, that he had heard "on the grapevine" that the funds for the conversion of the derelict house into a new museum were about to be voted through by the Borough Council. He had been asked to head the committee they were intending to appoint to oversee the progress of the project. Reading between the lines, I guessed he had been warned that there would be no place for an honorary

"Curator" in the new organisation, and was leaving before he was pushed. All the same, it was a load off my mind. I wondered, briefly, which of the councillors had given him the nod.

The party went on until well after midnight. By that time there were only a handful of us left, but that handful would have gone on revelling indefinitely if Nathan hadn't pointed out that the people who lived in the houses nearest to the Village Hall might "get a bad impression" of the Re-enactment Society and its members if we didn't all go home and let them get a bit of sleep.

I'd offered overnight accommodation in my attic to several of the party-goers, but none of them took me up on it. Joe and Tina were staying overnight with the Eatons, and Nathan had been offered a bed by Colonel Montgomery. Some of the other Society members were staying at the Dog and Drake, some were camping in a nearby field, and a small, but determined, group set off to spend the night in the graveyard.

I DIDN'T THINK about Edward Long again until after I got home. While I was getting undressed, I noticed that one of the shoulder seams of my blouse was beginning to come apart. I decided against sending him the bill for a replacement. Later still, when I was lying in bed, the memory of his clumsy attempt at seduction came seeping back into my mind. Given a few more minutes, I thought, I could have taught him a thing or two about kissing.

Chapter 25
An Apology

That Saturday was unusual in that I wasn't working. This had been carefully planned since the date of the party had been decided. "You'll be worn out," Herbert had warned (overlooking the fact that all the volunteers were likely to be equally affected), but he could never have predicted the events of the week that had led up to my rest day.

You'll recall that we hadn't been able to have the battle itself on that particular day, because of the Society's other commitments and the need for the museum volunteers to attend. As it transpired, Herbert had to make do with a much depleted staff, because Jonathan had decided to go and spectate at the battle the Society was putting on that afternoon, in the next county. It was a much larger affair than the Battle of Barrow End was going to be, but it didn't have the same cachet, because it was an "imaginary" battle in a field that wasn't an authentic battle site.

I looked forward to a leisurely day with my feet up, but first I had to go out and do the week's shopping. I was at the supermarket before nine, to avoid the worst of the rush, and back home in time for my elevenses. I put away most of the groceries, leaving out some salad which I set aside for my lunch, then I sat down with the newspaper at the kitchen table.

My doorbell rang. This wasn't an unusual occurrence, but during the daytime most of my friends would have gone to the museum to look for me. Expecting either a door-to-door salesperson or a religious extremist, I went wearily downstairs, mentally preparing myself to be rude or, at best, off-hand.

It was a total surprise to see Edward Long standing there. The rain had come on since my return. He was wearing an overcoat, but nothing on his head, and the water was trickling off his short fringe. It struck me that he looked rather cute with wet hair.

He didn't say anything for a moment, and neither did I. We just looked at each other. Then his eyes moved down my figure, taking in my scruffy Saturday-at-home look. It must have been obvious I wasn't going anywhere.

"May I come in?" he asked.

He wiped his feet carefully on the mat before following me upstairs to the flat. I led the way, leaving him to close the doors behind us. Opening the living room door, I ushered him in, but didn't invite him to take off his coat. He stood, dripping, on the threshold.

"I've come to apologise for my behaviour last night," he said.

Finding that I couldn't meet his eyes, I walked into the room ahead of him, and didn't pause until I was standing by the window, with my back against the radiator.

"There's no need to apologise," I said.

He was still standing over by the door, and looking slightly disappointed at my lack of reaction. It was obvious that he had been prepared for a good telling off. Given my track record, it was an understandable expectation.

"I don't know what I could have been thinking of," he went on.

"It doesn't matter," I said. "Worse things happen at sea." I don't know what I meant by that. It was just something to say, to deflect attention from the blush that I knew was spreading over my cheeks.

I waited for a moment, expecting that he would take his leave, but when I saw he hadn't yet managed to get out everything he wanted to say, I went back on the offensive. I couldn't let him know what was really going through my mind.

"Was there something else?" I asked.

"Are you having an affair with Peter Markham?"

The question took me completely unawares. I had been so sure that Peter and I had done nothing to give ourselves away.

"I don't think that's any of your business." As an attempt to avoid answering the question, it was worse than useless. It told him everything he could possibly want to know.

"You're right, it's not," he said, "but I'm still asking."

I stared at him, hard. It seemed to have no effect. On the contrary, it was me who was thrown by his steady gaze.

"As a matter of fact," I said, after a few seconds, "I'm not." It was the literal truth.

He seemed to be expecting further information, but as far as I was concerned, he wasn't going to get any.

"I beg your pardon," he said, coldly. "I must have been mistaken."

I didn't know how to take things forward from here; and, it seemed, neither did he. He didn't cross the room towards me, but neither did he make any move to leave. Who knows, perhaps he sensed that I didn't want him to go? Like me, he may have wondered why not.

"Would you like a cup of coffee?" I asked eventually, my natural politeness getting the better of me.

"That's very kind of you," he said, stiffly. "I don't want to put you to any trouble."

"It's no trouble," I said, remaining torn between a sneaking desire to sound welcoming and the more primitive urge to throw him out. That air of vulnerability about him was winning over my usual intransigence.

I went into the kitchen, expecting him to follow me, but instead he took off his wet coat and sat down on the settee. In a way, I was glad. Although I generally preferred to use the kitchen table and stools for informal entertaining, Edward Long wouldn't have looked quite right in that setting.

He made no attempt to carry on a conversation while I was boiling the kettle and getting out the cups and saucers. Mugs wouldn't do for a councillor, I thought.

I rattled things around in the kitchen for longer than was strictly necessary. When I couldn't delay the inevitable any longer, I put everything on a tray and brought it into the living room, setting it down carefully in front of him. Feeling the need to maintain a physical distance, I sat down on one of the threadbare armchairs, at the opposite side of the coffee table.

Now that I looked at him properly, I noticed, to my surprise, that he was wearing a navy V-necked jumper over his collar and tie, in place of a jacket. It made quite a difference to his appearance.

When the formalities of offering milk and sugar were done with, I settled back into the chair with my cup, not feeling inclined to risk further discussion of Peter Markham.

Edward—I was beginning to think of him by his first name at last, mainly because of the way he had kissed me—was unforthcoming, and I needn't have worried about a continuation of that line of questioning.

"How's your mother?" I asked, after a few moments.

"Much as usual," he said. "You know her, I take it?"

"She comes into the library often. Sometimes she comes into the museum as well."

"Ah yes, of course. Does she give you much trouble?"

He was getting very good at throwing out these surprise questions, designed to catch me off guard.

"What makes you think that?" I retorted. When you can't decide whether to tell the truth, answering a question with another question is always a good fall-back.

He smiled slightly, stirring his coffee and tapping the spoon on the edge of the cup to remove the excess drips. "I know her," he said.

It pleased me to discover that he did have a sense of humour after all, but I continued to avoid the question.

"Is it just the two of you, in the house?" I asked.

"That's right." He paused to sip his coffee. "I have two elder brothers, but they don't live locally. My father's dead."

I thought of the body, hanging in the garden shed. He must have thought I didn't know. I wondered how much it hurt him to mention it.

"Are you quite recovered from the other night?" he asked, presumably in an effort to steer the conversation away from his family history. "Your a-accident, I mean."

"Yes, thanks," I said, holding out one hand, palm upwards, to show him how the grazes had diminished. "All gone."

"The men the police apprehended," he persisted, "did you know them?"

"Not personally. But I gather one of them is a close friend of Mrs. Farmer's."

He didn't say anything immediately, just peered into his cup.

"Is that coffee all right?" I asked, worrying that I was failing to meet his high standards.

"What? Yes, I beg your pardon. But I think I should be going now."

He put down his cup, which still had a few dregs in the bottom, and picked up his wet coat. I got up as well, waiting until he had passed by my chair so that there was no danger of our coming into physical contact. I watched him open the door.

"Thank you for calling," I said, aiming for an effect somewhere between courtesy and sympathy.

He turned suddenly in the doorway. "I don't suppose there would be any point in my asking you out to dinner?" he said.

Chapter 26

A Great Night Out

For an instant, I really thought I was imagining things.

It took me a few seconds to get my breath back.

"Wha... ? How...? I...," I said. Or something like that.

"No," he said, frowning slightly. "I didn't think so."

He was halfway down the stairs before it occurred to me that there was anything I could do about it.

"Edward!" I called out.

At last, I had done it. I had called him by his first name, to his face.

He stopped on the stair, and half-turned, crossing his free hand onto the rail. There wasn't much natural light, and I couldn't see his expression properly.

"Could you...repeat what you just said?" I asked. I didn't mean the bit about him not thinking so. I meant the bit before that. He seemed to understand.

He came slowly back up the stairs, resting his hand on the top of the banisters. I could see his face now, for all the good it did. He wasn't looking at me, but down at his feet.

"I asked if you would come out to dinner with me," he said.

"When?"

His gaze travelled slowly from the carpet, up my body, to my face. Only when it arrived there did he reply.

"Tonight?" he said.

"That would be... nice." I was treading as cautiously as I knew how. I still wasn't even sure what I wanted.

"Seven?" he ventured.

I nodded. "Yes. Fine."

"I'll collect you." I got the impression he had chosen his words carefully. Most men said, "I'll pick you up."

After he had gone, I could hardly believe what I'd done.

Later in the day, when I realised I had no idea where he was taking me or what I should wear, I began to panic in earnest. It had been a foolhardy decision, even without my failure to double-check the arrangements. Perhaps, I reflected, there would have been no point. It must have been a spur-of-the-moment invitation on his part, surely, and he might not even have decided where we were going. (Even as I was thinking this, the idea crept into my mind that he had come to the flat specifically to ask me out.)

He knew nothing about me. He couldn't know what kind of food I liked. Knowing Edward Long...

But I didn't know him. I had been assuming that he was a certain sort of man—conventional, formal, reserved—when he had already proved, several times over, that he wasn't. What was that phrase Nathan used? "Look beyond the obvious."

For example, I now knew that Edward had never meant to help the Farmers force through their planning permission. He had never intended to be anything but impartial. He simply regarded it as his responsibility to ensure that they got a fair hearing. It was clear that, despite being their accountant, he didn't like them any more than the rest of us did.

My remaining preconceptions suggested that Edward would choose to take me to a restaurant in town, probably one of the more upmarket ones, like Hathaways or The Olive Garden. There was some evidence for this. He had said "dinner," which gave me a certain amount to go on. He wouldn't have used that word if he just meant a drink and a snack in a pub. It didn't fit with an Indian or Chinese meal, either.

I knew the kind of people Edward Long associated with, Conservative Party faithfuls, businessmen, the golfing fraternity, the well-off. They were the kind of people who ate in Hathaways and The Olive Garden, even if Edward himself wasn't. So that was bound to be the kind of place we were going, I decided.

After an hour hunting through my wardrobe, I selected the nearest thing I had to a little black dress. Actually, it was dark red, not exactly the best colour to wear when you're going out with a Tory, but he surely knew enough about me not to expect me to turn up in blue.

As I got ready, I started to think what signals I was going to be giving out. I was tempted not to wear any make-up. To allow him to think that I had taken trouble over my appearance would be tantamount to an invitation on my part. He had already accused me of adultery. Granted, I was guilty, but that didn't make me a pushover. On the other hand, to meet him looking like something the cat dragged in would not only be insulting to him, but would do nothing for my own self-esteem.

My dress was sleeveless, but not low-cut, so that was all right. As I smoothed it down and looked at myself in the mirror, I noticed that my hands were trembling. There was gooseflesh on my arms, yet my palms were perspiring.

He arrived at seven on the dot. The first thing I noticed was that he was wearing a suit. I almost sighed out loud with relief, because that meant I had made no major mistake about the nature of our dining experience. It wasn't quite conclusive, since he almost always did wear a suit; but he'd abandoned the V-necked jumper look of this morning. He must have *had* other clothes, I thought, reserved for informal occasions such as a drink in the pub.

The suit wasn't the same kind he usually wore, I observed. It was light grey, the sort of thing you don't wear to the office or a business meeting, but to an evening out. It wasn't the same suit he had been wearing the previous evening, when he had kissed me, either.

It was all coming back to me now. The suit Edward had worn the night before had been a very dark navy, cut in quite a different style. I remembered the feel of the lapels, under my hands, as he pulled me close. The one he was wearing tonight was double-breasted and comparatively baggy. It made him look more relaxed.

I said *more* relaxed, meaning less uptight than usual. Just as well he's feeling more relaxed, I thought, because I had enough adrenaline pumping around my system for both of us. You can guess what I was thinking.

I was wondering how long it would be before he tried to kiss me again.

His car—the big, silver one—was outside in the road. It was spotting with rain, but I didn't put up the hood of my coat, because I didn't want to spoil my hair. It had taken me ages to get it looking just right. That sounds wrong. I don't mean that I wanted to look perfect, I mean that I didn't want to look *too* perfect. Not that I needed to waste my time, because Edward made no comment on my appearance. I could probably have got away with wearing jeans, he wouldn't even have noticed.

We went down the stairs without saying a word. He opened the passenger door for me, seeing me safely seated before he went around to the driver's side. I watched him through the windscreen as he looked out for traffic—a pointless exercise, in a place as quiet as Barrow End. His face was as solemn as ever, but I hadn't looked at him from this angle before, and I noticed how clear the skin was on his neck and jaw. It astonished me that I could ever have mistaken him for a man in his forties.

He didn't look at me as he started up the car.

"I've booked a table at the Flying Goose," he said. "I hope that's all right?"

I had never heard of it.

"Where's that?" I asked.

"Little Wildmarsh," he replied, looking slightly surprised at my ignorance. "Don't you know it? It's a small place, but the food's very good."

It was a ten-mile drive, down narrow winding country roads, to Little Wildmarsh. I wondered if he had chosen it specifically for that reason, so that there would be plenty of time to talk during the journey. If that was the case, he made little use of the opportunity. We fell into silence until we were about halfway to our destination.

"We seem to have moved on a little," Edward said suddenly. "I think you once said you would never get into a car with me."

It was lucky that it was such a sunless evening and the interior of the car was dark, because I blushed at the recollection.

"I was out of order," I said. "I didn't understand you."

He shrugged. "You certainly gave me pause for thought. I've never had such a violent reaction when I've offered anyone a lift."

It sounded like a joke, but he wasn't smiling. I looked out of the window at the passing trees.

"Would you like the radio on?" he asked, after a while.

"No, thanks," I said.

There was no more conversation until we reached the Flying Goose. The place really was in the middle of nowhere. If we should quarrel in the course of the evening, I reflected, I wouldn't have the option of walking out, because I would never be able to find my way home. Perhaps that was all part of his master plan.

The Flying Goose certainly looked like a pub, albeit a slightly posh pub. When we went in, however, I realised that it was one of those places where gourmets and very rich people go when they want to avoid the formal atmosphere of a High Street restaurant. The car park was already very full.

The food was so expensive that the prices weren't listed on the menu. I was rather grateful, because I would have felt obliged to choose the cheapest thing in every category, even though it obviously didn't matter to Edward.

We were shown to a table in a quiet corner. I wondered whether he had asked for it specially, being a regular customer, or if it was mere chance that we were tucked away cosily like this. The manageress, or head waitress or whatever you would call her, seemed to know Edward quite well. She fawned all over us, pulling out chairs and rearranging cutlery to reassure us of her attention. I was glad I'd worn something smart.

The woman went over the menu with us, dwelling on the detail of each item and pointing out tonight's special dishes. I was practically slavering by the time she moved away and left us to our choice, lighting the tall candle on the table to create a pseudo-romantic atmosphere. She had particularly recommended the duck.

"I think I'll have the seafood pancake," said Edward, refusing to be led. "What would you like, Rose?"

He hadn't often called me by my name, and I was certain he had never called me by the shortened version before. He was looking at me earnestly, as though unsure whether he had already gone too far.

I chose the lamb. To the slaughter.

"I'm afraid I don't drink when I'm driving," said Edward. "I'm sure you'd like something, though, wouldn't you? They have a lot of good wines here that come by the glass. Or perhaps you'd prefer a half-bottle."

"Are you trying to get me drunk?" I said, inanely.

"Of course not." He looked quite shocked at the idea, and I realised he had taken me seriously.

I opted for a glass of house red.

Before the main course came a fan of melon, for me, and soup for Edward — broccoli and Stilton. Picking up the maraschino cherry that came with the melon, I sucked it sensuously off its cocktail stick, conscious as I did so that he was watching me with fascination. I hadn't intended to be provocative. If I had been with Joe, the look of patent lust wouldn't have taken me by surprise, but I hadn't expected someone like Edward to be turned on by the usual things.

He couldn't have been aware of the messages he was sending out. Loud and clear. I put down the cocktail stick quickly at the side of my plate. Reining himself in suddenly, Edward picked up his spoon and gave his attention to the soup. We didn't speak again until we had finished the starter.

"That was really nice," I said, unimaginatively. "How was the soup?"

"Very nice," he answered, equally unimaginatively, wiping the corner of his mouth with his napkin. I could see that embarrassment had got the better of him now, and I was almost as bad.

Some time passed before the main course was ready, and we were hard pressed to make conversation to plug the gap. I asked again about his mother, forgetting that I had only done so a few hours earlier, and he repeated that she was very well. He asked if I'd heard that detailed plans for a new District Museum were about to be put before the Council. I said I had. I asked if we had him to thank. He said, not him personally. For once, I wasn't sure that he was being completely truthful.

When the food came, we were able to stop talking about awkward topics such as life and start talking about food again. It was good food, just as he had promised, but I found I didn't have much of an appetite for it. I even passed on dessert, which is almost unknown for me.

Edward seemed disappointed. He said that if I didn't have one, he wouldn't have one either. He suggested a liqueur coffee instead, and I agreed. I sipped the creamy froth off the top of the glass, watching him over the rim. That ardent look had crept onto his face again, but at the same time he was keeping up a pretence that he didn't mind the evening coming to an end. So was I.

Chapter 27

Secrets and Lies

It was dark by the time we came out of the restaurant. The string of twinkling lights threaded through the trees that surrounded the car park gave an air of enchantment to our progress, but Edward remained silent as he unlocked the car. There was failure in the atmosphere. The nearest he had come all evening, physically, was when he had helped me on with my coat.

The journey home seemed only half as long as the journey there, though I was quite sure Edward wasn't driving any faster. I sat back in my seat, and watched him. There was still time to notice the way he drove. Not like Joe, who always drove far too fast and too close to the car in front. Not like Peter, who drove over-cautiously, in the style of a granny. Edward just drove, efficiently, smoothly, and carefully. I always think it tells you something about a man.

When we got to Barrow End, he pulled up outside the house and looked uncertain whether to switch off the ignition.

"Aren't you coming in?" I asked.

He looked at me for a couple of seconds before turning the key and cutting off the purring noise. Then he leaned across me, very deliberately, and opened the passenger door. That was all he did.

It had stopped raining. I was still fumbling with my front door key when Edward caught up with me in the porch, and for a moment I thought he was going to take advantage of our close proximity to try and kiss me, but he disappointed me again.

We went up to the flat, still not speaking, and I hung up both our coats on the hooks at the top of the stairs.

I offered him a cup of coffee. He refused politely. I offered him a drink, and he refused even more politely. I asked him to sit down, and he did, taking off the glasses he'd been wearing to drive, and putting them back in his breast pocket. I couldn't think where we were going to go from here. Then he remarked that it was a warm evening. And I asked him if he would like to take his jacket off.

Edward looked at me, very doubtfully, then stood up and began to slip the jacket off his shoulders. Underneath it, he was wearing a pale blue shirt and a grey tie, and they looked remarkably good on him. He had very broad shoulders, I noticed, even for a man of his height. He was a bigger man than I had thought, in every sense.

From the look on his face, though, you would have thought I'd asked him to perform a striptease. I considered the possibility. While I was still thinking about it, he sat down again, on the settee, right next to me.

I edged up closer to him, so that our bodies, from shoulder to thigh, were touching. Edward flinched, as though he'd been slapped. Perhaps a slap was what he'd been expecting. Recovering his composure quickly, he eased back into his seat, but he was still tense, his body rigid. I felt his unfamiliar warmth, radiating through his shirtsleeves.

He turned his head towards me, and again I noticed the colour of his eyes. I smiled at him. Recognising an invitation to intimacy, he slipped a tentative arm around my waist, but it didn't feel quite right. He was only doing what he thought was expected of him. His hand made awkward contact with my bare arm.

"Are you going to watch the battle tomorrow?" I asked matter-of-factly, trying, with little success, to settle into a comfortable position, leaning back against him.

"I haven't quite decided," he replied. "It might be entertaining." For a moment, he seemed to be pondering on some problem. "You know," he added after a few seconds, "when those people first turned up here, I used to think they looked ridiculous. But after a while, I realised — *I* was the one that looked ridiculous."

He didn't intend to sound pathetic. It just came out that way.

"You're not ridiculous, Edward," I said. "You're different." His name still sounded strange in my mouth. I liked the way the two soft "d"s came together. It was a name that would lend itself to being whispered.

"I'm that, all right," he said, with a grim smile. "I could hardly be more different from your...um...your *other* admirer."

He meant Joe. I tried to overlook the word "other." This was all getting too complicated.

"Joe's an old friend," I said. "That's all he is."

Hearing the truth from my own lips like that came as a bit of a shock, but I felt much better for having said it.

It didn't help. Edward had retreated back into himself. I couldn't even tell whether he was pleased.

"I'd like to come and watch the, er, the battle," he said, returning to the ostensible topic of conversation. "On the other hand, I have a lot of work to catch up with..."

"All work and no play," I interrupted.

"Quite," he said. "Incidentally, I wouldn't want you to think that I'm just going to stand back and let that planning application go through. I do intend..."

"Don't talk about it now," I said. I wasn't sure, at the time, why I said that. Later, I realised it was because I was afraid of getting into an argument, and I didn't want to spoil things.

"Very well," he said.

There was silence, for about a minute.

"The Markhams weren't at the Village Hall last night, were they?" Edward remarked suddenly. It seemed that no sooner did we get off one difficult subject than we got onto another.

"They've gone away for the weekend," I said. "It's their wedding anniversary. Why are you so interested in the Markhams?"

When he didn't reply, I turned my head to look at him properly. Our faces were dangerously close.

"Old wounds," he said. The corner of his mouth twitched, but not with amusement.

"You know Hilary well." It was half a statement, half a question.

"I was at school with her."

Of course he was. Just as I was at school with Joe Payne. But I had always had difficulty imagining Edward as a schoolboy.

"Childhood sweethearts?" I suggested.

"Hardly that," he said. "I worshipped from afar."

Yes, I could see them now, in my mind's eye, clear as day. The blossoming thirteen-year-old girl. The gawky fourteen-year-old boy, still wondering why his father hadn't loved him enough to stay alive. The words of sympathy, the crumbs of comfort, breaching the wall of his loneliness.

I tried not to descend into sentimentality. "Was that all?"

"No. I didn't see much of her while I was doing my university course, but when I'd finished, she was still around, and we became more friendly. I was still... attracted to her. In fact, I was in love with her."

I could see almost exactly how it had been. I felt a mild surge of jealousy.

"Did Peter take her from you?"

He gave a short, sharp laugh. "She wasn't mine to take."

"Are you still fond of her?" I asked.

"Yes, I am."

"Are you still in love with her?" I pressed.

Edward took his arm away from my waist, and stood up. "No," he said, with his back to me. "No, I'm not. I'm in love with *you*."

He picked up his jacket from the chair, and started to pull it on.

"Where are you going?" I asked, my voice lost somewhere at the back of my throat.

"Home." He glanced at his watch. "My mother will be wondering where I've got to. She can't be left, unfortunately."

He was just going to leave me sitting there, after saying a thing like that. I couldn't believe it. By the time I had struggled to my feet, he was already at the door.

"I'll see you tomorrow, no doubt," he said. "Or failing that, at the planning meeting on Monday. Stay where you are. I'll see myself out."

Chapter 28

Church Parade

When someone has just told you he loves you, you're bound to see him in a different light. I'd realised a couple of weeks earlier that I no longer hated Edward Long, but I hadn't realised how deeply attracted to him I was until the moment he took his jacket off, in my living room, and I got my first good look at his physique. Yet I couldn't think of a single thing I'd ever said or done to merit his affection.

Under normal circumstances, I would have spent the next twenty-four hours going over and over what had been said, wondering what I could have done to make things turn out differently, but Sunday happened to be the day of the long-awaited Battle of Barrow End, and that gave me no shortage of other things to think about.

It hadn't been very late when Edward and I got back from our evening out, and I hadn't had much to drink, so I had no difficulty in getting up early on Sunday morning.

Joe arrived at about ten o'clock, with Tina in tow, and started unloading piles of stuff from his car. "Necessities," he called them. In the Re-enactment Society's own private patois, that meant cans of beer. Joe had talked me into letting him and his mates use the flat as a general depository and a place to get a wash and change in slightly more comfort than allowed by their campsite. Only his closest mates, you understand—about fifty of them.

They included a rather high proportion of women. Some of them were participating actively in the battle, mostly as musketeers. There was one notable exception, a ginger-haired girl called Mo, who was apparently the only female "pikeman" in the whole regiment. You've heard of Little Mo. Well, this was Big Mo. The rest of the girls were camp-followers, but they still got the chance to go on the field during the battle. Their jobs included carrying water bottles for the men to refresh themselves at intervals. I felt a bit left out—as a non-member, I wasn't insured, and I would have to watch from behind the safety barrier.

To my surprise, Mrs. Murphy, instead of complaining about the noise from the flat, actually offered to let some of Joe's mates use the downstairs facilities. That relieved the pressure on my bathroom a little. She quickly developed a soft spot for Wally, and spent ages being told about the details of his uniform. I think he was the first person she'd ever met who could out-talk her.

The reason so many of Joe's particular friends turned up early was that they had agreed to participate in the special commemorative service at St Catherine's that morning. Peter Markham wasn't taking the service; he and Hilary were scheduled to arrive back from their weekend trip at about lunchtime, just in time to watch the re-enactment.

In Peter's place, we had acquired the services of a curate from the next parish, who had expressed an interest in the whole concept of the battle. It was, in fact, at his suggestion that the Re-enactment Society were taking part in a kind of "church parade" in celebration of the day's special events. I was surprised at the enthusiastic response they made.

When it was nearly time to walk over to the church, I changed out of my jeans and into my seventeenth-century costume. Today was almost certainly the only chance I would ever have to wear it without attracting strange looks, and I couldn't resist. After the battle, I thought regretfully, it would have to be returned to its rightful owner, a girl called Penny, to whom I'd been introduced earlier.

The curate had recruited Nathan Pendragon to help him decide the order of service, and I soon realised that this was the key to so many of the Re-enactment Society having turned up at the church. St Catherine's was "low" at the best of times, but today's service was so informal that we could have dispensed with the Book of Common Prayer altogether.

Instead of the curate giving a sermon, Nathan gave a kind of short lecture about the religious strife that played a part in the English Civil War. I had been expecting something similar to what we had heard at the Village Hall, earlier in the summer, but Nathan turned out to be even more versatile than we all thought. His talk was deeply moving, as well as informative, dwelling on the deep religious convictions felt by both sides in the War, and ending with a plea to us all to understand the importance of tolerance between fellow Christians.

I knew for a fact that Nathan himself was an atheist, but he somehow contrived to come over as a cross between a clergyman and a mystic. He concluded with readings from contemporary sources about the Battle of Cheriton, which Joe had once told me about when we were sitting in the Lamb & Flag having lunch, that first day the two of them had come to the museum.

Nathan's commanding tones rang out through the nave as he began to read: "Now was the enemy constrained to betake himself and all his forces to the church." He described how the Roundheads, under Sir William Waller, had driven the Royalists into Alton churchyard, and had even pursued them into the church itself. The Royalist Colonel, Richard Bolle, had been killed in the pulpit, refusing to surrender his sword. Eyewitnesses made this sound like an act of gallantry, but there was no doubt, from the way Nathan put it, that he regarded it as a piece of profound stupidity and pointless self-sacrifice.

You could almost see tears glistening in his eyes as he concluded his performance by reading Bolle's epitaph from Winchester Cathedral:

"Alton will tell you of that famous fight,
Which this man made, and bid this world good night.
His virtuous life feared not mortality,
His body must, his virtues cannot die,
Because his blood was there so nobly spent,
This is his tomb; that church his monument."

After the service, the congregation filed out of the church and headed off in various directions. Some of the Royalists and Roundheads had a bite of lunch in the Dog and Drake, while others went back to the campsite, from where they would form a procession to arrive at the battlefield at half past two in the afternoon.

I went back to the flat for a sandwich, then helped Joe and Tina carry some of their essential equipment down to the field. Some car parking for spectators had been organised in the pub yard and the church car park, but that was nowhere near enough for the number of visitors we were hoping to attract.

The weather was fine, Saturday's showers had dispersed, and it seemed as though we would get a good crowd. There was already a row of cars parked all the way down the narrow main street. The Village Hall had its own car park, which had been marked out as an overspill, and the school yard had also been opened up for parking. Beyond that, there were fields available for people who didn't mind walking that bit further from their cars.

I was surprised how many families, with children in tow, had turned up to participate in the battle. There were lots of kids—from small babies up to teenagers—dressed in miniature versions of their parents' costumes. They wouldn't go onto the field during the battle, but they were obviously enjoying being part of it all.

Nathan was acting as the "commander" of the Royalist forces for the purposes of the exercise. The Parliamentary side were led by a man called Daniel Stowe, a blond-haired schoolteacher from somewhere north of Sheffield, who had travelled down specially to help christen the Velvet Vale battlefield. He was talking openly about making this an annual event. I hoped his optimism would prove justified.

NATHAN'S MASTER-STROKE had been achieved on Saturday, while I had been occupied with Edward Long. Nathan had told the Farmers, in no uncertain terms, that he intended to give the field a good going over with metal detectors before staging the battle. That way, he said, there would be little danger of replica equipment belonging to the Society being mistaken for the real thing at a later date—in an excavation, for example.

Nathan was bluffing. He would have been able to tell, at a glance, whether something found in the field was an original piece of seventeenth-century history (like the belt buckle he'd already identified for the police). For one thing, it would be *rusty.* This was where the Farmers betrayed their ignorance yet again. They told Nathan to go ahead, doubtless hoping that he would not only find something of value but also spare them the effort of getting an expert in to look at it. But the word "value" meant something quite different to the Farmers from what it meant to Nathan.

What they found, that morning in the field, was a lot of little round pieces of lead. Balls. Or bullets to you. Musket balls, proving beyond reasonable doubt that there had been considerable military activity in that field.

Some people—not the Farmers, who would never have dreamed that he might be as devious as they were themselves—claimed that Nathan had planted them, just to make a better case for the battle. Even some members of the Re-enactment Society were saying as much. If the musket balls had been there all along, they argued, why hadn't the night hawks found them?

There was a multitude of possible answers to that. The most likely was that the night hawks, limited in their activity by the lack of daylight and the time available, simply hadn't explored the parts of the field where the bulk of the musket balls were found. It was also possible that there had been so many of the damn things that, even after they had taken a lot of them away, there were still plenty left for Nathan to find. Perhaps the Battle of Barrow End had been more than a skirmish after all.

I never believed Nathan had planted the musket balls. I believe he *would* have planted them, if it had suited his purpose, but I don't believe he did. He really cared about that field, and to him, planting false evidence would have been just as bad as not finding any.

CHAPTER 29

The First Battle of Barrow End

Nathan Pendragon led his troops onto the field at precisely two thirty, looking splendid in his buff and scarlet uniform. He was mounted on a grey horse which, according to Joe, was an ex-police animal. It looked docile enough, but I suspected Nathan of being a skilled horseman, capable of controlling almost any steed. Let's face it, what animal would have dared to play him up?

There were only about twenty men on horseback on each side. The three ponies borrowed from the Farmers weren't going to be allowed into the thick of the battle, Joe had explained. They would simply be paraded round the perimeter of the fenced-off area, looking authentic. It would be too much of a risk to let them participate fully, since they would be unused to the noise and tumult of a mock battle, and might panic.

Nathan was representing Sir Henry Kinkade, the real-life leader of the Royalist faction. I have to mention that his costume bore no resemblance to the get-up worn by the freshly-painted figure of the "Mad Dog" on the pub sign.

The proceedings began with a set-piece, intended to instruct the spectators in the background to the forthcoming conflict. A selection of uniformed Society members lined up on the field, and their clothing and equipment were described in detail by a disembodied voice coming over a loudspeaker.

A couple of small cannon—they may have been "drakes," for all I know—were wheeled on and shown off to the crowd, without being fired. Then there was a description of the various types of weapons, and a demonstration of a musket being fired. The crowd enjoyed this display for a while, but started to become restless as the time wore on, eager to see some real fighting.

As a warning that things were about to get serious, Nathan had removed his feathered hat and replaced it with a helmet. Dropping the visor, he gave a signal to the artillery, and a cannon was fired.

The leader of the opposing "army," Daniel Stowe, looked almost as dashing as Nathan, though his costume was slightly less elaborate. Nathan had decided on a total of about five hundred fighting "men" for the battle, not counting the camp-followers and other hangers-on. The participants had come from several different "regiments," groups of Society members from various parts of the country who, for one reason or another, liked to associate themselves with particular leaders from the real Civil War. Each had its own standard, and they made a colourful, fluttering display as the armies trooped onto the field.

Right in front of where we were standing, a fair-haired girl in a low-cut dress, carrying a basket of oranges, displayed her wares to the crowd. The oranges, I mean.

"Is that supposed to be Nell Gwyn?" asked Molly.

"About thirty years too early," corrected Herbert. He was wearing the Cavalier hat that Nathan had presented to him at the party.

Doris and I each bought an orange from the vendor, more as a gesture of friendliness than because we were hungry or thirsty. Doris had a cool bag at her feet, crammed full of sandwiches, crisps and drinks to keep us going.

Herbert and Doris were the kind of people who never went anywhere unprepared. They had even brought along folding stools to sit on while they watched the battle. Joe had estimated it would last about an hour and a half, but that wasn't counting the waiting time beforehand and the clearing up afterwards (which I had, needless to say, been drafted in to help with). It was going to be hard enough for someone of my age to remain standing for that length of time. For Herbert and Doris, it would have been unthinkable.

"Ooh!" squealed Doris, as the first volley of cannon-fire went off. "Is that a *real gun*?"

"Don't worry," said Herbert. "I'm sure they won't be using live ammo."

I smiled at he way he had unconsciously adopted the pseudo-military jargon of an earlier decade.

I looked out for Joe throughout the battle, but didn't catch sight of him after the initial parade of troops onto the field. I spotted Wally once or twice, not in the thick of the fighting, but dodging around in the background apparently shouting instructions to his "team," like the scrum half on a rugby field.

It wasn't easy for a lay person to follow what was going on, once the battle really started, or it wouldn't have been if we hadn't had a running commentary over the loudspeaker system Nathan had thoughtfully organised. Apparently, the Society's events were always "scripted," so that everyone knew in roughly what order things were going to happen, and which side was going to come out the winner. But there could still be a few surprises.

The commentary was done by a retired member of the Society who specialised in these things, and he did a remarkably good job. Just as the battle was starting, Colonel Montgomery came to stand alongside us.

"Good show," he commented. "Excellent turn-out. Commentator chappie seems to know what he's talking about."

When the fighting got into its stride, I began to see why the safety barrier and the insurance were necessary. This really was a—potentially—dangerous business. A pike, in the right (or perhaps I mean the wrong) hands, can be just as much a lethal weapon as a gun. In this case, the pike was more threatening than the muskets, which could do little damage in the absence of what Herbert would have called "live ammo." Unless someone left their ramrod in, which wasn't likely. Everyone had heard that horror story.

Nathan himself had scripted the battle, and in case you're curious to know how he went about it, I'm going to tell you exactly what he told me when I asked him.

For a start, there were no official records of the battle. Warfare in the seventeenth century wasn't the "sophisticated" business it is nowadays. Sir Henry Kinkade, or "Mad Dog" if you prefer, was an experienced soldier who had fought on the Continent in the Thirty Years' War, but his followers were a different kettle of fish — a motley crew of retainers, farm labourers and the like, many of whom had never used a pike in anger before October 1642.

The other side were much the same. It must have been a bit of a shock to their systems when the Royalist cavalry came charging towards them.

Nathan confided in me that he didn't believe there had actually *been* any cavalry at the real Battle of Barrow End. It was a piece of poetic licence, to enhance the effectiveness of the re-enactment. He justified it by saying that the presence of horses in our version of the battle would help to prove or disprove his theory.

Nathan's major problem in trying to piece together the sequence of events after three and a half centuries was the lack of consistency in the eyewitness accounts. There were good excuses for this—it didn't necessarily mean that anyone was telling porkies.

You see, the first thing that would have happened was not, as ignorance had led me to expect, a cavalry charge, but an artillery bombardment. This would result in clouds of smoke that would obscure the progress of the battle. Once the musketeers got started, there would be even more smoke blowing around, not to mention the noise. Add to that the sheer difficulty of telling the two sides apart, with their similar uniforms, and you can see why confusion reigned.

The cannon would have done a certain amount of damage in the real battle, but for the purposes of the re-enactment, there were no cannon-balls, just a lot of good solid bangs and a few puffs of smoke. Instead of real casualties, one or two people made screaming noises and lay down on the field. They were supposed to stay there, but I've a sneaking suspicion that some of them got up again when no one was looking and carried on fighting. They didn't like the thought of missing out. "Dead" people were dragged into the shadow of the hedge, where they lay looking pathetic for the rest of the battle.

In real life, the nature of the injuries would have been much more horrible than anything the Society could attempt to portray. Arms and legs would have been shot off by the cannon. Nathan's demand for authenticity didn't go so far as to ask his members to make a sacrifice of this magnitude.

After the cannon volleys, the fun really started. Musketeers marched forwards in formation, their black powder carried in bandoliers that hung across each of their chests like a row of little wooden bells. The barrels of the flintlock muskets held powder with wadding rammed down on top of it, to make sure that they went off with a loud report rather than a feeble pop. Once they got going, it was really quite frightening. You could almost believe you were in the middle of a real battle.

The pikemen were advancing inexorably towards one another. Two groups of opposing forces clashed, and I witnessed the first pike push at close quarters. Previously, I'd only seen Joe and his friends drilling with pike, and though I had been full of admiration for their skill in handling the things, the implications for the conduct of battle had been completely lost on me.

The pike push was spectacular, like a sea of porcupine needles that twisted, and turned, and suddenly lay down flat.

"We don't know for sure that they did it *precisely* like that," commented Herbert. From the far-away smile on his face as he watched his dream become reality, you would never have expected him to come up with any criticisms.

"I haven't seen Jonathan for about half an hour," I said. "Where's he gone? Is he over on the other side of the field?"

"Oh, he'll turn up," said Doris, laughing, "like a bad penny."

Chapter 30
The Battle Lost and Won

The rest of the battle was very much a repetition of what I've just described, only that there were multiple clashes going on in different parts of the field. I could certainly sympathise with the eyewitnesses who had recorded their contradictory impressions of the original battle. For a lot of the time, I couldn't tell what was going on at all, except for the details that the commentator was relaying over the loudspeakers — which regiment was which, and so forth.

Midway through the battle, he interrupted his commentary to ask his listeners to look out for a lost child, which had strayed from its mother somewhere near the entrance to the field. From what we could gather, it was a little boy aged about two, wearing a green tee-shirt and yellow shorts. He ought to stand out in a crowd, I thought to myself.

The commentary proper resumed. My inability to follow the armies' progress without it didn't affect my enjoyment of the battle. I only wished I had someone to watch it with, other than three senior citizens.

At other times, I wished I was on the field with the rest of the girls. They seemed to be having a good time, watching those hot sweaty men giving it what for with the pike at close quarters. All they had to do themselves was stay out of the way and occasionally administer a drink of water to a hot sweaty man.

While I was thinking about it longingly, I noticed a flurry of activity centring on the Parliamentarian cannon. By the look of things, the Royalists were about to capture their opponents' guns. There was a bit of mock sword-fighting and a few of the artillerymen got run through, then came a whoop of triumph from what I thought of as "our side," and the cannon were wheeled jubilantly away by the Royalists.

All was now confusion in the Roundhead ranks. Scripted confusion, of course. You can't have people going their own way in a battle, even if it is all acting, or it might end up with someone getting hurt.

The Royalist cavalry charged down from one corner of the field which was a little elevated, and the opposing forces scattered. Although the Society could only supply small numbers of suitably-trained horses and experienced riders, they looked pretty impressive when they waded in with swords drawn and some bloodthirsty yelling.

Then the musketeers let loose with their black powder again. One of the riders on Nathan's side made a dramatic business of "falling" off his horse, fatally wounded, and was dragged to one side of the field by his comrades, one of whom immediately appropriated the riderless horse for his own use.

There was a sudden commotion around the point Nathan and his cavalry had reached. From where we were standing, we had a good vantage point which enabled us to see roughly what was happening in that area, though most of the crowd would have been oblivious to it.

There was a lot of shouting, and even a few screams—but they didn't sound like scripted screams to me. I could see a little knot of people converging on the spot.

"It's a child!" exclaimed Doris.

As soon as she said it, I could make out what was happening. There was indeed a small child—it looked like a boy—no more than three years old, standing in the middle of the press of horses. Disaster was imminent. The cavalry were going full tilt, so that to stop or swerve would have been just as dangerous as to do the same thing in a car travelling at high speed. The little boy wasn't doing anything in particular, just standing there staring about him. He was wearing a green tee-shirt and yellow shorts.

As we watched, our hands in front of our mouths, speechless with fright, the nearest pikeman ran forward, grabbed the child, picked him up and ran with him across the path of the charging horses, carrying him out of danger. It was a heart-stopping moment.

Only a small proportion of the spectators had witnessed the incident. The commentator hadn't seen it, and didn't draw attention to it. The pikeman had already disappeared from view, taking the child off the field, but he had been in our line of vision long enough for me to recognise the now-familiar cut of the uniform, the unmistakable figure.

"Was that who I think it was?" asked Herbert, the only other person who seemed to have recognised him.

"Yes," I said. "That was Joe."

For the second time in five days, he was a hero.

You could tell that both armies were getting tired now. It was a hot day, and they would have been sweltering in all that gear, even if they hadn't had to exert themselves. It was one area where Nathan's quest for authenticity had not been fulfilled, as the real battle had happened on a cold day in the late autumn; and the real battle would have gone on longer than an hour and a half.

Daniel Stowe came forward alone, and offered his sword to Nathan. Nathan accepted it graciously, and made no attempt to run Daniel through with it, as I think everyone had been hoping.

It was only then that I realised the battle was over.

THE TROOPS FORMED a kind of rough procession to leave the field. Some marched in formation, others made a show of being wounded, with "blood-soaked" bandages round their heads and various other parts of their anatomy. As they passed in front of the spectators, the commentator once again named the successive regiments, and we all applauded.

As Joe passed close to the safety barrier, our little group clapped and cheered more loudly, in recognition of his potentially life-saving effort at the climax of the battle. In response, he tipped his helmet at Herbert and Doris, but the wink that accompanied it was meant for me alone. He made a gesture with his elbow, clearly signifying an intention to partake of alcoholic refreshment and presumably inviting me to join him. I smiled, nodded, and threw him a packet of crisps which he caught deftly. He grinned, and blew me a kiss.

Another of the Royalist soldiers had detached himself from the procession, and was coming towards us. He ducked under the safety barrier, and had got within about six feet of us before we saw who it was.

"Jonathan!" we chorused simultaneously.

Jonathan was almost unrecognisable, until he took off his helmet. Flushed and happy, he carried himself like a hardened veteran, and wore a streak of dirt across his cheek like a war wound. His hair was sticking up in tufts, and there was a dazed look in his eyes, as though he had been in another world—which, in a manner of speaking, he had.

"Did you see me?" he asked. "Did you see me, in that pike push?"

"N—," I began.

"Yes, dear, we saw you," said Doris. "It was wonderful, just wonderful. I hope you haven't hurt yourself." Opening the cool bag, she brought out a carton of semi-chilled fruit juice, which he poured thirstily down his throat in record time.

Something told me that we wouldn't be seeing much of Jonathan in the museum the following summer.

When the field had cleared, we all went back to my flat for a cup of tea. When I say "all," I mean Herbert, Doris, Verity, Molly and me. Those who had been involved in the battle went straight to the pub. Later, Molly and I went back to the field and helped to pick up litter. We could hardly leave the Farmers' property in a worse condition than we'd found it.

Molly had volunteered to help, simply because she hoped to see Nathan again. I feared she would be out of luck, but in fact Nathan, as befitted his rank, was supervising the clearing-up effort, and came over to thank us for our contribution. Molly glowed with pride when he addressed her, but I suspected he didn't even know her name. Afterwards, I gave her a lift home, then went to the Dog and Drake to meet Joe and the others.

Joe made absolutely nothing of the rescue of the little boy from in front of the horses' hooves, though several of the cavalry men involved in the charge congratulated him heartily on his action. I felt so proud, not just of his courage, but of the modesty with which he conducted himself afterwards, that once again I found myself regretting the fact that my attempts to form a relationship with him had foundered.

There was no going back. Joe was very affectionate towards me that evening, but he was equally affectionate towards Tina, and rightly so. We sat, one either side of him, and later on, when we were all starting to feel tired, I even dozed off on his shoulder for a while. The warmth of his body under my cheek reminded me of what I'd been doing, less comfortably, the night before, but I tried not to dwell on it.

When I opened my eyes, after a few minutes, stretched and sat up straight, I saw Nathan, at the other side of the table, smiling at me in a fatherly way. I had to force myself to remember that he did this kind of thing every weekend, in summer, as did Joe and Tina and Wally and Daniel Stowe (who, by the way, had done me the honour of chatting me up for about quarter of an hour before getting into his car for the long drive back up north). The novelty had long since worn off for them, so I felt it was a compliment to me that they appeared to find such pleasure in my company and were prepared to listen to me enthusing about the battle for several hours after it had ended.

As I was leaving the pub, Nathan asked me to walk out to his car with him, "to fetch something." He opened one of the passenger doors, rummaged around on the back seat in the dark, and handed me a thick envelope.

"I thought you might be interested in this," he said. "A draft chapter from my book. It won't be out till next year, of course, but there'll be an acknowledgement for you."

"What have I done to deserve an acknowledgement?" I asked, genuinely mystified.

"You found the pub sign, among other things," he said. "All the museum staff will get a mention anyway, but I do feel you made a special contribution. As far as I know, no one else got beaten up in the cause of historical research."

I smiled at the thought. "Will you include Molly?" I asked. "By name, I mean."

"Molly," he said thoughtfully, as if trying to put a face to the name. "Why Molly, in particular?"

"She's got a crush on you."

"Ah." He didn't sound surprised. I guessed this kind of thing happened to him all the time. "I wish I'd known. Of course, I'll make sure she gets a special mention."

"Thanks. She'll be thrilled. And thanks for letting me see this. Do I have to send it back to you when I've read it?"

"No, it's just a draft. But I'd appreciate any comments you may have."

"I can't see that I'm likely to be able to add anything to your analysis," I said, surprised by his apparent respect for me.

"Rosemary," he said, gently, "don't underestimate your intellect. It's been a pleasure to make your acquaintance." He extended his right hand.

"I have to leave early in the morning, but I hope to meet you again some day."

I think I floated home on a cloud. To think that Nathan Pendragon valued my opinion! I looked back on that day, a few months earlier, when I'd met him for the first time, in the Lamb & Flag, and had wanted nothing more than for him to go away so that I could be on my own with Joe. So much had changed in that time. All my assumptions had been challenged, all my preferences overturned.

When I got home, I started getting ready for bed, but I ended up drinking hot chocolate at the kitchen table and reading Nathan's draft. Though it was late, and I was desperately tired, my brain was still buzzing with excitement. I knew I wouldn't sleep for hours.

The chapter Nathan had chosen to give me concerned the background to the battle, the build-up of the military campaign and the way both sides would have gone about recruiting in the area. It didn't deal with the actual battle. He was obviously still working on his analysis of that. It was interesting, nonetheless, and made me feel part of something bigger than a mere battle re-enactment—or even a piece of "reconstruction archaeology," as Nathan might have described it.

When I finally got under the duvet, at about half-past one in the morning, I felt quite pleased with myself for what Nathan had referred to as my "contribution" to the effort. Whatever happened about the planning application, I would always have this to look back on. My name would be in print, in the acknowledgements at the front of Nathan's book, and he had promised me a complimentary copy when it came out.

It had been a fantastic day. There was really only one way it could have been improved on.

Chapter 31

The Second Battle of Barrow End

I really had thought Edward would be there that afternoon. Though I would have been ashamed to admit it, I had been looking out for him. Several times, I'd caught a glimpse of a tall man among the crowd and had wanted it to be him, then been disappointed to find, on closer observation, that it was some total stranger.

I felt terribly let down by Edward's failure to appear. I'd given him as much encouragement as I felt able. During Sunday morning, I had begun to give credence to a brief fantasy in which, admiring me in my camp-follower's costume, he would approach me in a totally relaxed and affectionate manner and we would resume our acquaintance on a more informal basis.

On the Monday, I still half-expected him to ring me, or to slip across the road from his office and come into the museum to seek me out, but he didn't do that either. I resigned myself to not seeing him until the evening, and I wasn't sure that I would even get a chance to speak to him then, with all the council business going on. It was just as well, really, because I had no idea what to say. What was worrying me most was the thought that I had somehow frightened him off.

Pride prevented me from going over to his office to look for him during my lunch hour. If he wasn't going to make the first move, I certainly wasn't. After all, he was the one who had walked out on me, wasn't he? At least, that's how it seemed to me at the time. I took refuge in the idea that there was still the whole afternoon for him to make contact. But the afternoon came to an end, and he hadn't.

I tried not to dwell on it. Men just aren't the same as us, and what a dull life it would be if they were. I went back to the village for my tea. Joe had taken a couple of days off work, and hadn't gone home since the battle. I'd given him a key to the flat, and he and

Tina were making themselves at home when I arrived. A couple of pizzas had appeared from somewhere, and it was just as well, because I felt too physically and emotionally drained to prepare anything. We all went back into town together for the planning meeting at seven o'clock.

There was such a crowd that we could hardly get in through the door of the Town Hall. The number of spectators who could be seated in the council chamber was severely limited, but the Velvet Vale Action Committee went to the front of the queue, and the crowd also parted for Peter Markham and some senior officers of the Re-enactment Society who had come along to represent Nathan. Peter was just ahead of me, and Joe just behind me, as we jostled our way through. Consequently, we had the best seats, in the front row of the gallery, looking down on the assembled councillors.

It was a shame that Nathan couldn't have come to the meeting and made the kind of impassioned speech, in opposition to the development, that had been so effective earlier in our campaign. But members of the public aren't allowed to speak or participate in planning meetings, so it would have been pointless him staying. The main purpose of our presence was as a reminder to the councillors of the tireless lobbying we had been doing in the lead-up to the meeting.

We had all hoped that the planning application for Velvet Vale would have been withdrawn before the meeting, but the word had gone around that it was still to be considered. That made Edward's attendance at the meeting vital. I was sure I knew what his intentions were. He wouldn't be able to speak in the debate, but just by showing his face, he would be sending a clear message to the Farmers that they risked exposure if they continued with the application.

The Farmers were present, sitting almost alongside us. I don't know how they had managed to get to the front of the queue, but they had even better seats than we did.

"I can't see Councillor Long," I remarked to Peter, taking care to avoid any use of Edward's first name. "Where is he?"

Peter shrugged, and looked at Hilary, on the other side of him. She didn't respond.

The meeting began. There was still no sign of Edward.

I didn't have to wait long to find out why he wasn't there. When apologies for non-attendance were called for, the Secretary reported that he had received a letter from Councillor Long, who was indisposed and could not attend. Edward had chickened out.

That was my first thought. I disregarded it almost immediately. Whatever else Edward might be, he wasn't a coward, nor was he a liar. He had said he didn't intend to let the planning application go through on the nod. If he claimed to be ill, then he was ill. It would have to be something pretty serious, to keep him away from such an important meeting, but it could be fatal from the campaign's point of view. As for the implications for our relationship, they didn't bear thinking about.

The first three-quarters of an hour was taken up with mundane procedural stuff. I wondered if the Borough Council did it this way deliberately, in the hope that anyone who'd come to a meeting with the idea of making trouble would have lost interest by the time the important matters got their turn.

At long last they got onto the subject of the planning application that had attracted the large audience. The sight of Trevor and Valerie Farmer in the gallery had put paid to any faint hope we might have had of their having withdrawn it at the eleventh hour. Several of the councillors looked as if they had something to say on the subject of Velvet Vale, which made us feel hopeful. It wasn't a foregone conclusion.

Sally Maplethorpe, whom I had once thought of as Edward's partner in crime, was first to get up. "Councillor Long has been unable to attend tonight, but he's sent this letter, to be read out to the meeting, with the Chairman's permission."

The Chairman looked surprised. "Councillor Long has declared an interest in this application. I thought he wasn't intending to participate in the debate."

"No," she said, "this isn't exactly a contribution to the debate. Councillor Long said it was only to be put on the table if the Velvet Vale application wasn't withdrawn. It's a... point of order?"

The Chairman looked even more bewildered. "I don't think I understand, Mrs. Maplethorpe."

Sally Maplethorpe looked as serious as I'd ever seen her. "I think you will when you hear the contents of the letter."

The Chairman nodded. "You'd better carry on, then."

The letter started off with a brief summary of the facts. People were starting to look bored by the second paragraph; but luckily, that was where things took off. I watched the faces of the individual councillors as recognition dawned. Briefly, Councillor Long was reporting an attempt to interfere with the course of the application for planning permission, by offering bribes to interested parties. Needless to say, the word "bribe" wasn't used. Neither was the word "corruption."

I admired his style. His literary style, that is. It was a particularly well-written letter—tactful, specific and to the point. Much clearer than the letter he'd sent Mrs. Challoner, all those weeks ago. No names were mentioned, and yet no one in the room was left in any doubt as to the identity of the people involved in the corruption. The Farmers turned to look at one another in dismay, then quickly covered up their confusion by turning their pink faces back to their copies of the agenda.

When Sally Maplethorpe sat down, there was a general murmur of indignation from the members of the committee, and an even louder one from the uninvited audience.

I glanced at Peter and Hilary. Edward's letter had made no mention of the vicar's role in the episode, but some of the other people in the gallery must have had an idea he was involved. He was doing his best to look as if the whole thing was nothing to do with him, and Hilary was playing along. I had no wish to see Peter humiliated, and I turned away from them again.

The Chairman consulted hurriedly with the colleagues nearest him. Their private confab went on so long that it seemed doubtful whether they would ever get around to the remainder of the meeting's business.

"Why don't they hurry up?" whispered Joe.

"This is an important matter, Joe," said Herbert, who was sitting on the other side of him. "It has to be given proper consideration."

Finally, to everyone's relief, the Chairman raised his head again and addressed the meeting.

"Councillor Long's letter raises some very serious issues," he said. "I've consulted with the Vice Chair and the Secretary, and I must say we feel this matter should be referred back to the relevant authority. I don't think we should continue to discuss this application tonight."

There was muttered agreement from the other councillors, and a burst of applause from the more unruly members of the public—in other words, the Re-enactment Society.

We spilled out of the Town Hall, onto the pavement, and I temporarily lost sight of all those who had been sitting next to me in the gallery. The Farmers, I noticed, had remained in their front row seats, obviously waiting for the crush to die down so that they could sneak out without attracting attention. Joe and his mates would be bound for the Lamb & Flag, I suspected. I headed in that general direction, and came upon Peter, Hilary, Herbert and Doris, standing further along the pavement, in deep conversation.

"Food poisoning, apparently," were the words I caught as I came up to the little group.

"Are you talking about Councillor Long?" I asked.

Peter turned and saw me. "Oh, Rose, there you are. Yes, it seems Edward Long's in a really bad way, that's why he wasn't here tonight."

"Did I hear you say food poisoning?"

Peter nodded. "That's right. He's been ill since yesterday."

The seafood pancake. It had to be.

Joe and Tina stayed over with the Eatons that night. Tuesday was my day off from the museum, as usual, and they came to see me in the morning, before they left for home.

"Seemed like the meeting went well," said Joe, repeating what he had said several times the previous evening in the pub. He probably couldn't remember saying it.

Jonathan and I had tried hard to persuade him to let us give the local paper the "exclusive" story of his rescue of the little lost boy during the battle. There was going to be a write-up in any case, but a sensational story like that, with a "human interest" angle, would help to maintain public enthusiasm for the Battle of Barrow End.

Joe ignored our pleas. He wouldn't accept any plaudits for his action. The most he would agree to was Jonathan's suggestion that we give them the story of the rescue, but say that it had been carried out by a "mystery man" whom no one could identify. Jonathan already had the details of the child's attractive young mother, and would prime her to describe how a dashing cavalier had returned her child to her and then vanished into the crowd.

And now Joe was leaving, and I would have to look around for another hero. The irony was that I didn't know how close I was to finding one.

"I'm really pleased for you all," said Tina, as she climbed into the passenger seat of Joe's battered old Mini. "You're such a nice bunch of people. You don't deserve to have some horrible housing development on your doorstep."

I thanked her for her concern. The two of them got into the Mini, and drove off noisily down the village street, disappearing round the corner by the Village Hall, on the road home.

A tear came to my eye as I continued to wave, not accepting for several minutes that they weren't going to turn around and come back.

That was the last time I ever saw Joe Payne.

IT WASN'T UNTIL Thursday morning that we received official confirmation that the Farmers had withdrawn their planning application. They had little choice. It didn't mean they couldn't re-submit when all the fuss had died down; but somehow I didn't think they would. For the moment, their name was mud.

And there was still no sign of Edward Long.

Throughout the week, the idea of going round to see him kept insinuating itself into my mind. Once or twice, I was on the verge of getting into the car and driving over there. Only one thing stopped me—the thought of Edward's mother. My guess was, he hadn't told her he was seeing me, so he wouldn't thank me for turning up on the doorstep. If I could have been sure of arriving at a moment when she was out, I would have been there like a shot; but it seemed likely that she would only be out during the day, and the only time I could reasonably go was in the evenings.

The thought of him lying there vomiting his guts up did arouse some kind of feeling in me—other than disgust, I mean. It's horrible to be that ill, and it's worse when the only person you've got to look after you is a fussy old bag like that, even if she is your own mother. I couldn't help thinking how much better off he would have been if I had been there to sit with him and apply cold flannels to his forehead, or whatever you do with a food poisoning victim. I wondered if he was thinking the same, or if he'd already forgotten me.

It wasn't that I felt under any obligation to him, just because he had said he was in love with me.

But yes, guilt—or shame—played a part in my growing desperation to see him again. When I considered the events of recent months, and the catalogue of deliberate rudeness and wanton cruelty that I'd inflicted on Edward, I couldn't recognise anything that might have inspired him to fall in love with me. Was the man some kind of masochist?

Later that same Thursday morning, the police telephoned me at work, and asked me to call in at the station. This time, I was able to get there during my lunch hour. I didn't have great expectations of my visit. The police hadn't been outstandingly helpful up to now. My statement had been signed and handed over the previous week, so I was at a loss as to what they might want me for.

The desk sergeant asked me to wait, and I did so for about a quarter of an hour, getting more and more frustrated, until I was ready to start making a fuss. Another officer appeared, in the nick of time, and called me into a small private office. His tone was confidential, and I began to have some apprehensions about the reason for my being called in. I nearly collapsed when he told me that they knew which of the men they had "caught" had attacked me the other night. All they wanted from me was my agreement for them to proceed with a simple caution, rather than a prosecution for assault.

The man had never been in any trouble before, they told me. If I insisted on charges being pressed, he would plead guilty and get off very lightly, so there was hardly any point in taking the matter to court. As a taxpayer, I could surely appreciate, et cetera et cetera...

Needless to say, I accepted their suggestion. I'm not vindictive—well, not usually. What bowled me over was the revelation that the man had come forward of his own accord and confessed to his misdeed. I could barely believe the explanation that was offered—that he was a previously law-abiding citizen who had been overwhelmed with guilt by his action and the thought that he might have caused me an injury.

His excuse for knocking me over was that he had mistaken me for a man, in the darkness, and had thought I was there to try and steal the metal detecting equipment! The police officer had the grace to look apologetic while telling me this exceedingly tall story. I was insulted, as much as anything, that anyone could believe in the possibility of *me* being mistaken for a man. Even in the dark.

All the same, I couldn't bring myself to reject the solution being proposed. If my attacker were to change his mind about pleading guilty, no one would be able to prove anything against him and he would get off scot free.

What I continued to puzzle over for the rest of the day was *why*. The man's name, by the way, was Brian Pratt. His surname might have caused me some amusement if I had even half-believed his version of events, but it hardly explained his willingness to own up to a crime he could never otherwise have been convicted of.

When I told other people that had happened, they were all equally incredulous, with one exception.

ON FRIDAY NIGHT, Peter came round to see me. It was quite unexpected. He hadn't been alone with me in my flat since the day he told me it was over between us.

I hadn't spoken to him since the night of the planning meeting. I wasn't sure if he knew it was me who had spilled the beans to Edward about the Farmers' donation to the restoration fund, but in any case I didn't care.

Peter told me that the Bishop had insisted on returning the Farmers' money, all five thousand pounds of it. He had got to hear—from the auditor, presumably—that the accounts had not been properly kept and that there could be accusations of corruption. Peter seemed resigned. He obviously felt he was getting off lightly.

Peter told me something else, too. He told me that Edward Long had made up the shortfall of five thousand pounds in the fund, out of his own pocket.

But that wasn't the main reason for this private visit to my flat. What Peter had really came for was to let me know that he was "moving on."

"I didn't want you to hear it from anyone else," he said. What he meant was that he wanted to witness my reaction. I think he may have been disappointed.

The Markhams were going to another parish, in another diocese, a hundred miles away. Peter didn't say that it had anything to do with the planning fiasco, but I assumed it did. Whether he had decided to go to avoid personal embarrassment, or whether the Bishop had made the decision for him, it made no difference. He would be out of my life, for the foreseeable future, and any danger that might have remained of us resuming our relationship was finally removed.

My feelings were ambivalent. Looking at Peter, even after everything that had happened and all the stupid things he'd done, I couldn't help feeling something for him. He looked lost, as though he didn't understand what was happening to him. He might have brought it on himself, but that didn't stop me feeling sympathetic. He would never be the Mayor's Chaplain now.

"What about Hilary?" I asked. "Doesn't she mind leaving her home town again, so soon?"

"Actually," he said, "I think she's secretly pleased. She knows about you and me."

I could have fainted on the spot, if I hadn't been sitting down.

"You didn't tell her?"

I had been so sure he wouldn't hurt her by letting her find out about it.

"Certainly not." He was more indignant than I'd ever seen him. "I had actually been wondering whether *you* had told her."

"Me?" I squealed. "You must be off your trolley!"

I could see how his mind had been working, though. The rejected mistress, taking her revenge by rubbing the wife's nose in it.

"In that case," said Peter, reflectively, "I can't think how she found out. I suppose she must simply have guessed."

I wondered about Edward. Might he have known, even though I hadn't confessed to it? Might he have told Hilary, perhaps as a way of causing a rift between her and her husband, in the hope that he could step into the breach?

"How long has she known?" I asked.

"I'm not sure. At least three months."

That more or less settled it. Edward had only asked me the question a few days before, and he hadn't seemed sure. Three months ago, he had scarcely known my name. And, thinking about it, he must have heard it from someone else in the first place. That same person who had told Hilary, perhaps. It was probably all over town by now, what I'd thought of as our little secret. What a fool I'd been, to think we could conceal something like that.

Then I remembered what Edward had said about his long-standing friendship with Hilary, and I realised it was the other way round. It was Hilary who had told Edward.

"What did she say?" I asked Peter. "Did she confront you with it?" There was nothing I could do; but I still felt I needed to know.

"Not at first. She started dropping little hints. "Are you going to see Rose?" —that kind of thing. Eventually I twigged. But I didn't admit it until she finally came out and asked me."

"You admitted it?"

Peter looked surprised that I should even ask. "Of course I admitted it. Hilary's my wife, she has a right to expect the truth from me. I would have preferred her not to find out, but I couldn't deny it when she asked me. I told her it was over, I asked her to forgive me, and she did."

I had been going to meetings of the Action Committee with a woman whose husband I had slept with, and she had known all along.

"What about me, Peter? Did you ask her to forgive me, too?" I asked indignantly.

"Don't be silly, Rose. She doesn't blame you, any more than she blames me. She knows about our previous relationship, she always did. She understands how it started up again. In fact, I think she blames herself more than anyone. She thinks it only happened because we weren't getting on well at home, and she feels it was her fault."

That didn't seem fair, either.

"So you're going to make a fresh start."

"That's right. I'm hoping it'll be easier this time. As soon as we've made the move, we're going to the doctor to see about IVF."

I hadn't even realised they had been trying to start a family. Peter had never mentioned it, when he had been going on about how unhappy they were and how he still cared for me.

Poor old Hilary, I thought, as I saw him off. On reflection, Peter was probably right when he said that she had simply guessed his guilty secret.

Men aren't usually very good at subterfuge. Peter had proved that by letting the cat out of the bag about the Farmers' donation. He hadn't even had the gumption to swear me to secrecy.

I felt no trace of envy for Hilary as Peter's wife, if I ever had. He wasn't such a bad person, but he was nowhere near good enough for her. She would have been better off with Edward Long.

NEEDLESS TO SAY, next day in the museum the main topic of conversation was the Markhams' imminent departure. The news had got around remarkably quickly, no doubt speeded on its way by well-wishers. I was pleased to note that no one seemed to suspect it had anything to do with me. The general opinion seemed to concur with what I had originally thought—that the Bishop, displeased by allegations about the attempted corruption of one of his parish priests, might have had something to do with it.

We had a quiet day, only twenty-five visitors between the morning and afternoon sessions. Jonathan and I went and tidied up some of the displays. While we were dusting down the Victorian kitchen utensils, he asked me if I fancied going out for a drink after we closed. I turned him down, on the pretext that I felt like a quiet night in. It wasn't a lie, but I admit there were other things on my mind.

When I had told Jonathan about the confession that had enabled the police to single out Brian Pratt from the list of my potential attackers, his response had been as straightforward and logical as Jonathan's always were. Everyone else had tut-tutted about it and said they couldn't understand it.

Jonathan just said, "Sounds like someone's leaned on him."

It made perfect sense as soon as he said it, but the only people who could have leaned on Brian Pratt were the Farmers. Why would they have done that?

I voiced the question, and Jonathan's next response was equally sane.

"Maybe they've got something to hide. Maybe someone else has got something on *them*."

Who would have that kind of information, I wondered, and why would they use it for my benefit? The word "gallant" sprang to mind. And of course, at that point, there was only one person I could think of.

Herbert came over to us, just as we were packing up to leave.

"I've written a letter to Councillor Long," he said, "thanking him for his role in getting the planning application withdrawn and exposing the attempted corruption. I thought he might have been in today to see us, but I expect he's still not well. I suppose I'd better just leave it in his pigeonhole."

The Longs lived in a large, rambling house on the edge of the town. I knew it well. It was *almost* on the road that led to Barrow End.

"I'll drop it off on my way home," I said.

Chapter 32
My Hero

After all the prevaricating I'd done during the week, I was still nervous about approaching the Longs' house. I didn't give much for my chances of conducting an intimate conversation with Edward, what with his mother hovering over us. Or maybe even hoovering. I probably wouldn't get past the doorstep. As I drove up their street, I noticed a "For Sale" sign outside the house next door. Perhaps it was a bit much to conclude that the neighbours were moving out because of Mrs. Long. All the same, I didn't envy any unsuspecting buyers.

I was startled, on getting out of the car and opening the front gate, to observe that the sign did not refer to the house next door, but was attached to the Longs' own gatepost.

As I walked up the drive, I still had half an idea of putting Herbert's envelope through the door and running away quickly; but that seemed a mean thing to do under the circumstances. Besides, I really did want to see Edward.

It took so long for the door to be answered that I had forgotten about the For Sale sign by the time it opened. I waited patiently, reasoning that, if Edward had been very ill, he was probably still convalescing and it might not be easy for him to get to the door. His mother might—God willing—be out, but even if she wasn't, she wouldn't be very quick on her feet. I just hoped Edward wouldn't answer the door in his pyjamas and dressing gown. (There was no doubt at all in my mind that he *did* wear pyjamas — probably stripey ones.)

I knew he'd been ill, so I wasn't expecting him to look that great; but I wasn't expecting him to look as awful as he did. It had been nearly a week, after all, and he should have been on the road to recovery.

He didn't look particularly pleased to see me.

"Oh, it's you," was all he said.

"Herbert gave me something for you." I proffered the envelope. "How are you feeling?"

Even in a week, he'd managed to lose weight. He was terribly pale, too. But at least he was dressed.

He was wearing brown cords and a worn-looking checked shirt. I'd never seen him dressed casually before, and the contrast with his usual style was striking. If he'd been suffering from sickness and diarrhoea all week, he would probably be scraping the bottom of the barrel by now, in terms of clean clothes. On his feet were beige canvas shoes. That colour wouldn't show up vomit easily, I thought.

"I'm okay," he said briefly, not quite looking me in the eye. "Thanks." He took the envelope out of my hand.

Reluctant to walk away now that I had made the effort, I looked for a way of prolonging the conversation.

"Is there anything I can do for you?" I blurted. "I would have come before, only..."

He stood back suddenly. "Would you come in?" he said, with a sweep of his arm in the direction of the interior.

After a moment's hesitation, I stepped across the threshold, into the dingy hall. As we passed through, I noticed a door standing ajar. Through it I glimpsed the book-lined walls of what appeared to be a little study. No wonder Edward never needed to patronise the library.

Having closed the front door, he manoeuvred delicately past me and led the way into what I supposed he and his mother would refer to as the sitting room. Or maybe even the drawing room. It looked like something out of the 1930s. It was plain that there had been no young people in this house for many years—unless you counted Edward.

There was no sign of the old lady.

"Where's your mother?" I asked.

"She's at Geoff's."

I looked puzzled.

"My brother," he elaborated. "My eldest brother. I couldn't look after her this week, the state I was in. I couldn't even take her out in the car." He gestured to an armchair. "Sit down, please. Can I get you anything?"

I felt guiltier than ever now. I could have been there with the cold flannels after all. "No, please, isn't there anything *I* can do for *you*?"

I protested. "You don't mean to say you've been here on your own all week?"

"Pretty much. I rang Geoff on Monday, and he came down that evening, stayed overnight, and took Mum back to Droitwich on Tuesday morning. Where, I hope, she'll remain."

I wasn't sure which to be more startled by, the use of the term "Mum" to refer to Mrs. Long, or the statement that she was staying in Droitwich.

"Will you please sit down?" Edward repeated.

I obeyed.

"Was it the seafood pancake?" I asked.

"The what?" He looked confused for a moment, then recognition dawned. "Oh, the food poisoning. No, I'm fairly sure it was the chicken portion I had for Sunday lunch. I started to feel ill immediately afterwards. My mother cooked it, but I don't think she defrosted it properly first. It wouldn't be the first time."

"Was she ill, too?"

"Oh, no. She didn't have the chicken herself. We rarely eat the same thing at mealtimes. She's very particular about her diet."

I was about to lean back into the chair and make myself comfortable. Then I remembered where I was. I hadn't come here to be comfortable.

"Anyway," he added, "that's why I didn't come to the re-enactment. Or perhaps you didn't notice that I wasn't there?"

He didn't look as if he intended sarcasm.

"I did notice," I said. "I thought I'd done something to put you off."

He grimaced slightly, a look not intended to be shared with me.

"It was so stupid of me," I went on, "not to come and see you earlier in the week. I just assumed your mother was here to look after you. I didn't think of you being on your own. How have you managed?"

He almost laughed. "Don't worry about me, I'm used to taking care of myself. The washing's piled up a bit—what with me throwing up all the time—but I'll soon get it back under control. And I don't have to concern myself with my mother any more."

Had he really meant it, when he said she wouldn't be coming back?

"So she's at your brother's now?" I probed.

"Yes. I rang him on Wednesday and told him I wasn't prepared to live with her any more. I suggested she should go into some kind of residential home, sheltered housing or something. He flew off the handle at first, said it wouldn't be right. But I said, if he wasn't willing for that to happen, then he would have to have her to live with him for a change. Or Adrian would."

"Adrian's your other brother?"

"Yes, but I knew what *he'd* say. He and my mother have barely spoken for the past few years. So, in effect, it was Geoff or no one."

"Did he come round in the end?"

This time he really did laugh. Only a little laugh, but a laugh nevertheless. "I wouldn't exactly say that, but he called me back next day and said there were suitable places near him and he would check it out, provided I was willing to sustain half the cost. Naturally, I said yes. The house is my mother's, of course, so there'll be the proceeds from that to help pay for her keep. I've already had the estate agent round. You might have noticed the board. I'll find myself something smaller."

He must have interpreted my silence as disapproval, because he added, "I suppose you think I'm heartless."

"No, not at all. I just didn't realise you were having a problem with your mother." Conscious that I wasn't being completely truthful, I added, "I thought she seemed pretty active for her age. Of course, I don't know how old she is..."

"She's seventy-eight." I was still doing the mental calculation when he added, "She was well over forty when she had me."

"In that case, I suppose it couldn't have gone on indefinitely."

"No." His face had closed down. He got up and moved purposefully away from his chair, towards a wall cupboard. "Will you have a drink? Sherry or something?"

Concluding that he was offering alcohol only because there was no milk in the house, I decided not to embarrass him by asking for tea or coffee. All the same, I hesitated before deciding that one small sherry wouldn't affect my driving and might help oil the wheels of conversation.

"A small one, then," I agreed.

He poured it quickly, followed by a measure of scotch for himself, and handed me the glass, taking care that our fingers didn't touch.

I sipped the sherry in a manner that was intended to be ladylike, sitting back in the chair now that I was more sure of myself.

Edward sat down again, took a nip of his drink, then leaned forward suddenly, startling me out of my complacency.

"It's not that I don't love my mother," he said, "but you see, I haven't had a life of my own for years."

He looked as if he expected me to comment.

"No," I said quietly, "I can see that. It must have been difficult."

"Extremely." He stood up again, went to the window, and looked out into the garden, hands in pockets. "I couldn't even have a woman here," he said, slowly.

I weighed it all up in my mind before speaking again. He was trying to tell me something. At the same time, he wasn't underestimating the extent of the obstacles remaining between us. Several of them were of my making. They needed to be removed if we were ever going to be anything to one another. The question was, did I want us to be?

I thought of telling him that I knew about him making up the shortfall of five thousand pounds in the restoration fund, but it didn't seem like the right moment. I thought of telling him that I knew he had "persuaded" the Farmers to deliver up the man who had attacked me. The dear, sweet fool. Edward, that is, not Brian Pratt.

In the end, I didn't say either of those things. Instead, I stood up, put down my drink on an occasional table, and moved closer to him. Not close enough to touch, but close enough to deliver the message. He turned around to face me.

"Do you remember what you said to me the other night?" I asked.

He nodded gravely. "Of course. I've had nothing much to do all week but lie here and think about it."

"Did you mean it?"

I didn't need to be more specific. He knew exactly what I was talking about. He looked me straight in the eye. "Absolutely," he said.

"Then there are a few things you ought to know."

Edward didn't look particularly curious, or anxious, or any of the things I was expecting. He just looked indifferent. His eyes moved across my face, but I was confident of not giving anything away until I opened my mouth.

"Shall we sit down again?" he asked, eventually, giving up on his attempt to mind-read.

I did as he asked, and he sat down in the other armchair, almost facing me. There was a few moments' silence, while I tried to work out how to begin. I looked down at my hands.

"Remember when you asked me about Peter Markham? You asked if I was having an affair with him."

I glanced up, for his response. He nodded again, but said nothing.

"I wasn't then, and I'm not now," I said. "But I'm not completely innocent either. I've known Peter a long time. I was at college with him."

"I know that," he said.

"I mean, I was his girlfriend."

"I guessed that," he said.

"When he came here as vicar, and we met again, I hadn't seen him for a few years, but naturally we resumed our friendship."

There was still nothing much in the way of a reaction from Edward. He didn't seem surprised by anything I'd said so far. But then, I hadn't come to the interesting bit yet.

"I had a kind of a fling with him," I said.

Edward looked at the carpet. The pattern was truly hideous, but he wasn't really seeing it. "Go on," he said.

"I slept with him, once, after he came here. I didn't mean to do it. That is, I didn't plan it. But I knew what I was doing, I understood the significance of it."

He didn't raise his eyes.

"It only happened once," I repeated, realising that the tone of my voice was imploring him for forgiveness. "The blame was equal, I think, but afterwards, if it had been up to me…" I paused for a few seconds, waiting to see what Edward would say, if anything. He still didn't react.

"I would probably have done it again," I finished.

He sniffed. At first I took it for a contemptuous noise, but then I realised it was nothing but a sniff.

"Do you think I'm a slut?" I asked.

He looked up, shocked. "Of course not!" he said, adding, "I suspected there'd been something of the sort."

"I suppose Hilary told you."

Edward looked ashamed of himself, as he nodded. He gave a deep sigh. "She said I was making a fool of myself over you."

The meanness of Hilary's action killed any sympathy I might have been feeling for her. She had been given the choice, between Edward and Peter, and she had rejected Edward. And I knew that, when he had said he had worshipped her from afar, he really meant that word "worshipped." But when she saw him taking an interest in someone else, Hilary couldn't resist trying to exert some influence. She didn't want him herself, but she didn't want anyone else to have him. Or at least, she didn't want *me* to have him.

I lingered over my response, watching Edward closely, noting how his mask had slipped. This man had been hurt, over and over—so many times that he had come to expect nothing else. All I knew was that I didn't want to be the cause of any more suffering. He didn't deserve it.

"You won't tell anyone else about me and Peter, will you?" I pleaded.

Once again, he looked shocked at the suggestion. "What kind of man do you take me for?" he asked.

"One with impossibly high moral standards," I replied quickly.

He appeared stunned.

"I think I ought to go now," I said, getting to my feet. "Will you be all right?"

He nodded dumbly. I picked up my bag and moved towards the door. "Thanks for the drink," I added, still trying desperately to make the leave-taking last long enough for him to say something else; but he chose not to reply.

I took one last look around the room, then turned my back on him and opened the door. I walked out into the hall, as slowly as I dared. I put my hand up to the lock and began to turn the knob.

With a swift, graceful movement, Edward placed his body between me and my exit. His long arms encircled me, and the front door remained closed.

9 781588 320094